OUT
IN THE
COLD

TREVOR DOUGLAS

vinci
BOOKS

By Trevor Douglas

The Bridgette Cash Mystery Thriller Series

Cold Comfort

Cold Trail

Cold Hard Cash

The Cold Light of Day

Out In The Cold

Hot And Cold

*This book is dedicated to Harper Anne.
The circle of life continues...*

Vinci Books

vinci-books.com

Published by Vinci Books Ltd in 2025

1

Copyright © Trevor Douglas 2022

The author has asserted their moral right to be identified as the author of this work in accordance with the Copyright, Designs and Patents Act 1988. This work is a work of fiction. Names, characters, places and incidents are the product of the author's imagination or are used fictitiously. Any resemblance to actual persons, living or dead, places and incidents is entirely coincidental.

All rights reserved. No part of this publication may be copied, reproduced, distributed, stored in any retrieval system, or transmitted in any form or by any means, including photocopying, recording, or other electronic or mechanical methods, nor used as a source for any form of machine learning including AI datasets, without the prior written permission of the publisher.

The publisher and the author have made every effort to obtain permissions for any third party material used in this book and to comply with copyright law. Any queries in this respect should be brought to the attention of the publisher and any omissions will be corrected in future editions.

A CIP catalogue record for this book is available from the British Library.

Paperback ISBN: 9781036702038

Printed and bound in Great Britain by Clays Ltd, Elcograf S.p.A.

Map

The island for this story exists purely in the writer's mind even though there are some similar examples along the Fraser River in British Columbia. The following map may assist readers in understanding the island's layout, which is a key part of the story.

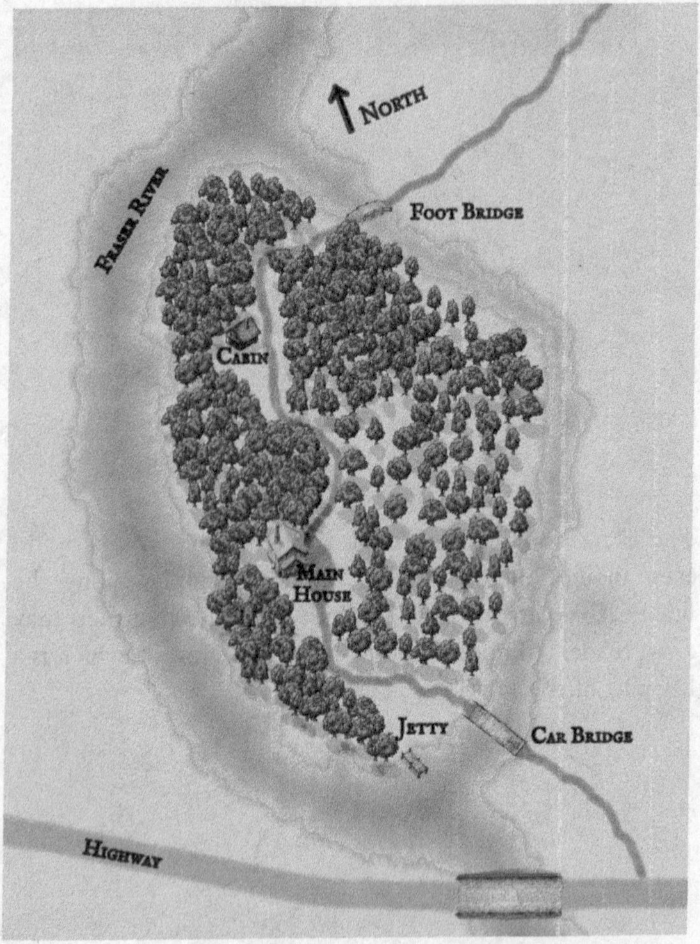
North
Fraser River
Foot Bridge
Cabin
Main House
Jetty
Car Bridge
Highway

Thursday 2:02 AM

Detective Bridgette Cash felt her heart race as the silhouette of the man came into view. She tried adjusting the focus of her binoculars to get a sharper image of the man's face, but the steady stream of misty rain made it impossible for her to recognize any of his facial features.

A voice to her left said, "Do you think that's Anderson?"

Keeping her binoculars steady on the man, she responded, "I'm not sure. He's about the right height and build. But he's got the hood up on his jacket and I can't get a good look at his face."

"He's staying in the shadows and away from street lights. I think it's him."

Bridgette lowered the binoculars and studied the man as he continued his journey. She too, had noticed he was staying close to the buildings, but she was not about to jump to any conclusions.

"He might be just trying to avoid getting wet."

"If he wanted to avoid getting wet, he'd be walking a lot quicker than that."

The voice reached out a hand.

"You mind if I take a look?"

Without taking her eyes off the man, Bridgette handed the binoculars to her partner, Levi Frost.

At just over six foot three, Frost found it hard to stay comfortable for long periods in a car, and shifted in the driver's seat as he raised the binoculars. After attempting to adjust the focus for several seconds he lowered them and growled, "You can't see squat with these."

Bridgette smiled to herself as she glanced at her partner. They had gotten off to a rocky start but eventually found a way to work as a team. Now on their second murder case together, they weren't exactly friends, but they'd worked out each other's strengths and weaknesses and settled into a routine. While she was reserved and considered, Frost was the exact opposite, a trait which caused some within the Vancouver police department to label him as reckless.

She turned back and followed the man's progress as he walked along the inner-suburban street.

Frost rubbed his hand across the interior of the windscreen.

"Bad enough that it's raining but now we're fogging up as well."

Bridgette estimated the man had closed to within about thirty yards of the apartment block.

Parked on the opposite side of the street between two delivery vans, they had a good view of the front of the building without being too conspicuous. She was reasonably confident they wouldn't be spotted as they slumped lower in their seats to follow the man's approach. Bridgette knew they would have their answer soon enough as the man slowed his step to a cautious walk.

Frost remarked, "He's definitely checking out the place. It has to be Anderson."

Bridgette held her breath. If the man stopped in front of the building, there was a high probability Frost was right.

As if reading her mind, Frost said, "It's just after two in the morning. Nobody in their right mind would be out walking around in this unless they had to be."

Bridgette murmured, "I agree," as the man she now believed to be Gerrit Anderson slowed his step and glanced into the dimly lit lobby of the apartment block. Until recently, Anderson had run a successful business importing air compressors for the construction industry. But the relationship with his business partner had soured in recent months when he had accused Anderson of embezzling company funds.

She watched as the man quickened his step again and walked on.

"He's not stopping," said Frost.

"I think he's just being cautious."

Bridgette frowned as the man stopped in the shadows of the next apartment block on Haro Street and pulled out his phone.

Frost asked, "What's he up to?"

"Maybe he's calling the girlfriend. If he doesn't have a pass to the building, she'll need to buzz him in."

The man abruptly turned and started walking back.

"He still on the phone?"

Bridgette nodded. "I think she's going to let him in."

Keeping low in their seats, they watched the man retrace his steps to the front of the apartment block. He paused with his hand on the front-door handle and glanced back up the street to see if he had been followed. Bridgette got her first good look at the man face.

3

"Bingo," she said. "That's definitely Anderson."

Frost asked, "So, do we call this in?"

Bridgette barely heard the question as she watched Anderson push on the front door and slip inside. She was already thinking ahead. Gerrit Anderson was a prime suspect in the murder of his business partner, John Goldsack, who had been reported missing three weeks earlier. The case had been upgraded to murder when his body had been discovered in a shallow grave in parklands outside the city. Bridgette and Frost were assigned to the case at the beginning of the week. Anderson had been cooperative in his first interview, but had come across as cold and calculating. Their suspicions were further heightened when Anderson went to ground and did not show up for a second interview or return any of their calls. Unlike his business partner, whose accounts had not been touched, Anderson was still withdrawing cash and shifting large sums of money from business to personal accounts.

Afraid that he was getting ready to disappear for good, they had interviewed Anderson's girlfriend in her West End apartment. She swore she hadn't seen him in more than a week but told them little else. After an hour of questioning she finally conceded that her boyfriend's business had some cash flow problems, then she requested a bathroom break. While the woman was in the bathroom, Bridgette noticed two laptops on a side table in the living room. One was a slimline Mac Book in a pink case and the other was a high-end Dell laptop in a black ruggedized case designed for outdoor use. It was the case on the Dell that caught her attention. It was almost identical to the case on Goldsack's laptop that the Vancouver police had seized shortly after they had found his body. Bridgette was suspicious and wondered if the laptop belonged to Anderson.

She quickly powered up the device and while the prompt for a password prevented her from exploring any further, the background picture of Anderson holding up a marlin on a large fishing boat was all she needed to confirm her suspicions.

Bridgette had wondered if Anderson was deliberately hiding it at his girlfriend's place. Rather than getting a search warrant for the girlfriend's apartment, Bridgette had convinced her boss to establish a stakeout team to watch the apartment and a second team to follow her. Two days in, her hunch that Anderson would return had proven right.

Frost repeated his question, "Are we going to call this in?"

"Yes, we…" Bridgette paused and focused on the front of the apartment block. "Can you lower your window, Levi?"

"Why?"

"I think he still in the foyer. It looks like there are two people in back near the stairs, but I can't be sure."

Frost held down a button on the console until his side window was almost fully open.

Now with a clear line of sight to the front of the building, Bridgette focused the binoculars on the shadows and two figures came into view.

"There are definitely two people. It looks like they're just talking."

"The girlfriend?"

"I think so but it's hard to… wait… one of them is going back upstairs."

Bridgette dropped the binoculars. "We need to move now, I think he's going to leave through the back exit."

Thursday 2:08 AM

Bridgette signaled Frost to head to the right side of the apartment block as she sprinted across the street. With her SIG Sauer pistol drawn, she cursed herself for allowing Anderson a way to escape as she raced down a walkway to the left of the building.

She had discussed the rear entrance to the apartment building with Frost when they had first set up surveillance. The door was always locked and only accessible from the outside by a key. Her boss had offered her an extra team to stake out the rear lane as well, but Bridgette declined. Extra cops increased the risk that Anderson would realize he was walking into a trap and no one wanted to scare him off. Besides, the rear door led directly into the foyer, making it impossible to get to the elevator or stairs without being seen through the building's front windows. Now, as she sprinted down the paved walkway, her decision looked flawed. She hadn't counted on Anderson coming in through the front entrance and then leaving by the back.

Bridgette paused at the rear of the building and looked

into the lane behind the apartment block. The access way was dimly lit and barely wide enough to allow cars to pass. As the light rain continued to fall, she scanned for any sign of Anderson. Her view of the rear entrance was partially blocked by two parked cars and a dumpster. She couldn't see any sign of her quarry, and wondered where Frost was.

Bridgette glanced to her left. The lane opened onto Jervis Street and provided Anderson with multiple directions for escape. But he only had a few seconds' head start on her. The lane was quiet. No telltale sound of footsteps of someone fleeing the scene. She frowned—surely he couldn't have got out that quickly? Was he still here? Hiding close by? And where was Frost? They had arranged for him to come around the right side of the building and he should have been at the other end of the lane by now.

Bridgette looked past the two parked cars and the dumpster and focused on the rear door that led into the building. It was possible Anderson was already out of the lane and escaping down a side street. But it was also possible he was still inside—hiding in a rear corner of the building that couldn't be seen from the front. Using a double-handed grip, Bridgette brought her SIG up into the combat firing position and took two steps forward. She barely noticed the light rain falling as a lump formed in her throat. It was quiet—too quiet. She moved three steps forward and stopped between the two cars. The poor light made it hard for her to distinguish shapes from shadows.

Bridgette sensed movement in the shadows behind her as she turned to check the dumpster. She pivoted in time to see a dark figure rushing forward. The stillness of the night was broken by a low whooshing sound as the man swung a two-by-four length of timber at her.

She had no time to react as the two-by-four struck her

pistol. Bridgette felt the force of the blow jolt through her hands and wrists as her weapon discharged. The subsonic boom shattered the night as it echoed across the lane, drowning out the clattering sound of her SIG as it skidded across the pavement.

Now defenseless, she kept her focus on the two-by-four as Anderson feigned a second swing. Once a junior champion in Taekwondo, Bridgette still took at least one night a week off from CrossFit workouts to practice the martial art. It had been drilled into her that observation was one of her primary defenses. Being able to discern your opponent shifting their weight forward or backward, or from left to right, invariably gave you an advantage as they telegraphed how they were going to attack. But in the lane's gloom it was impossible for her to see the almost indiscernible shifts in Anderson's body weight as he readied himself to strike again.

Bridgette stepped back on her right foot to balance her weight as Anderson moved out of the shadows. He feigned another swing, which Bridgette flinched at but stood her ground. The standoff lasted three seconds before Anderson lost his patience and swung the two-by-four again, this time using a baseball swing. Bridgette was better prepared. She bent her knees and ducked forward in one motion without taking her eyes off her opponent. As the weapon fizzed harmlessly above her head, she knew Anderson was off balance. That fraction of a second it took for him to regain his footing was all she needed.

Pivoting on her right foot, Bridgette turned her hips and swung her left foot around in an arc parallel to the ground. The roundhouse was her favorite kick and a move she had practiced thousands of times and executed regularly in competitions. At five-feet-ten, Bridgette's long legs gave her a reach advantage over many of her female opponents. Although Anderson was close to six feet tall, his forward stumble had placed him well inside her range and she caught him flush on his rib cage. It was not quite a perfect execution, but good enough to see him drop to the ground in agony. Bridgette turned him onto his stomach and, with little sympathy for his discomfort, handcuffed him.

Frost appeared a moment later.

Bridgette looked up and asked, "Where were you?"

"Sorry, I saw somebody take off when I got to the other side of the building so I gave chase—turned about to be some homeless guy."

Feigning disappointment with a shake of her head, she responded, "Some help would've been nice."

Frost repeated his contrite apology before asking, "Where did you find him?"

"He was hiding behind the dumpster," replied Bridgette. As she rose to her feet, she added, "I haven't questioned him yet, but I'm wondering if he spotted us across the road?"

Frost looked down at Anderson, who was still writhing in agony on the ground, and asked, "Does he need to go the hospital?"

"Probably. I think I broke some ribs."

Thursday 8:03 AM

Bridgette stifled a yawn as she knocked on the door of Chief Inspector Felix Delray's office. Now thirteen months into her career as a detective, she had become very familiar with her boss's quirky mannerisms and management style.

When Delray's booming baritone voice responded, "It's open, come on in," she glanced at Frost and murmured, "He's in a good mood," and opened the door.

Delray headed up the Homicide Unit within the Major Crime section of the Vancouver Police Department. Despite his senior position, his twelve-by-twelve office on the fourth floor of police headquarters was barely large enough to accommodate his scarred wooden desk, three filing cabinets and two visitors' chairs.

Bridgette, whose neatness bordered on a disorder, always struggled with Delray's desk. This morning was no different when she walked in for their eight o'clock appointment. Despite the department embracing the digital age, Delray was proud to be 'old school'. His preference for paper-based reports and using his desk as a filing cabinet made him look disorganized, but Bridgette knew nothing could be further from the truth.

Peering over a brace of files, he commented, "You two look like you're ready for bed."

Bridgette managed half a smile. "I guess."

"Well, that was great work last night. Getting Anderson off the streets is a great outcome for the department. So let's make this quick so we can get you both out of here."

Frost chimed in as he settled into his chair, "No argument from me, Chief."

Delray leaned back in his chair and stifled a wry smile.

"I gotta hand it to you two—when you first came to me with the idea of staking out Anderson's girlfriend's place, I thought it was a long shot."

Frost held up his hands, palms out. "Bridgette's idea, not mine."

Bridgette frowned. "It could have all gone south so easily. If he had gotten out of that lane, we may have never found him."

Delray waved her off. "Don't beat yourself up over it. It's all a trade-off. Cops staking out the lane might also have tipped him off." Delray paused and raised an eyebrow. "I hear he's got a couple of broken ribs?"

"He tried to cave my skull in with a two by four."

"It sounds like he got off lightly."

"I thought so."

"Did you get a confession out of him?"

Frost responded, "No, Chief. He clammed up as soon as we arrested him and we're now dealing with his lawyer."

"The doctors currently have him sedated," added Bridgette. "I don't think we'll get a shot at talking to him before tomorrow."

Delray nodded. "Well, that probably works out for the

best. It will give us more time to build a case against him before the first interview."

"I'm looking forward to round two with Gerrit Anderson."

Delray grimaced. "There's been a change of plans, Bridgette. It will be Detective Frost and I doing the interview tomorrow."

Bridgette frowned. "Why?"

"Alex Hellyer's trial has been postponed."

The mention of the name Alex Hellyer sent a shiver down her spine. Bridgette and Frost had arrested Hellyer a month earlier on a murder charge, but it hadn't been without incident. It had been the first case she and Frost had worked together as a team and almost their last. She felt her heart race as she thought back to the midnight shootout on the roof of the Saint Joseph's Hospital.

Delray broke through her thoughts as he continued, "The judge assigned to hear Hellyer's case had a heart attack yesterday. It's mild and they expect him to make a full recovery, but he's on two weeks' medical leave. All his cases are being shifted back."

"So how does this affect the Anderson investigation?"

Delray looked down at an open file on his desk. "I've been reading your file... specifically the psychologist's assessment following the shootout on the roof of Saint Joseph's."

Bridgette nodded as she realized there would be another assessment coming today. It was now mandatory for all Vancouver police to undergo a psychological assessment after every life-threatening police incident they were involved in.

Her boss added, "While the report says you were mentally fit to return to work, they warned if there were any more incidents it would trigger mandatory leave." Delray held her gaze and then added, "Last night qualifies, Bridgette…"

"I feel fine, chief."

"That may be so, but it's out of my hands. I might have been able to get your leave suspended if the trial was going ahead, but now that they've postponed it…" Delray removed his black-rimmed glasses. "When I joined the force thirty years ago, there was no counseling and nobody ever used the words mental and health in the same sentence. Times have changed—not everything for the better, but this is one change I believe in." He leaned back in his chair and added, "I've organized counseling appointments for both of you at nine. I expect they will allow Levi to continue to work, but I doubt you will be so lucky."

Bridgette let out a long breath. Frost had put his life on the line to save her during the Hellyer arrest. She had been forced to shoot at Hellyer, severely wounding him in the process. Despite her bravado, she still had nightmares about the incident.

Trying to push Hellyer to the back of her mind, she said, "I would have liked to see the Anderson case through to its conclusion."

Delray waved her off. "You've done the hard yards on this. We have Anderson in custody and with the added charges of attempting to kill a police officer and resisting arrest, we have more than enough to hold him while we close out the Goldsack murder investigation. You two have done a great job."

Silence descended on the room for a moment before Delray looked at his watch. "Treat this like an extra week's paid holiday leave, Bridgette. Get away somewhere and put your feet up. God knows you deserve it."

Bridgette stood up. "I guess I don't get any say in this?"

Delray shook his head. "None of us do, Bridgette. The board is all over the Chief of Police on health and welfare. Even *he* couldn't overturn this."

"I've got some paperwork to finish," said Bridgette with a sigh. "I'll use the rest of the time before my appointment to get it squared away."

Delray responded, "I think that's wise."

Frost stood and asked, "So what happens to Hellyer? Does he get another two weeks in hospital?"

"No. My understanding is he's recovered enough to go back to prison. They're shipping him out tomorrow."

Bridgette paused in the doorway and looked back at Frost talking to their boss. Suddenly she was back at Saint Joseph's in the early hours of that morning a month ago. After setting fire to part of the hospital, Hellyer had tried to escape via the hospital roof. Frost and Bridgette had given chase but had become separated. It had been a tough night. She recalled Hellyer holding a gun on her, screaming at her to drop her weapon just as the door to the rooftop was flung open.

The distraction provided by Frost had given her enough time to get off one clean shot at her adversary. Despite part of the hospital building being on fire, doctors at Saint Joseph's performed emergency surgery on Hellyer, saving his life. She was forever grateful to the medical team. Despite being a monster who had killed multiple people, she was thankful not to have Hellyer's death on her conscience for the rest of her life. She drew comfort knowing that when convicted, he would spend the rest of his life in prison.

Delray's voice broke through her thoughts again. "There's one more thing you need to know about Hellyer for the trial."

"What's that?"

"When the prosecutor called about the trial date shifting, he told me Hellyer's lawyer is changing his plea."

"He's going to plead guilty?"

"No. He's pleading not guilty by reason of insanity."

Frost exploded, "But that's crazy. He's not insane, he's just a monster."

Delray shrugged. "Maybe so, but that changes everything for the trial."

Bridgette thought through the repercussions. "It's no longer about proving he committed the crimes, but that he was sane at the time."

Delray nodded. "The trial just got a whole lot harder for everyone."

Thursday 8:15 AM

Alex Hellyer lay in his bed pretending to be asleep. Before being shot by the bitch cop he only needed five hours sleep a night. But after the surgery to remove the bullet from his chest, he found himself needing at least fourteen hours of rest each day. Hellyer considered sleep an annoying interruption. Now, almost a month on from surgery, he was back down to six hours per night, although he pretended he still needed more. The illusion of sleep gave him time to plan without distraction. He could disappear into his own world for hours—a world where he was not shackled to a bed or pacing around an eight-by-ten cell.

He opened one eye and glanced at the guard who was sitting in a chair on the opposite side of the room. Hellyer had become familiar with the routine of each guard who had been assigned to watch him. Lance Connor had been here since the beginning on day shift. He was the senior guard and preferred the chair inside the secure hospital room to the one in the corridor which was usually occupied by his partner, Harvey. Harvey was addicted to Snickers bars and coke and regularly got into trouble from Connor for spending too much time at the vending machine. Harvey was not very bright, a trait Hellyer was already using to his advantage.

Connor's morning routine had not deviated in the past three weeks. He and Harvey arrived at seven each weekday to relieve the two guards from the night shift. Connor would do a quick visual inspection of Hellyer's room before settling into his chair. He rarely uttered a word and would spend the first hour reading a newspaper. At around eight-fifteen each morning he would take his first bathroom break and return with a cup of coffee from the vending machine. Hellyer knew Harvey was supposed to come in and watch him while Connor was gone, but that rarely happened.

After glancing up at the electric wall clock which read 8:06 AM, Hellyer closed his eyes again. Above the silence that was punctuated occasionally by voices in the surrounding rooms, Hellyer listened to the clock as it ticked off the seconds. The math was simple—it was nine minutes until 8:15 AM when Connor normally took his first break. That gave him five hundred and forty seconds to count down. Hellyer was nothing if not patient.

Today, he only got to four-hundred and twenty-two before he heard Connor stretch and then rise from his chair. He listened to the guard's footsteps as he walked out of the room and waited until he heard the door open before lifting his head a fraction off the pillow. The guard's conversation was brief as usual, with Harvey declaring there was no need for him to leave his post if the prisoner was sleeping. Hellyer smiled as the security door clicked shut again. The guard detail had settled into a predictable routine that made it easy for him to work around. He knew he would have between four and five minutes of unsupervised time in the room. On previous days, he had used almost every second. Today he was relaxed, as he knew he would only need a few.

Conscious of the security camera in the room, Hellyer pretended to roll over in bed to face the wall. While he didn't believe the camera was being actively monitored, he was not about to take any chances. He waited a few more seconds before shifting his sleeping position slightly to allow his unshackled right hand to rest on the side rail of his bed. When he had first commenced his planning, he knew he would need a hiding place. Inside the hollow metal tubing of the side rail was an obvious choice. It provided easy access to what he was hiding, but it was unlikely to be discovered by a guard during a spot search of his room.

At first the plastic end cap on the side rail had been difficult to remove. But accessing his hiding place regularly had worn the edges of the cap down, and it now gave him little resistance as he deftly removed it with his fingers. Hellyer breathed a sigh of relief as he slipped the cap under his pillow. With his left hand shackled to the bed, dropping the cap could have proven disastrous if it had rolled out of his reach and been discovered by a guard. Hellyer continued to count down the seconds in his head as he inserted a finger into the hollow rail and withdrew a plastic shiv.

The shiv had started out life as a pair of disposable plastic forceps. The nurse who came to dress his wounds each morning always carried at least a dozen of them in sealed plastic bags in her cart along with the bandages, dressings and medications. Hellyer immediately saw the device's potential, but he knew stealing a pair wouldn't be easy. Every part of his life was supervised. Even toilet breaks weren't private with the guards insisting the door to the adjoining bathroom only ever be partially closed.

But he was smarter than the nurses and guards and knew he would eventually get an opportunity. Six days earlier he got his break when the nurse who had arrived to change his dressing realized she had left some bandages she needed back at the nurses' station.

It was one of the rare occasions when Harvey was on guard duty in the room. The nurse was out of the room for less than two minutes, but two minutes was too long for Harvey. After a minute of diligently watching his prisoner, Harvey wandered over to the window and peered outside. It was all the time Hellyer needed. While pretending to cough, Hellyer bent down and grabbed a set of the forceps off the cart with his free hand and slipped them under his mattress. The nurse returned oblivious to what had happened, and changed his dressing without incident.

After breaking the forceps in two like a turkey wishbone, he kept them hidden in the side rail, removing them whenever he was alone for a few minutes to sharpen one end against a rough edge on the underside of the bed frame.

Hellyer felt the tip. It was now as sharp as a needle point and while the weapon was small and looked innocuous, in the right hands—his hands—it could kill within seconds. After replacing the plastic stopper in the side rail, he moved the shiv under his bed sheets. He felt around his pajama bottoms for the small hole he had made earlier in the seam of the garment and then pushed the shiv through the opening until it was completely hidden.

He glanced back up at the clock which now read 8:18 AM and then closed his eyes again. Hellyer allowed himself a smile as he began to count down the seconds to 9:30 AM.

The nurse would come to change his dressing then, completely unaware of his plans. He could hardly wait.

Thursday 10.29 AM

Bridgette looked up when she heard the clank of keys dropping on the desk in the cubicle next to hers. Despite being six-foot-three, the angular frame of Levi Frost moved quietly through the homicide office and she hadn't heard him approach. Now well after 10 AM, the room was abuzz with the noise of detectives hard at work. With quiet conversations now impossible, she got up from her chair and leaned on the pod wall that separated their two work areas.

"How did it go?"

"OK, I guess."

"Just okay?"

Frost grimaced. "I'm on notice. The psychologist said any more violent episodes with criminals and I'll be on mandatory leave as well."

"But Anderson was almost in handcuffs when you arrived."

"I pointed that out but it fell on deaf ears."

Bridgette surveyed the room. At any one time there

were at least forty detectives, analysts and assistants working in the office. She knew from experience that most modern-day investigation work was done in front of computer screens and in the lab.

"I wouldn't worry too much. The chances of you being involved in another incident like last night's any time soon are fairly low."

"What about you? I guess you weren't so lucky."

Bridgette shook her head. "No. Just as the chief predicted, I'm on a week's leave and then I'll be reassessed."

"Well, that sucks. So what are you going to do?"

"I don't fancy sitting around in my apartment for a week feeling sorry for myself, and I can't spend all my time at the gym, so I've been on Airbnb."

"You found something you like?"

"A cabin up near Kawkawa Lake. It overlooks a river and there are lots of walking trails nearby."

"Sounds perfect. I'm surprised you got a booking at such short notice."

"There was a cancellation. A big storm is coming through and potentially a lot of rain…"

"You sure you want to go up there if there's a big storm coming?"

"I'll be fine. I've got four paperbacks on my reading list, so if it's raining I'll stay inside and curl up in front of the fire."

Frost nodded and then added, "When do you leave?"

"I'm going home now to pack. And then I'll grab a couple of hours' sleep. It's about a two-hour drive and I'm planning to get there before nightfall."

"Is there anything you need me to do while you're away?"

"No. I've finished the report and I've sent the chief an email, so I'm all squared away."

"What about at home? You need someone to pick up your mail or anything?"

Bridgette shook her head.

"Thanks, but I'm all sorted. I've called my neighbor. She's going to take care of my mail and water my plants."

"It sounds like you've got everything covered."

"I hope so. The psychologist said I needed at least a week's rest before she would consider a re-assessment. I'm hoping a week in the woods will be enough."

"Enough?"

"She won't guarantee my return to work. If she thinks I need more time off, I'll be forced to take another week's leave."

"Something you want to avoid."

"I don't want to miss the Hellyer trial. So I figure a week out of the city in a remote country location shows I'm serious."

"I agree."

They were quiet for a moment before Bridgette said, "I see the chief's got the team hard at work."

"They're searching Anderson's girlfriend's apartment as we speak and the lab guys are going through his laptop."

"Let's hope they find something else to link him to the crime. So what's he got planned for you?"

"I'm going home shortly. I'll get a few hours' sleep and then I'll prep for the interview with Anderson tomorrow. The chief's going to be my backup, so I want to make sure I'm fully prepared."

"He's very experienced. Anderson will no doubt have a lawyer present and getting any straight answers will be next to impossible."

Frost nodded.

Bridgette added, "I wish I could stay and help, but I'm technically not even supposed to be here now."

"Then you should go."

"I feel guilty... like I'm letting down the team."

Frost held her gaze. "You of all people have nothing to feel guilty about."

Bridgette thanked Frost for his show of support before returning to her computer. She checked her emails, turned on her out-of-office message, and then powered down the device. She had never been good at taking holidays, particularly when forced to take them on her own. She sighed as she gathered up her phone, charger and keys from her desk before stowing them in her leather tote bag.

After saying a brief goodbye to Frost, she headed for the elevator wondering what the week ahead would bring. The weeks normally flew by for her, but she feared the next one would feel more like a month. She hoped her decision to head to the quiet surrounds of Kawkawa Lake had been the right one as she pressed the elevator button to head down to the parking lot.

Thursday 10:35 AM

Alex Hellyer stared at the clock on the wall as he counted off the seconds. It was now 9:37 AM—four-hundred-and-twenty seconds past the time when the nurse normally came into his room to change his wound dressing. He was not the type to panic. Routines in hospitals were constantly being disrupted by sick people and emergencies. He took one deep calming breath as he looked across at the guard. Connor was still reading his newspaper and seemingly unconcerned by the lateness of the nurse.

Hellyer went through the plan in his head one more time. This was his first—and last—opportunity for freedom. He had spent hours going over each detail of the plan in his mind, looking for weaknesses. He had played out every scenario he could think of: how the guards might react, how the nurse might react, and even how he might react under pressure. The plan was far from foolproof, but he had refined it as much as he could. He was a realist and considered the odds of its success were fifty-fifty. Not great odds, but worth the risk. After all, what did he have to lose?

He returned his gaze to the clock. Four-hundred-and-sixty seconds had now elapsed and still no sign of the nurse.

Connor broke the silence as he got up from his chair and barked an order, summoning his partner. Hellyer made no pretense of sleep as he watched Harvey saunter in to the room.

Connor said, "I've got a phone call I need to make about my house insurance and I'm not making it here in front of him. You need to stay and watch him until the nurse comes."

Harvey frowned.

"How long are you going to be?"

"Not long, unless they put me on hold."

"What do I do if the nurse comes while you're away?"

"He's handcuffed to the bed and he's not going anywhere. You follow the routine we've been over and let her do her work."

Harvey didn't look convinced as he nodded.

Connor raised an eyebrow. "If you don't think you can handle it, I'll make the call later…"

"No, I'm all good. I got this."

"I shouldn't be long. If anything happens out of the ordinary, call me straight away."

Connor turned and walked from the room. The click of the door shutting was dwarfed by the thump Harvey made as he slumped into the guard's chair.

As if by magic, a Snickers bar appeared in Harvey's hand.

Harvey looked across at Hellyer as he peeled the chocolate bar like a banana and snapped, "What are you looking at?"

Out In The Cold

Hellyer counted off another eight-hundred-and-six seconds in his mind before the door to his secure hospital room opened again. He could barely contain a smile as the nurse walked in pushing the same trolley she pushed every other day on her rounds.

She said a brief good morning and asked about his partner. Harvey explained that Connor had to make a call and that he was in charge until his return.

The nurse nodded and then asked Harvey to fix Hellyer's handcuffs before she approached.

Harvey stepped forward and took another pair of handcuffs out of his back pocket. He used them to handcuff Hellyer's left hand to his right hand before unlocking the handcuff that had been used to secure him to the bed. He checked his work and gave the nurse a thumbs up. "All good."

The nurse moved the trolley forward and positioned a chair near the bed. "Can you please sit up?"

Hellyer sat up and swung his legs over the side of bed just as he had done every day for the previous three weeks. He felt his heart race at what was about to unfold. He cautioned himself that now was not the time to break the routine.

The nurse turned towards Harvey. "Lance normally stands beside me—I feel safer that way."

After mumbling a, "Sure, no problem," Harvey stood up and shuffled over next to the nurse.

The nurse looked at Hellyer and said, "You can remove your pajama shirt now."

Hellyer obliged even though it was difficult with his two hands cuffed together. He grimaced as the nurse pulled off the soiled dressing. The routine was always the same, and he waited for her to clean the wound.

After spending less than a minute on the task, the nurse declared, "The wound is looking really good. I'll wait for you to shower and then I'll apply the dressing."

Harvey stammered, "Wait a minute, nobody said anything about a shower."

The nurse glared at Harvey.

"The prisoner always has a shower before I dress the wound. Keeping his body clean helps minimize the chance of infection."

Harvey swallowed. "Maybe we should wait for Lance to get back?"

The nurse looked at her watch.

"I don't have time to wait. You're the guard—surely you train for this? You leave his feet shackled, but take the handcuffs off. He goes into the bathroom, showers and dries himself. It's not as if he can go anywhere—the room has no windows."

Hellyer watched as Harvey's eyes darted left and right seemingly looking for answers.

After taking a deep breath, Harvey unfastened the safety strap that held his Glock in its holster. To Hellyer's surprise, Harvey removed the weapon and pointed it at him.

"Is that really necessary?" demanded the nurse.

"I'm not taking any chances," growled Harvey. "This guy has killed before and I don't intend being his next victim."

Harvey paused and lobbed a small set of keys at Hellyer before adding, "You can unlock the cuffs yourself and no tricks."

Hellyer smiled as he caught the keys.

"Just take it easy there, Harvey. I've got one bullet hole in me already. I don't want to make it two."

Out In The Cold

Holding the key out in front of him, Hellyer added, "I'm going to insert the key into the lock now. Is that okay?"

Harvey swallowed again. "No tricks."

Hellyer undid the handcuffs and then stood up slowly.

"I'm going into the bathroom now if that's okay?"

Harvey nodded. "Don't take too long in there and leave the door open so I can see what you're doing."

Hellyer looked at the nurse and put on his best confused frown.

"I need to take a dump. Can I have a little privacy?"

Harvey went to protest, but the nurse said, "Lance always leaves the door just a little ajar. We can hear what's going on, but we don't need to see him taking a shower or using the toilet."

Harvey conceded, "OK, but make it snappy in there. The nurse doesn't have all day."

Hellyer shuffled forward as Harvey kept his gun trained on him. The cuffs around his ankles were joined by a thick chrome chain that was about ten inches long. He could only take small steps and while he was now practiced in walking with them, he moved slowly to keep Harvey calm.

After shuffling into the small six-by-six white-tiled bathroom, he looked at the nurse and asked, "Can you close the door, please?"

The bathroom door opened outwards to prevent prisoners from barricading themselves inside. The nurse moved forward and pushed the door forward until it was only open about an inch.

Hellyer smiled as he sat down on the toilet bowl without lowering his pajama pants. He disliked enclosed spaces, and the musty smell of the windowless bathroom had made him nauseous on more than one occasion. He carefully maneuvered the shiv out of the pajama seam, before pulling several sheets of toilet paper off the roll and flushing them down the toilet. Over the sound of the flush and the cistern refilling, he reached in behind the bowl and pulled out a tightly folded plastic bag that he had stolen from the medical supplies trolley a few days earlier.

He called out, "I'm turning on the shower now," and then reached up and turned on the faucet. After unfolding the bag, he held it up towards the shower stream, allowing a small amount of the water to fill the bag without disrupting the sound the stream made as it splashed on the tiled floor. When the bag was about two-thirds full, he removed the bag from the stream and tied a knot in the opening.

Satisfied with his work, Hellyer shuffled towards the door, careful to keep his legs as far apart as possible to keep the chain taught. He was fairly sure any sound the chain made wouldn't be heard over the sound of the shower, but he was not about to take any chances.

When he was about a foot from the door, he peered out through the crack. His visibility of the room was limited and he couldn't see either the nurse or Harvey, which meant they couldn't see him either.

Hellyer mentally stepped through the rest of his plan as he gripped the plastic shiv.

Holding the plastic bag out with his left hand, he lobbed it up into the air and was satisfied with the loud pop it made as it burst open on the floor.

Hellyer started groaning over and over above the sound of the shower and turned to face the door again. He dropped his shoulder, ready to charge forward as heard the muffled voice of the nurse outside.

"Oh my God, I think he's fallen."

Thursday 10:43 AM

Bridgette was about three minutes from her apartment in Richmond when her cell phone started playing the song, *I'm Just A Girl*, by the group, 'No Doubt.'

She had programmed in the favorite song for each of her girlfriends as their ringtone so she knew it was Renée Filipucci, a sub-editor at the Vancouver Post, who was calling.

Her friend's husky voice filled the car.

"Hi, BC—just checking in on you."

"Hi, Renée. I'm in the car, heading home."

"Are you okay to talk for a minute?"

"Sure. I'm hands free, so all good."

There was a moment's pause before Filipucci said, "I guess if you're heading home that means the assessment didn't go so well?"

In an earlier call, Bridgette had shared a few details of what was likely to happen. Despite Filipucci's job with a newspaper and always being on the lookout for good stories, Bridgette trusted her. They had been close for more than a year and regularly leaned on each other for support. "It went as expected, I guess. I'm on a week's leave and then I'm up for re-assessment."

"Are you okay? I mean, if a psychologist thinks…"

"I'm fine, Renée. They're just being cautious."

"Well, I guess… so what are you going to do?"

"I've booked a cabin up near Kawkawa Lake. I'm heading home now to pack and get a couple hours sleep before I leave."

"Well, I guess that's preferable to hanging around your apartment for a week."

Bridgette laughed. "I'd go stir crazy, I think."

"Hey, I worked last weekend and I've got next Tuesday and Wednesday off. If you want some company, I could always drive up?"

"That sounds great. The cabin's up near the mountains and I'm not sure how easy it will be to find. I'll call you tomorrow with some directions."

"Perfect."

"So how's the news room?"

"Slow-news day so far. I much prefer it when it's crazy busy."

Bridgette glanced at the clock on the dashboard of her '66 Mustang as she responded, "It's not even 11 AM Renée—plenty of time for the news day to heat up."

"Here's hoping, BC."

"Hey, I'm going to be home in a moment. I'll speak to you tomorrow."

"Sounds good. Travel safe."

Bridgette disconnected and peered up through the windscreen at the dark storm clouds that were forming above Richmond. She had heard the weather forecast on the radio and decided she would pack, fix herself a strong espresso and get on the road straight away. Sleep could come later when she was settled in her cabin and out of the storm.

Hellyer's plan relied on a guard opening the door. If the nurse opened the door, he knew his chances of escape would drop considerably.

After hearing the nurse cry out, "Oh my God, I think he's fallen," the room went quiet.

Keeping his right shoulder low and his knees bent, he focused on the door looking for any sign of movement.

He kept the groaning up as he heard Harvey's muffled voice, "I'm going to call Lance."

The nurse said, "We need to check on him. He could be badly hurt."

Hellyer lowered the volume of his groaning to better hear Harvey as he responded, "He's also a murderer. I'm not going in there without backup."

"Just open the door a little so we can see inside," demanded the nurse.

The room went quiet. Hellyer continued his soft groaning as he imagined Harvey moving towards the door.

He held his breath for close to ten seconds, his body coiled and ready to spring.

The door opened a fraction more—the moment of truth.

Using every ounce of energy he could muster, Hellyer sprang forward, crashing his shoulder into the door. He had rehearsed the move over and over in his mind, planning for multiple outcomes. He hadn't planned on his bullet wound hurting as much as it did, but he blocked out the searing pain as the door made a loud thump as it sprang open.

Hellyer's reflexes took over as he stumbled forward. Initially, he could see no sign of Harvey as the nurse stood frozen in the middle of the room with her mouth open.

In a blink he was on her as she turned to run. He grabbed her hair with his left hand and pressed the shiv against her right ear, hissing, "Quiet bitch, you're not going anywhere."

With the nurse now under his control, Hellyer spun her around in front of him as a shield and then turned to face Harvey.

He allowed himself a brief smile as he gazed down at the prone figure of the overweight guard. His shirt was covered in blood which continued to pour from his broken nose. Hellyer realized Harvey was no threat as he tried to get up before collapsing on the floor again. He spotted Harvey's gun on the floor about four feet in front of him. Knowing Connor could return at any moment, Hellyer shoved the nurse forward. As she collapsed on top of Harvey, Hellyer bent down and picked up the gun which he pointed at the nurse demanding, "Get the keys off his belt and throw them to me!"

The nurse's eyes widened as she pleaded, "Please don't hurt me."

Hellyer motioned her with the gun, "Do as you're told now and I might let you live!"

The nurse unbuckled a ring of keys from Harvey's utility belt and lobbed them at Hellyer's feet.

While Harvey continued to groan, Hellyer shuffled through the keys until he found the one that unlocked the ankle bracelets. He allowed himself a second to take his eyes of his prisoners while he reached down to unlock the shackles.

Now free, he stood up to his full height and said to the nurse in a calm voice, "Get the handcuffs off his belt and cuff his wrist."

With one eye on the door for any sign of Connor's return, Hellyer watched the nurse cuff Harvey and then said, "Get him to his feet."

The nurse protested, "He's barely conscious."

Hellyer studied the guard. His eyes were swelling rapidly and turning black.

"Harvey, I know you can hear me—get your ass into the bathroom now or I'll shoot you."

Harvey tried to protest, but the gurgling sound he made was incomprehensible.

Hellyer stepped forward and grabbed the nurse by the hair and dragged her off the guard. He twisted her body around and shoved her hard through the bathroom door. She landed hard on the tiled floor and skidded into the wall.

As she lay on the floor sobbing, Hellyer went to move towards Harvey, but paused as the door opened.

Connor took two steps into the room before he realized what he was walking into.

As he stared into the barrel of his partner's gun, Hellyer said, "Good of you to join us, Lance. Close the door behind you and don't make any move for your gun."

Connor's face was stony as he replied, "You won't get away with this."

"And you won't be alive if you don't shut the door, now!"

Without taking his eyes off Hellyer, Connor reached back with his right hand and swung the door closed.

Hellyer nodded once and said, "Come in here and lie face down."

Connor balked. "What are you going to do?"

"I'm going to escape, you moron—now get your hands up."

Hellyer kept the gun trained on Connor as he lay down on the floor. Hellyer moved forward and pressed the gun into Connor's left ear.

"I'm going to take your gun. Any false move by you and your brains are going to be spread all over this floor. Are you going to do anything stupid?"

Connor shook his head.

Hellyer responded, "Smart play, Lance," and then he reached down and unfastened the guard's gun holster. After removing the weapon, Hellyer backed up a couple of steps and dropped it on the bed.

Keeping his gun trained on Connor, Hellyer demanded, "Take off your uniform—and make it quick."

Connor looked up. "Why the hell do you want me to do that?"

Hellyer smiled and said, "I can't exactly walk out of here in pajamas," before taking a step forward and adding, "You've got sixty seconds. After that I put a bullet in your fat friend."

Connor undressed quickly. When he was down to his underwear, Hellyer motioned the guard with his gun. "Get me Harvey's wallet and then drag him into the bathroom."

Connor removed Harvey's wallet and then went to lift his partner, but Harvey protested with a nasal twang, "I can walk."

Hellyer watched as the two guards shuffled into the bathroom.

He called out, "Sit down next to the nurse."

Hellyer stood in the doorway with his gun trained on his three prisoners. He was satisfied with the three terrified looks that returned his gaze.

Pointing to the nurse he said, "Slide the free handcuff on Harvey through the shower railing and clamp it over your wrist."

Through tears, the nurse obliged.

Hellyer lobbed Connor's handcuffs back to him and demanded, "Handcuff yourself through the railing too."

Satisfied that his prisoners were now secure, Hellyer dressed himself in Connor's uniform. They were both close to six feet tall and Hellyer was happy enough with the uniform's fit.

After removing the cash from each guard's wallet, he demanded Connor tell him where he had parked his car. Connor looked back at him with a stony face which prompted Hellyer to hold up his wallet.

"I know where you live, Lance. Don't make me pay you a personal visit."

After getting the information he needed, Hellyer spent a couple of minutes using bandages from the hospital cart to gag each prisoner. Happy with his work, he closed the door to the bathroom and then walked out of his secure room and into the hallway. He turned right and walked casually to the end of the corridor. Without looking back, he opened the door that led to the fire stairs, pleased that his plan was working so far.

Thursday 2:08 PM

Bridgette changed down to second gear as she pulled off the highway and turned onto a narrow unsealed road. As she drove down through a forest of Western Hemlock trees towards a single-lane timber bridge that spanned the river, she was confident her journey was almost complete when she caught glimpses of a white colonial house on the other side of the river.

Her Mustang's tires pattered across the treads of the bridge, making her wonder how well the decking boards were bolted down. After crossing the bridge, she gently accelerated up a steep rise before coming to a halt in a circular gravel driveway in front of the house. If the directions on Airbnb were right, she was now close to her home for the next week.

She allowed herself a tired smile as she sat admiring the backdrop of trees that surrounded the house. This was the perfect spot for her week off, she thought. She peered up at the angry black clouds through the windscreen as light rain began to fall. The weather might be less than ideal for the next couple of days, but that didn't dampen her spirits.

Bridgette stifled a yawn as she switched off the engine. The caffeine hit from her espresso had long since worn off and she was ready for bed. After grabbing her duffel bag from the front passenger seat, she got out of her car and walked toward the front of the house. The house was two storey, with white clapboard siding, a charcoal-gray roof and trim. It looked well maintained and had a homely feel which complimented the rural setting. She stepped up onto a wide timber porch and knocked on the front door. The house had a narrow, ornamental glass window next to the door. Bridgette could see through the sheer curtains and noticed a figure working in the kitchen at the back of the house. As soon as she knocked, the figure turned and headed through the open-plan living area towards the front door.

A slim woman dressed in jeans and a black woolen sweater opened the front door. She had shoulder-length dark brown hair that was pulled back in a ponytail. Based on the traces of gray in her hair and wrinkles around her eyes, Bridgette guessed she was in her late forties.

The woman put on a cheery face as she said, "Hi, you must be Bridgette," but the greeting didn't mask the pain in her eyes.

"Yes, and you must be Monica?" replied Bridgette.

"Monica Poole," said the woman, extending her hand and coming out onto the porch. "Welcome to our little part of Hope."

After shaking hands, Monica closed the door behind her and pointed to a pathway at the side of the house.

"The cabin's about a hundred-and-fifty yards back that

way through the woods. Unfortunately, this is as close as you can get your car, so you'll have to carry everything from here."

"That's all right. All I have is my duffel bag for now."

Monica frowned. "No groceries?"

"Not yet. I pulled an all-night shift at work and haven't been to bed yet. I thought I'd get here ahead of the storm and grab a couple of hours' sleep first and then head back into town later."

"Well, don't sleep too long, most of the shops close here around six. But let's get you to the cabin."

As they walked, Monica looked up at the dark clouds as light rain continued to fall. "Normally I give everyone a grand tour of the island when they arrive, but that can wait until tomorrow."

Bridgette raised an eyebrow. "Island?"

"Yes. Technically, my property is an island." Monica made a sweeping gesture with her hand as she added, "Even though you can't see it from here, the Fraser River splits in two at the northern end of my property and then joins up again at the southern end."

"So, your property is the land in the middle?"

"Yes, all twenty acres of it. So technically because we're surrounded by water, it's an island."

"You didn't mention that on Airbnb."

"No," said Monica with a shake of her head. "When I first started renting out the cabin I tried marketing the place as an island, but people complained because it's not what they expected of an island, so I stopped. So what are your plans while you're here, Bridgette?"

Bridgette decided Monica didn't need to know the exact reason she was having a week off and replied, "I have a week off, so I thought it would be good to get away from the city. I've packed some books to read and I plan on exploring some of the walking trails around here."

Monica looked up at the black sky through the canopy of Western Hemlock trees as the rain started to get heavier. "There's a lot to see around Hope, but I'm glad you've got some books to read because I don't think you'll be getting out on the walking trails for a couple of days at least. The storm front that's coming through looks like a monster."

The trail veered right and Bridgette caught her first glimpse of the cabin through the trees. "We're almost there," said Monica.

They walked another fifty yards until they came to a clearing. The cabin was just like the pictures Bridgette had seen on Airbnb. She smiled to herself as they approached the sturdy low-set structure. The cabin had a pitched tin roof with Cedar shingle siding. Bridgette noticed a puff of smoke wafting up from the cabin's stone chimney.

"I started the fire for you to warm up the cabin. There's plenty of firewood out back so no need to be cold."

Bridgette thanked Monica for her thoughtfulness and then turned to her right.

She could see glimpses of the Fraser River about eighty yards in front of her and murmured, "It's perfect."

"Come on inside and we'll get you settled."

She followed Monica onto a timber veranda that ran the length of the cabin.

Monica handed Bridgette a set of keys before opening the unlocked front door.

"I never bother locking it as we're eleven miles from town and nobody ever comes here. But most city folk find habits hard to break, so here are keys if you need them."

Bridgette thanked Monica and then spent a moment looking around the cabin. Apart from a small room at the rear, which she presumed doubled as a bathroom and laundry, the cabin was one single room with a double bed at one end and two leather sofas set around the stone fireplace at the other. The cabin had a small kitchenette set against the rear wall with a wooden table and four chairs in front of it. It was simple—almost primitive—just what she wanted.

As she looked up at the raked ceiling, she commented, "It's just like the pictures on the website, Monica. This is just what I'm after."

"I'm glad you like it. My husband built this just after he bought the property twenty years ago. This was where he lived until I came along and we got married."

As she admired the craftsmanship of the exposed beams, Bridgette replied, "Your husband is very talented."

Monica let out a sigh as she looked up at the ceiling. "Was… we lost him nine months ago."

"I'm sorry for your loss, Monica. This must be very hard for you."

"Yeah, it's taking some getting used to." After managing a weak smile, Monica said, "There's no TV or internet, but I'm sure you know that from the description we have on Airbnb."

"I was hoping to get away from all that for the next few days."

"There's a small bathroom and laundry in the back and plenty of hot water."

"It feels like home already," Bridgette responded, as she noticed a large framed photograph on the front wall.

"That's an aerial view of our property. It was taken before we built the main house, but you can see the cabin clearly enough."

Bridgette took a couple of steps forward to study the photograph in more detail. The land mass of Monica's property was just as she had described it—a diamond shaped island surrounded by the Fraser River.

Bridgette pointed to a small bridge in the photo on the cabin side of the river and said, "You have a second bridge onto the property?"

"Yes, a footbridge. My husband... Clint, built it six years ago. The river's a lot narrower on this side and he decided it would be nice to offer folks who stayed in the cabin a quick way to get to the forest walking trails that surround us."

"I'll check it out later."

"The trail that we walked up continues down to the bridge and the river. You can't miss it."

Bridgette looked around the room again. "I plan on having a very relaxing week here."

"Well, unless you've got any other questions, I'll leave you to get settled."

Monica pointed to an old-fashioned wall phone, complete with crank handle and two chrome bells near the front door. "If you need anything, you can call me on that. Clint rigged it up last year. Just wind the crank handle a couple of times and it will ring."

Bridgette marveled at the device which looked in keeping with the rest of the decor. "So, it's connected to your house?"

Monica nodded. "Yes, but that's as far as it goes. Cell reception isn't great out here, and we wanted people staying to have a way of communicating with us without having to walk back to the house. We thought having something old was more in keeping with the cabin's theme than anything modern."

Bridgette nodded as she glanced around the cabin again. "It feels like I've stepped back in time."

"Well, you look tired, so unless there's anything else, I'll let you get some sleep."

Bridgette looked longingly at the bed. "A couple of hours should tide me over." She looked at her watch and then added, "I'll get up around five and head back into town to get some groceries and something for dinner."

Monica stepped out onto the porch and looked up at a darkening gray sky as the rain got heavier. "The weather forecast says the big storm is coming tomorrow, but maybe it will be here sooner than that. I best get going before I get soaked."

Bridgette said goodbye and then closed the door behind her. She closed her eyes and massaged the back of her neck, debating whether she would unpack now or later.

After opening her eyes again, she stared at the bed and murmured, "Later," and kicked off her boots.

Bridgette crawled up onto the bed and covered herself with a blanket. The bed was firmer than she expected, but she didn't care—she would have slept on the floor if she had to. After setting a timer on her phone to wake her in two hours, she closed her eyes.

Within seconds, she drifted off to sleep.

She dreamed of a cabin in the woods by a gentle flowing river.

She could hear a voice calling out her name and got up from a chair on the porch to investigate. After taking a few steps forward, she stopped to listen again. The voice was faint, like it was a long way away. She stood still and listened some more. It sounded like her partner, Levi Frost, but she couldn't be sure as the voice called out her name over and over. She felt cold and exposed, like someone was watching her.

She heard an enormous bang behind her and whipped around. The cabin was gone...

Levi Frost was getting ready to leave work when the call came through on his desk phone.

Delray was as concise as ever. "Got a minute?"

Frost had been with the Homicide unit less than six months, and while he was still learning the ropes, he was now reasonably attuned to the nuances of Delray's voice. He could easily pick his three main moods: frustration, anger, and happiness.

The tone in his voice suggested something different. Frost told his boss he would come straight away and checked his watch as he walked to Delray's office. It was close to 6 PM and he wondered why his boss wanted to see him at this hour of the day. Perhaps a new case?

The door was open and Frost could see Delray sitting behind his desk reading something on his computer screen.

As a courtesy he knocked once and said, "You wanted to see me, Chief?"

"Have a seat, Levi."

Delray waited until Frost was settled and then said, "I just had a call from Operations. Alex Hellyer has escaped."

Frost's mouth fell open. No words initially escaped and then he said, "What?"

"Apparently he jumped a guard."

"How did that happen?"

"I'm not sure of all the details yet, but apparently the guards were separated. He had a shiv and managed to overpower one of them while he was supposed to be taking a shower."

"But surely he was in shackles and handcuffs?"

"Apparently they take the handcuffs off prisoners when they shower but leave the shackles on."

Frost shook his head in disbelief. "Have they caught him yet?"

"No. He's been on the run for six hours."

"He could be anywhere by now."

"Every patrol cop in Vancouver is on the lookout for him. We're confident he'll be caught soon. We believe he's still driving the guard's car that he stole so hopefully he won't be too hard to find."

"So did he get a gun as well?"

Delray grimaced. "Yeah. He got the guns of both guards, in fact."

"We need to tell Bridgette."

"No. She needs a holiday."

"She might not be safe, Chief. You know what that psychopath is capable of."

"I rest easy in the knowledge she's two hours' drive from here camped up in the mountains. If we don't know where she is, he won't either. Besides, Hellyer will be focused on getting out of the city without being recaptured."

"I'd feel better if we contacted her."

Delray mulled it over for a moment. "Let's leave it to the morning. If he hasn't been recaptured by then we'll call her."

Frost spent another five minutes in Delray's office discussing the situation before his boss announced he was heading home. As Frost returned to his desk to process the news he became increasingly uneasy. Delray was down playing the significance of the escape—probably because he had been instructed to by his superiors. Knowing that Alex

Hellyer was now out roaming free sent a shiver down his spine.

He mulled over Delray's directive not to call Bridgette but he decided she needed to know. If the situation was reversed and a psychopath he had arrested had escaped, he would want to know. Over the next twenty minutes he tried calling her three times, but each call had gone through to voice mail. At 6.30 PM, he decided there was nothing more he could achieve in the office and packed up to head home.

He tried calling her number again as he walked towards the elevator and swore as his latest call also went through to voicemail. After pressing the elevator button to head down, Frost did something that was rare for him and composed a text message. Texting was a skill he had never really mastered and he kept his message to Bridgette brief.

'Call me ASAP.'

Alex Hellyer pulled the car to a gentle stop opposite an EasyPark in Gastown. He was still driving the car he had stolen from the guard earlier in the day. Careful not to speed, he had obeyed every road rule to avoid attracting the attention of any Vancouver cop. But he knew it was too risky to continue driving the guard's car. He was sure every cop in Vancouver had his physical description by now and the car's details as well.

He scanned both directions of Abbot Street looking for any sign of cops. The street looked quiet and nobody was paying him any attention, so he figured it was safe enough. He pulled the remaining cash out of his pocket and counted it—forty-six dollars. It had started out as more than double that amount when he had stolen it from the guards before escaping from the hospital. But a trip to a Walmart to buy clothes and a burger for lunch had eaten into his cash reserves. He figured he would spend another thirty dollars in a drugstore on some bandages for his bullet wound and some hair dye to change his blonde hair to something darker.

The math was simple, he needed more cash. Hellyer glanced up again to make sure no pedestrians were walking near his car while he unwrapped the two handguns he had stolen from the hospital guards. He picked up one of the guns and admired it—a Glock 22. He was not sure exactly what it was worth on the black market, but figured it should bring in at least five hundred dollars, maybe more. He had already been on a website on the Dark Web recommended by his hacker friend and had found a potential buyer. He had decided to only sell one of the guns and they had agreed to meet at seven that evening on the third floor of the EasyPark. Selling one gun would give him the extra cash he needed to get out of Vancouver.

Hellyer checked his appearance in the rear-view mirror. He planned to spend a night in a cheap motel, partially to sleep and partially to change his appearance. His blonde hair would be dark brown before he left the city. He focused on his eyes. They were light blue—the striking color due to an absence of melanin. But he barely noticed their color. All he saw was resolve. He allowed himself a smile as he thought back to his escape from the hospital. His weeks of planning had worked out almost better than he could have hoped for. His one regret was not killing the nurse and the guards. But he liked to take time when he disposed of people. Quick kills brought him no satisfaction, and there was too much risk that his escape would be discovered if he had stayed to do the job properly.

Out In The Cold

He looked up at the EasyPark again as he started the engine. He would dump the car several blocks away and then walk back. It was about two hours until he was due to meet the buyer. Plenty of time to scout the EasyPark and memorize its layout, security cameras and exit points. He hoped the deal would be quick and clean. He had his plans all laid out—glorious plans—months in the making. After the deal, there were two things left for him to do and then he would be out of Vancouver for good.

Thursday 6:29 PM

The dream lingered for Bridgette. After the cabin disappeared, she ran on through the forest. She sensed she was being chased but was too afraid to turn and look back. She could feel hot, dank breath on the back of her neck. She dodged and weaved as she ran deeper into the woods.

No matter which way she turned, or how fast she ran, the presence followed her. She screamed for help, but no sound escaped. She kept running—now hopelessly lost—but she still couldn't get away. A roaring sound pounded in her head. She looked back over her shoulder as she ran. The sound that started in her head was now all around her.

Bridgette jolted awake and stared wide-eyed at the rafters above her. She breathed in deeply to control her panic. The roaring sound continued. She cocked her head and realized the sound was heavy rain falling on the roof. She blinked several times, then recognizing the fire in the fireplace, remembered where she was. She cursed as she realized she had overslept and then started rubbing her eyes.

Out In The Cold

A few seconds passed and then she heard the wall phone ring. Bridgette muttered, "Coming," and got up off the bed. She pulled her shoulder-length, dark brown hair off her face and then picked up the handset. "Hello."

A young female voice greeted Bridgette. "Hi, is that Bridgette? Oh. My bad, of course it is. This is Amy, Monica's daughter, up at the house."

"Hi Amy, how can I help?"

"Mom asked me to call you to see if you'd like to come for dinner. She said you were planning on going back into the grocery store, but she doesn't think that's a good idea, seeing as how heavy it's raining."

Bridgette peered out through the cabin's window into the darkness. The rain was coming down in sheets. It had been years since she had seen rain this heavy and thought Monica's advice was wise.

Amy added, "Mom says the grocery store will close early tonight, anyway. And the roads are pretty slippery and dangerous."

"Well, thank you, Amy. That's a kind offer, but I don't want to impose."

"You wouldn't be imposing. And we don't have many people over, so this would be a treat for Mom and me."

Bridgette thought about the remaining two protein bars she had in her duffel bag, and realized if that was all she ate, she would be starving by morning.

"Thanks, Amy, that would be nice."

"Mom's cooking chicken and vegetable pie. It's my favorite—wait, you're not a vegetarian, are you?"

Bridgette let out a short laugh. "No, I'm not a vegetarian. I rarely eat read meat, but fish and chicken are fine."

"Good. If you look in the cupboard next to the kitchen

sink, you'll find a golf umbrella. It will save you from getting soaked on the walk to the house."

Bridgette peered out again at the raging storm and grimaced. "Thanks, Amy. I think I'm going to need it."

"We'll see you soon, Bridgette."

Bridgette yawned as she hung up the phone and then stretched as she stared at the coals in the fire. She would have preferred a quiet night on her own, but she was hungry and appreciated the Pooles' generosity in providing her with a home cooked meal.

After retrieving the golf umbrella, Bridgette stepped onto the porch. The roar of the rain was deafening, and she knew even with the umbrella that she was going to get wet. After sucking in a deep breath, she closed the door and set off down the path towards the house.

Alex Hellyer spent over an hour scouring the four-story EasyPark. With a baseball cap set low on his head to hide his face from the security cameras, he had walked the length and breadth of each floor of the facility. After committing to memory all exits and security cameras, he had formed a plan in his mind. No plan was foolproof—they all involved some risk—but he was happy enough.

The dialog with the buyer on the dark web had been brief. He got the sense this was not the first gun the buyer had bought, and perhaps not even the first time he had used the EasyPark for a trade.

After his reconnaissance, he understood why the location had been chosen. There were only two security cameras on each floor—one at either end. The buyer had assumed he had a car and had instructed him to park in the middle of level three. It was far enough from each camera that they would only capture a grainy image at best.

He was told to stay in his car and wait for the buyer who would park alongside. Neither party would need to leave their vehicle. Hellyer approved of the location. The parking lot worked in all weather conditions—snow, rain or heat. And it provided a certain level of security—like doing a drug trade in a bar.

He had only seen two patrons returning to their cars during the previous hour, but he figured that was enough of a deterrent. The venue would encourage a quick transaction—buyer and seller motivated to complete the deal without too much haggling, and be on their way.

Hellyer reviewed the EasyPark layout in his mind as he walked back along level three. He had checked every car on each floor. He had seen no one sitting in a car as a lookout, nor any other sign he was walking into a trap. Hellyer concluded the buyer was most likely operating alone. If he had done this before, he figured the deal would be quick—in and out in under five minutes. He wondered if the buyer operated with stolen plates on his car. He would have if the roles been reversed.

Hellyer stopped in front of a late model white Toyota sedan that was parked nose into the wall. He looked left and right. It was almost in the middle of level three and had vacant spots on either side. It was perfect for his purposes and he leaned against the trunk as if he owned the vehicle.

He checked the time on the phone he had stolen from the guard. It now had a fresh SIM card so he couldn't be tracked, but it had proven useful for much more than just telling the time. The buyer was late. He debated using the smartphone to access the dark web again to see if there were any messages for him, but decided against it. Until he left the EasyPark he needed to keep all his senses alert to what was happening around him and staring down at a phone screen only made him vulnerable.

Hellyer let out a calming breath. Criminals weren't known for their punctuality, and he was not too concerned. He had been a drug dealer prior to his incarceration and knew the value of patience to get what you wanted.

Staring off into space, he went over the plan one more time. He played out each scenario he could think of—from the very best to the very worst of outcomes. He had a plan to cover what he would do if the car showed up with more than just a driver. He had another if the buyer arrived on foot rather than in a car. And he had one for what he would do if an innocent bystander returned during the middle of the transaction. He nodded to himself—satisfied he had his bases covered. All that was left to do was wait… something he was very good at.

Thursday 6:48 PM

Bridgette was thankful for her coat as she ran to the Pooles' house. The umbrella offered little protection from the storm and her coat was sodden by the time she reached the front porch.

She heard yelling coming from inside as she closed her umbrella and stepped back from the front door. It was clear mother and daughter were arguing, but it was hard to tell what about over the roar of the rain on the porch roof. The argument continued for another minute before she heard a door slam.

Bridgette was unsure what to do. Knocking now would send a signal she had heard the exchange. And returning to the cabin would mean having to come up with an excuse later, and besides, she was hungry. In the end, she waited two minutes before knocking.

Monica appeared soon after, looking slightly exasperated. She opened the door and said with a forced smile, "Hi Bridgette, come on in."

Bridgette pretended she had heard nothing. "Thanks for the invitation, Monica. I really appreciate it."

Before entering the house, she removed her coat saying, "I'll just leave this here on the porch."

As she followed Monica inside, her host said, "Can you believe this weather?"

"I saw the forecast before I left the city, but I had no idea it would be this bad."

"I don't think anyone did."

They walked down a small hallway through to the kitchen where preparation for the evening meal was in full swing. The kitchen was modern, with a granite counter-top and a white-tiled splash back. It connected to an open plan dining and living area. There were two gray sofas set around a cozy fireplace and lots of pictures of family on the walls, which gave the house a homely feel.

As Bridgette sat down on a bar stool next to the kitchen's island bench, she said, "You have a lovely home, Monica."

"Thanks. It's comfortable and I couldn't imagine living anywhere else." Monica put an apron on and then added, "I'm really glad you decided to join us. I think the roads would have been treacherous tonight."

"I'm sure you're right." Bridgette found the smell of the chicken and vegetable pie baking in the oven distracting. As her mouth watered, she added, "This smells amazing."

Before Monica could reply, a tall, slim girl appeared in the entrance to the kitchen. She was wearing faded jeans, a khaki-colored woolen sweater, and had her hair swept back off her freckled face in a ponytail. Bridgette guessed she was about fourteen years old and noticed she had high cheekbones similar to Monica.

Ignoring the red rings around the girl's eyes, which were

telltale signs she had been crying, Bridgette smiled and said, "Hi, you must be Amy. I'm Bridgette."

Amy gave a bashful smile. "Hi. Did you get wet?"

Bridgette laughed. "A little. But the golf umbrella really helped."

Amy's attention was drawn to the food her mother was preparing as she walked into the kitchen.

Monica looked up at the wall clock and then asked, "How's the homework coming along, Amy?"

Leaning her long frame across the Island bench to examine an apple tart her mother was making, Amy replied absently, "It's almost done."

"We've got about fifteen minutes until we dish up. How about you go finish it?"

Amy scowled at her mother and left the room.

Monica waited until her daughter had disappeared down the hallway. "She's a good kid and very smart. But sometimes she's a bit lazy about homework. If you'd arrived a couple of minutes earlier, you would have heard us having a raging row about it."

Bridgette smiled. "I seem to recall I struggled with homework when I was her age as well." She watched as Monica cut the excess pastry off the apple tart and added, "Thanks again for the invite. I was down to my last two protein bars, and this looks awesome."

Monica said, "We're glad you could join us, Bridgette," as she used a fork to press down the pastry edges.

Monica stepped back to look at the tart and then declared, "I think it's ready for the oven."

Bridgette watched as Monica used oven mitts to remove the chicken pie and then replace it with the tart.

After placing the pie on the bench, Monica said, "This is going to be really hot. I think we'll give it ten minutes to cool. I normally don't drink during the week, but this storm has made me edgy. I'm going to have a glass of Australian Riesling—do you want to join me?"

Bridgette rarely drank on account of her training schedule. But with no plans for hitting the gym this week, she decided the invitation was one she couldn't pass up. "Sure. I've never had an Australian Riesling, so that would be nice."

While Monica poured the wine, she said, "You said you do shift work. What kind of work do you do?"

"I'm a police officer—a detective, actually."

"Really? That's what Amy wants to do when she grows up."

"I'd be happy to answer any questions she may have, if you like."

Monica took a sip of wine. "As long as you don't sugarcoat it. My brother used to be on the force. I know it can be dangerous."

"Sure. I won't hold back—it's the kind of job you need to go into with your eyes wide open."

"I presume you like it?"

"The work itself is very challenging—which I love. But the politics can be irritating."

Monica nodded. "You get that in most places. Selfish people with egos trying to prove they're better than everyone else."

She took another sip of wine and then asked, "What do you investigate?"

"Murder cases mostly, and some missing persons."

"That's right in the deep end."

"No two days are ever the same."

Monica walked across to the window and peered out. "I

can't believe this storm. You made a good call not to drive in this."

"You don't get many storms like this?"

"Never. I'm actually worried about flooding."

"But you're up on a rise. Surely you're safe here?"

"I'm sure the house and cabin will be safe, but it's the bridge I'm worried about. If the river rises and the bridge goes under, we'll be cut off."

"I have a girlfriend who is planning on coming out for a couple of days later in the week. Maybe I should call and warn her?"

"That might be wise. Excuse me for asking, but is she your partner?"

"No, she's just a friend."

"Well, if she makes the trip, I have a portable bed we can set up for her."

"Thanks, that's very kind." Bridgette paused and then added, "So, I take it, it's just you and Amy living here?"

Monica nodded as she turned back from the window. "Yes, it's just the two of us now, since my husband's death."

"I'm sorry for your loss."

"Thanks. We seem to cope okay most of the time, but if we're flooded in… that will be a whole new ballgame."

"I can't imagine how hard that must have been for you."

Monica nodded. "It's all still a bit raw. Clint's motorcycle accident was nine months ago, but it seems like only yesterday."

"I can't imagine how hard that must be."

"When I got the call to say he had been hit by a car, I didn't know what I would do. Amy came to the hospital with me and we never left his bedside. He had a major brain injury… he lasted five days before he finally passed."

"I guess that five days gave you and Amy a little time to prepare."

Monica glanced at the open doorway that lead to the hall and lowered her voice a little as she responded, "Clint and I had a fight the morning he died. It was over something trivial, but that's the last memory Amy has of her father and me being together. We never fought much, but she blames me for the accident even though we talked by phone after he got to work and patched things up."

Bridgette wasn't sure what to say as she saw Monica's eyes well up with tears. "I know this may sound trite, but I'm sure she'll come around in time."

Monica replied, "I hope you're right." She moved back from the window and sat on a stool next to Bridgette. "So, what do you do when you're not working?"

"I spend a lot of time in the gym. That's where most of my friendship group is."

"Friends are important. Sometimes as important as family."

Bridgette sipped her wine. "I don't have much family anymore. My mother and father have both passed, and so has the aunt who raised me."

"I'm sorry to hear that. It's good that you have a circle of friends then."

"I'm lucky that way, I guess."

Monica stared off into space. "It's funny…"

"What…?"

"I knew Clint from high school. We were just friends and nothing more. And we hadn't seen each other in years when we bumped into each other in Hope one evening. Both of us had just come out of bad relationships when we reconnected. Neither of us were interested in another relationship and we were just friends for over two years."

"What changed?"

Monica laughed. "One of my best friends was getting married, and I needed a date for the wedding. I didn't want to give anyone the wrong idea, so I asked Clint. I'm not sure what happened—Clint was as shocked as I was. But before we knew it, we'd fallen madly in love and were married less than twelve months later. And then Amy came along."

"She's a credit to you."

"She's a handful. But she keeps me young. I couldn't imagine life without her." She paused and then asked, "And what about you? Do you want kids?"

"One day. But I need to find the right guy first." Bridgette smiled and then added, "But, so far, he's eluded me."

"Well, you're a pretty girl and living in the city, I'm sure you get asked out on plenty of dates."

"I'm in no rush and right now I'm concentrating on my career."

Monica raised an eyebrow. "Cupid can strike at any time. Remember that."

Before Bridgette could respond, Amy burst into the kitchen. "Mom, the Internet's down."

Monica frowned. "What do you mean?"

Amy handed her mother her smart phone and said, "Look. No signal."

Monica examined the screen for a moment and then picked up her own phone from the bench. After checking its signal, she frowned and said, "You're right, we've got no cell signal."

Bridgette pulled her phone out of her pocket. "What carrier are you with? Maybe it's the carrier that's down."

"We're with Bell," said Amy.

Ignoring her four missed call messages, Bridgette replied, "I'm with Telus," and examined her screen. The signal bars she normally saw in the top right-hand corner had disappeared. She grimaced. "I don't have a signal either, so it's not the carrier."

Amy looked at her mother. "Maybe a phone tower got hit in the storm."

"You don't have a fixed line Internet connection?" asked Bridgette.

Monica replied, "No. Clint got prices for it some time back. But the cost of getting a cable across the river for just one house was prohibitive. We have a good deal on mobile broadband and that's all we've ever needed for phone and Internet."

Amy frowned. "So until this is fixed, we're cut off?"

Monica looked up from her phone. "It looks that way."

Alex Hellyer watched as a late-model, black Ford F150 pickup truck drove slowly along the third floor of the Easy-Park. Pretending to be cold, he kept his hands in his jacket pockets with his right hand firmly gripping the Glock. The tint on the windows made it hard for him to make out any of the driver's facial features. But as the truck crawled forward, Hellyer had no doubt this was the buyer.

Hellyer continued to lean on the trunk of the Toyota as the truck pulled to a stop next to him. The buyer kept the motor running as he lowered his driver's side window.

They studied each other for a moment. Hellyer guessed the man was in his early twenties. He had shaggy, light-brown hair and a pencil-thin mustache. The man looked inexperienced. Hellyer figured it was unlikely this was the same person he had communicated with on the dark web.

Hellyer could see the man's Adam's apple bob up and down as he swallowed.

Finally, the man managed, "Are you John?"

Hellyer remained relaxed and even managed a slight grin as he responded, "Yeah, I'm John."

"Is that your car?"

Without taking his eyes off the buyer, Hellyer shook his head. "I chose to walk."

The man frowned. "You were supposed to come by car."

Hellyer shrugged. "Change of plan. I have the gun. Do you want to see it?"

The man scanned left and right again and then said, "Let me pull in."

Hellyer waited until the truck rolled into the parking bay next to the Toyota and then walked around to the driver's door.

The man wound down his window a little more and said, "OK, let's see what you got."

Hellyer slowly removed his left hand from his coat and held the gun up to the open window. "It's not loaded."

The man took the gun and then switched on his interior cabin light. Hellyer watched as he deftly removed the magazine and then lifted a clip on the side of the weapon to remove the Glock's slider. After examining the weapon for a few moments, he reassembled it and dry fired it twice.

He murmured, "Hardly ever been fired," as he placed the gun on the passenger seat on top of a black cloth.

Hellyer heard the soft clink of metal hitting metal and assumed the buyer had a weapon of his own hidden beneath the cloth. He was neither surprised nor alarmed. He, too, would have brought a gun for security if the roles had been reversed, but he would have stuck it under the dashboard between his legs for easier access.

The man removed a folded wad of cash from his jacket pocket and held it up between his middle and index fingers. "Five hundred?"

Hellyer leaned in and snarled, "We had a deal—seven fifty."

The man shook his head as his Adam's apple bobbed up and down again. "That's all I'm allowed to offer you. Take it or leave it."

Hellyer whipped his right hand out of his pocket and stuck the other Glock through the open window.

As the man recoiled, Hellyer said, "You're not listening and this one *is* loaded. We had a deal. I came with the gun, so you need to give me seven-hundred-and-fifty dollars."

The man's eyes widened. He raised his hands and said, "Hey, man. I'm just the pickup and delivery guy. That's all I'm authorized to give you. This isn't even my truck."

"Switch the engine off now!"

The driver obliged and then responded, "OK, let's all relax here."

"Get out of the truck!"

"Hey, man, what are you doing? This is crazy! I…"

Hellyer shoved the gun hard into the man's cheek. "Get out of the truck now. I'm not going to repeat myself."

"Okay, okay… Just relax!"

Hellyer stepped back three paces and kept the Glock trained on the man as he got out of the truck.

"Take your jacket off and put it on the ground in front of you."

The man pleaded, "Please, man, don't hurt me. I'm just trying to get by…"

"Where's your wallet?

"In my back pocket."

"Take it out slowly and put it on top of the jacket."

The man obeyed. As he dropped his wallet on the jacket he said, "I don't want any trouble here. Like I said, I'm just a courier. Take the truck if you want—it's not mine, anyway."

Hellyer waved the Glock. "Move to the back of the truck."

The man kept his arms raised and pleaded, "Please don't hurt me. I've got a wife and kid."

Hellyer followed the man around to the back of the F150. Keeping a space of about six feet between them, he kept his gun pointed at the man's forehead as he said, "I can't afford to leave you here, just in case you contact someone."

"Please man, I'll be cool. I won't say anything. I'll just walk away."

Hellyer motioned with his gun, "Open the tailgate. You're coming with me."

The man's Adam's apple bobbed again as he responded, "Okay, okay, please don't hurt me."

Hellyer watched as the man unlatched and lowered the tailgate.

"Get in."

The man hesitated as he looked at the F150's hard fiberglass cargo cover.

Hellyer pointed to the cargo hold that was about eighteen inches high and said, "Last chance. Get in."

The man went to protest again and Hellyer shoved the gun up under the man's jaw near his left ear. "You wouldn't be the first asshole I've killed, so don't try my patience."

The man turned white as he sat on the tailgate and swung his legs up.

"Move in under the cover—all the way!"

The man protested as he inched back, "There's no air in here, I could suffocate."

As he pointed the gun at the man's temple, Hellyer replied, "I doubt that. You'd still need to be breathing," and pulled the trigger.

He watched the man's body instantly go limp, as the sonic boom of the gun's discharge reverberated around the concrete walls.

Hellyer lowered his gun and without looking around pushed the body further into the cargo hold and then raised the tailgate. After collecting the man's coat and wallet, he got into the truck and started the engine. Hellyer lifted the cloth on the passenger seat and wasn't surprised when he found it concealed a pistol, this time a Sig Sauer P220. Hellyer turned and looked into the tiny cargo hold behind the two seats. Mounted on the rear firewall was something a bit longer than a baseball bat and covered in a black cloth. Hellyer let out a low whistle as he lifted the cloth and stared at a hunting rifle complete with telescopic sights. He preferred handguns and didn't think he would have need of such a weapon, but it was always good to have options. Hellyer dropped the cloth back in place and put the truck in gear.

As he drove out of the EasyPark, he mentally went through the list of things he still needed to do before he left Vancouver. The list now included disposing of a body. He figured another few hours would be all he would need.

Thursday 9:22 PM

Despite the roar of the storm outside, Bridgette enjoyed the dinner. She found the Pooles to be good company even though Amy was preoccupied with checking her cell phone for a signal.

At the end of the meal Bridgette sat back. "Thanks Monica, that was delicious."

"You're welcome," said Monica as she took a sip of wine. "I can give you the recipe if you like?"

"That would be great."

"Do you cook much?"

Bridgette shook her head. "It's only me and because I work crazy hours, it's hard. But when I do cook, I like to try something new. This pie is definitely something I want to try."

Without looking up from her phone, Amy said, "Still no signal, Mom."

"I don't expect it to be back any time soon, Amy. I'm just about to clean up. Do you want to help, or would you rather do your homework?"

Amy blurted out, "Homework," as she rose from the table.

Bridgette couldn't hide her smile as she watched the teenager escape down the hallway towards her bedroom. Monica shook her head and raised an eyebrow as she mumbled, "Teenagers."

When Monica stood up to clear the table, Bridgette said, "Let me give you a hand."

"Thanks, Bridgette. I'd like to get the dishwasher on as soon as possible, just in case we lose power as well."

"Is that likely?"

"I have no idea. But if a storm like this can take out our cell phones, then I guess it can take out our power as well."

After they had packed the dishwasher, Monica said, "I'm really sorry, we've ruined your holiday."

Bridgette waved her off. "It's just a storm and my cabin is warm and dry."

"I'm not sure you'll sleep with the roar of this rain."

Bridgette laughed. "I've only had two hours' sleep in about the last forty hours. Right now I think I could sleep through world war three."

Monica moved across to the window and peered through the curtains again. "I can't believe it. This storm is relentless."

"Maybe we should turn the TV on and see if there are any news updates on what's happening?"

"Good idea, but I think I'd like to check the bridge first."

"You're worried about flooding?"

Monica nodded. "I think I'll sleep better knowing what we're up against. Also, I'd like to know what this means for you. I'll only be gone a few minutes. Why don't you pour yourself another glass of wine and relax on the sofa until I get back?"

"Would you like me to come with you? It might not be wise to be out there on your own."

"I don't want to put you out. You're a guest after all."

"It's no problem. I think I'd like to see for myself what we're up against, too."

Bridgette could see relief on Monica's face as she replied, "Thanks, Bridgette. I'd appreciate it. Give me a minute and I'll go let Amy know what we're up to and then I'll grab my coat."

Alex Hellyer opened the door to the motel room. After switching the light on, he paused for a moment to survey the dingy interior. The overhead light didn't work and the two bed lamps on the wall above the bed emitted a dim glow that left the room in shadows. The double bed was covered in a brown quilt with threadbare gold edging that may have been fashionable back in the seventies. In the gloom, Hellyer could see the teak bedside tables were scarred from years of use like everything else in the room. There was a matching wardrobe and a single chair to complete the decor.

Hellyer almost smiled. It was perfect for his needs. The room had cost him eighty-dollars cash; sixty for the room itself and twenty to the night clerk for not registering his attendance.

After closing the door behind him, he locked it then slid the safety bolt into place. He dropped the two guns on the bed along with a burger he had bought that was still in its brown bag.

Hellyer entered the bathroom. He ignored the cracks in the floral tiles on the walls and the smell of mold, and focused on the bathroom's small frosted window.

He figured it was big enough to squeeze through if he removed the sliding pane. After undoing the latch, he tried sliding the pane back a fraction, but it refused to budge. He checked for any sign of screws or welds holding the frame in position, but couldn't see any. This time, he pushed harder on the frame and the window moved a fraction.

Thirty seconds later, the rusted sliding pane yielded and came out of its frame. He placed it on the floor in the shower cubicle and then gingerly stood on the edges of the toilet seat and peered out through the window opening. He could see a narrow walkway covered in weeds about twelve feet below. Hellyer looked left and right. He hated sleeping in any building that only had one exit. Although the opening was small, he was confident he could squeeze through it in a hurry if he needed to escape. He was not expecting trouble tonight, but he always had an exit plan.

Hellyer walked back into the main room and peered out through the front curtain into the motel's parking lot. The motel was a two storey U-shape design reminiscent of the seventies. He had insisted on a ground floor room but had deliberately parked his truck on the other side of the complex as a precaution. The motel was about half full that evening, and he spent some time studying each car and motel room in his vision.

Satisfied that he was not being watched, he glanced at his truck again. He thought about the man he had killed less than two hours ago. He would have preferred to have gotten his money and simply walked away. But there was no way he was letting that young punk get the better of him. On his way out of the city he had cruised past several lanes between buildings before spotting one with a suitable dumpster and no security cameras.

He felt no remorse as he disposed of the body. Killing the buyer was simply solving a problem; like driving to a grocery store to pick up milk. He knew there was a risk in not abandoning the truck immediately, but he figured it was small. It was unlikely the buyer would be reported missing before tomorrow, and even more unlikely that whoever he was working for would report his truck as stolen.

Hellyer moved back from the window and pulled the burger out of its paper bag. He took a bite and reflected on his nine years in prison as he chewed on the bland mix of beef patty, mustard and bread. The brutal attack by a fellow prisoner in the shower block on his second night in the facility had proven fortuitous.

After spending several days in a coma, he had hatched a plan to use the incident to his advantage. Concealing his recovery, he continued to feign symptoms of paralysis and brain damage. Closely watched by the doctors for months, he eventually convinced them his injuries were genuine and spent the rest of his jail term in the infirmary away from the general prison population. Although a drug dealer before his conviction, he found it ironic that they had sentenced him to prison for a murder he hadn't committed.

Hellyer swallowed another mouthful of hamburger and placed the rest of the inedible meal back in its bag.

Tonight's murder took his body count to seven, but he didn't consider himself a serial killer. Three murders had been carefully planned revenge attacks—the others were just people who got in his way or threatened his business. He lay down on the lumpy bed and examined the smartphone he had stolen from the guard.

The man they had found him guilty of murdering was

also a drug dealer, a competitor who had disappeared and was presumed murdered. When the police searched his house after a tip off and found a knife with the missing man's blood on it, Hellyer realized he had been framed.

As he twisted the device around in his hands, he reflected on how powerful smartphones had become. After bribing a nurse to smuggle in a smartphone for him to use, he had spent almost every night of his nine years in the infirmary searching the Internet for any sign the other dealer was still alive. His need for revenge overshadowed his desire for freedom when he eventually discovered the dealer's new identity and location. Rather than immediately arranging for the man's location to be reported to the police to gain his freedom, he took his time and arranged for the man's murder and the discovery of his body. All from inside a prison, and all from a device similar to the one he now held in his hand.

Hellyer let out a sigh and punched in a phone number from memory. He held the device up to his ear and waited for his call to be connected.

A woman with a mature voice answered with a guarded, "Hello."

"Hi, Mom, it's me."

There was silence on the phone for a moment. Hellyer thought he could hear his mother sobbing before she replied, "Are you alright? I've been watching the news reports on the TV."

"I'm fine, Mom."

"Where are you?"

"Somewhere safe. I can't tell you, because someone might be listening to this call."

"When am I going to see you?"

"I'm not sure. I have to go away for a while. But when I get set up again, I'll come for you. I promise."

Hellyer could hear more sobbing before his mother said, "You're all I've got, Alex. After you were framed and sent to prison, I thought I'd lost you forever. And to think that I might lose you again, it breaks my heart."

Hellyer stared up at the ceiling for a moment. "If I could change things, Mom, I would. But I can't."

"You didn't hurt the guards, Alex. Or the nurse. That was good."

"No, Mom. You know I never want to hurt anyone. I just wanted to get away. I didn't want to go back to prison again. If it wasn't for those stupid cops meddling with matters that didn't concern them…"

"I know, dear. It's so unfair."

There was more silence before Hellyer said, "I love you, Mom. Promise me you'll never forget that."

"I won't, Alex. And I love you too."

"When I'm safe, I'll call again. But it might be a while."

Hellyer could hear his mother trying to mumble something through her tears.

In a firm voice he said, "I'll call you as soon as I get settled," and then disconnected.

Hellyer sighed then opened the Google maps application on the phone. There was one more person he needed to visit before he left town. He knew where they lived but he required a route that avoided major roads. He was confident that if he stuck to side streets, he could reach his destination in twenty minutes without being discovered by the Vancouver cops.

He studied the map for a few minutes until satisfied he had a safe route committed to memory.

Hellyer got up off the bed and grabbed the rickety

wooden chair. After carrying it over to the motel door, he wedged it underneath the handle. It wouldn't stop anyone getting in, but that was not the point. Nobody could get in without making a lot of noise and he would be awake with guns pointed at them as a greeting.

Satisfied that the room was now secure, he moved back to the bed. After getting comfortable, he pulled a stocky knife out of his pocket and ran his thumb across a razor-sharp blade that was barely two inches long.

He closed his eyes and allowed himself to visualize tomorrow's meeting. His expectations were high as he murmured, "We have a lot to talk about."

Bridgette and Monica walked side-by-side under the cover of the golf umbrella. Only seconds after they had left the shelter of the house, Bridgette's boots and the lower half of her jeans were soaked through from the driving rain.

To be heard over the rain, Monica yelled, "This is worse than I expected. Let's just go to the jetty. We can see the bridge and everything from there and we won't have to walk so far."

Bridgette responded with a thumbs up and then zipped her coat up higher to keep out the rain.

After another minute of walking, Monica said, "Just down through here."

She put her hand out in front of Bridgette as they emerged from the trees and shouted, "We have to be careful here. The bank is high above the waterline, but it's slippery and we don't want to fall in."

They came to a stop about three feet from the bank's edge. Monica pointed her flashlight over the edge and played the beam across the swirling torrent of water about twelve feet below.

Despite the driving rain, Bridgette could clearly see the river was full of sticks and branches and other debris that had washed down from upstream.

Monica exclaimed, "I can't believe it's already risen so much, and so fast!"

"The forecast said it was going to be bad."

Monica nodded and then shouted, "Let's check the jetty and then get out of this. We're going to be soaked to the skin if we stay out here any longer."

Bridgette followed Monica along the river bank until they reached the jetty. Monica pointed her torch onto the rustic timber platform. It was about twenty feet long and made of hardwood that she imagined could have been railway ties in a previous life. The jetty was supported by heavy wooden pylons with a wooden ladder at the end which Bridgette presumed led down to the waterline.

Monica grabbed the railing on the jetty and yelled, "Hold on and walk with me. We'll get a better view of the river upstream from out there."

Bridgette followed her host's lead and gripped the railing. With slow and steady steps she followed Monica out onto the slippery platform. When they reached the end, Monica pointed the beam of the flashlight upstream. She played the light from left to right across the river about fifty yards in front of her and said, "That's where the car bridge is. My guess is it's currently under about a foot of water."

"So there's no other way off the island?"

"Not in a car at least." Monica played the flashlight across the water further up the river and added, "Your cabin is about two hundred yards further up. If you keep going, you will come to the footbridge."

"Will it be underwater too?"

"No, it's set much higher above the waterline."

Monica focused the beam on a small tree that was being propelled down the river by the force of the current. "I think it's going to be days before we can drive off the island."

Bridgette shivered as she contemplated the gravity of her host's words. She stared at the river, finding it hard to comprehend that she had driven across the bridge just a few hours earlier. Monica swung the torch around to her right. The natural lagoon where the two branches of the river rejoined was now a swollen mass of churning water.

She yelled, "The highway bridge is a little further downriver, but it's hard to see in this driving rain. If this water keeps rising, it might go under as well."

Monica shone the flashlight down over the edge of the jetty. "This ladder leads down to a landing, but it's under water too."

She swung the beam of the flashlight further to her right and played it across a small wooden boat that was covered in a tarpaulin and tethered to one of the jetty's pylons.

Bridgette remarked. "I didn't know you owned a boat?"

Monica was going hoarse from yelling over the noise of the storm. "It was Clint's. When I heard about the storm, I came down and covered it. With all this rain, I'm surprised it hasn't sunk… yet."

Monica leaned down to check the tension on the tether rope. "It looks like it's going to hold."

She played the beam of the flashlight out across the junction of the river one more time.

They stood for a few seconds, each lost in their thoughts, trying to fathom the power of the storm and how it had turned the once peaceful river into an angry and unrestrained monster.

Finally, Monica said, "I'm worried about what's going to happen if the rain doesn't stop soon. This water is rising way too fast. Let's head back and see if there are any updates on the late news."

Thursday 9:43 PM

Bridgette was cold and wet by the time they returned to the house. She was keen to head straight back to the cabin to sleep, but Monica insisted she come in for a cup of cocoa while they waited for the late TV news.

After removing her coat and leaving it in the mudroom, Bridgette stood close to the fire to dry her jeans out and did her best to stay awake. They watched a crime show on TV with the sound muted while they waited for the news bulletin. Monica regularly lapsed into periods of silence—her furrowed brow suggested she was in shock as she came to terms with the extent of the flooding.

Every few minutes, Monica would look up towards the ceiling as she listened to the rain. "It's not letting up is it, Bridgette."

Bridgette grimaced. "Not so far."

Amy wandered into the room for the first time since their return and asked, "Any late news yet, Mom?"

"Not yet, dear. But I think it's safe to assume you won't be going to school tomorrow."

Amy let out a little squeal of delight, which prompted her mother to add, "But that doesn't mean you get to stay up late, young lady."

Bridgette listened to the interchange between mother and daughter, with Amy pleading to be allowed to stay up longer seeing as tomorrow was no longer a school day. In the end, Monica compromised by telling her she could stay up and read only after she got into her pajamas and brushed her teeth.

Bridgette moved back a little from the fire as a delighted Amy walked back to her room.

"Getting hot?" asked Monica.

Bridgette half smiled as she sipped her cocoa. "My jeans are starting to steam."

"You'll dry out soon enough."

To keep the conversation off the storm, Bridgette asked, "So how long have you had the cabin up on Airbnb?"

"Only a few months. Before Clint passed I used to do part-time bookkeeping and accounts. But the bills have piled up and the insurance company hasn't paid out on Clint's life insurance."

"Are they allowed to do that?"

Monica grimaced. "Not really. According to my lawyer, it's a straightforward claim. But insurance companies seem to like to hold on to their money. I didn't want to go back to work full-time on account of Amy, so I need to keep it rented."

"Well, it must be nice to have another income stream."

Monica nodded. "Truth be told, I need the insurance payout. We're still not earning enough to cover the mortgage. I haven't told Amy anything, but it's not looking great."

"Well, let's hope your lawyer comes through for you."

"Here's hoping. It's times like these that I really miss Clint. He never let things like this worry him. He always seemed to find a silver lining, but I'm not wired that way."

Bridgette went to respond, but a news bulletin update flashed across the TV screen.

Monica turned up the volume and said, "OK, let's see what we're in for."

They were quiet while a solemn anchorwoman took eyewitness accounts from reporters in the field. They learned the source of the rain had been unseasonal weather conditions that would dump three months' worth of rain over large parts of British Columbia in the next forty-eight hours.

Monica despaired. "Three months' rain!"

They watched as the bulletin cut to a series of live news feeds of the Fraser Valley showing houses in low-lying areas already being inundated by water and farmers moving livestock to higher ground.

Monica shook her head. "This is awful."

They were quiet again while they watched the rest of the bulletin. A grim faced meteorologist warned they did not expect the storm to ease until sometime tomorrow, before adding that residents along the Fraser River should prepare for significant flooding.

Monica muted the TV sound. "It looks like we'll be cut off for days, Bridgette. I'm really sorry."

"Do you think there's any chance of the house or cabin being flooded?"

"I doubt it. When Clint bought the land, that was one of the first things he checked. The buildings are on the highest part of the island, which apparently has never flooded."

"Then we just make the best of it and wait it out."

Out In The Cold

Monica looked up at the roof as she listened to the rain. "I think it's going to be a long wait."

Bridgette yawned. "I think I'm going to head back to the cabin, Monica. I really need to get some sleep."

"Sorry, I keep forgetting you've only had a couple of hours in two days. You must be exhausted." Monica frowned and then added, "You have nothing for breakfast in the cabin. When you wake up, come up here and we'll fix you something. I know that would make Amy very happy."

Bridgette thanked Monica for her generosity and added, "The whole idea of coming up here was to relax and get my mind off work." She looked up at the roof with a sleepy smile and added, "So far, it's working a treat."

Monica picked up the TV remote and said, "I think we're done with the news for tonight."

Bridgette frowned as she saw a news flash on the screen just as Monica switched off the TV.

"Something wrong, Bridgette?"

"That news flash. It said a prisoner has escaped."

"That happens from time to time."

"But the reporter was out front of a hospital."

"You want me to turn it back on?"

"Would you mind?"

"No problem."

Bridgette willed the TV to turn on quickly, but the device still took its usual twenty seconds to power up again.

The reporter was just signing off as the picture and sound returned. Bridgette focused on the background before the vision cut back to the anchorwoman in the studio.

As the woman started the next story, Bridgette said, "That was definitely Saint Joseph's Hospital."

"In Vancouver?"

Bridgette nodded as she chewed her bottom lip.

Monica added, "I didn't think they had prisoners in a general hospital?"

"They don't unless they need special care or surgery."

Monica muted the TV. "Is this a case you're involved in?"

Bridgette stared at the TV screen. The image of the reporter standing out front of the hospital building was now etched in her mind. "My last case, in fact."

"You look pale."

"Sorry. It's a bit of a shock."

"Is this prisoner dangerous?"

Bridgette nodded.

Monica turned up the sound again. "Let's check the other channels. Maybe we can get some more information for you."

While Monica flicked through TV channels, Bridgette pulled out her smartphone. She grimaced as she saw the 'No Signal' message still displayed. She realized she had unread text messages and opened them in the hope someone may have sent her information about the escape. There were two texts from Renée and one from another girlfriend, all sent much earlier in the day to wish her a safe trip. The only other text had come from Levi Frost while she was asleep in the cabin. It read, 'Call me ASAP.'

Bridgette frowned and cycled through her missed calls. Three were from Levi and one from Renée, and they had all come in while she was asleep.

It was the text message from Levi that worried her the most. It had come in after his third phone call, almost as a reinforcement to call her. She had never known Frost to use text messaging, not even to his own mother. She opened up his text again and felt a shiver run down her spine as she reread the three-word message.

Thursday 9:51 PM

Levi Frost dropped his apartment keys in a bowl on his coffee table and slumped down on his couch. He checked the time on his watch. The half-hour walk he had planned to clear his head had turned into a two-hour trek around the inner city streets of Vancouver. In that time he had repeatedly tried calling Bridgette, but each call had gone to voicemail. Frost sighed and picked up his phone again.

After punching in a number, he began pacing his studio apartment while he waited for the call to be answered. He had never spoken to Renée Filipucci before, but he knew she was Bridgette's best friend. Frost was confident that if anyone knew of Bridgette's whereabouts or how to contact her, it would be Renée.

Voicemail answered the phone on the third ring.

'Hi you've called Renée. Please leave a message after the tone and I'll call you back as soon as I can.'

Frost left a brief message explaining who he was, and that it was important that she call him back as soon as possible.

He sat on the couch again and picked up his TV remote. While twirling it around in his hand and contemplated his next move, his phone buzzed.

Frost grabbed the phone. "This is Levi."

"I got a call from this number a moment ago. Who is this?"

"Hi Renée, it's Levi Frost. I'm a detective; Bridgette's partner, in fact."

"How did you get my number?"

"I rang your paper earlier and said it was important. Your boss gave me your number."

"So, why are you calling me now?"

"I've been trying to get a message to Bridgette all day, but she's not answering my calls. Have you spoken to her?"

"Not since this morning. Is she okay?"

"I'm not sure. Have you heard about the prisoner escape?"

"The prisoner who escaped from the hospital?"

"Yeah… his name is Alex Hellyer."

"That was the last case Bridgette worked on. I hadn't joined the dots."

"I'm trying to get word to her that he's on the run."

"Do you think he'll go after her?"

"I spoke to the psychologist we used on his case earlier today. She doesn't believe he will simply disappear—he'll want revenge."

"Bridgette was the one who shot him when he tried to escape, so… it makes sense that she's at the top of his list, I guess."

"I was hoping he would've been caught by now, but it appears he's slipped through the net."

There was silence for a moment before Renée

responded, "I know she was going to a cabin about two hours west of here. Somewhere near Hope."

"That's what she told me too. But she didn't give me an address."

"She didn't give me an address either, but there could be any number of reasons why she didn't call back. BC likes to turn her phone off when she's out of the city. And cell reception isn't that great up there, either."

"I was hoping you might have an address or another phone number."

"Sorry, no. Do you really think she's in danger? After all, if we don't know where she is, then this guy isn't likely to find her either."

"Hellyer may be a psychopath, but he's also very intelligent and cunning. When he was released from prison, the first thing he did was go after the detective who arrested him twelve years earlier."

"I remember Bridgette telling me about that. The detective was lucky to survive."

"Personally, I don't think she's safe anywhere until he's re-captured. I just wanted to get word to her. Can you think of anyone else she may have told?"

"No one comes to mind. Hope is only a two-hour drive from here. Can't we just drive up and warn her?"

"I checked the area—there are too many bed and breakfast places. Without more details on where she went, we could search for days and not find her."

"Well, that's not going to work."

"I know from experience that Bridgette can look after herself. But still... this is not the kind of guy you want stalking you."

"Now you've got me worried. My paper did a profile on Hellyer about a month ago. He's screwed up and very dangerous." There was a pause before Filipucci added, "I'll call all our common friends now to see if they know anymore, but I think it's a long shot."

"Thanks, I appreciate it."

"If I get something positive, I'll call you back, If I don't have any luck, why don't we meet at her apartment tomorrow morning? I have a key and she may have left a clue as to where she was headed."

"Sounds good. She may already know, and this might all be an overreaction, but I'd rather be safe than sorry."

"BC's apartment is on my way to work. If I don't have any luck with her friends tonight, I'll text you. I can meet you there at eight o'clock in the morning if you like?"

"Thanks Renée. If I don't hear from you later, I'll see you at eight."

Bridgette listened to the roar of the rain on the cabin's tin roof as she lay in bed. Even though the cabin was warm and dry, she felt uneasy. She and Monica had trawled the late TV news bulletins until well after eleven for further updates on the prisoner escape, but every bulletin was focused on the storm and the flooding.

In the semi-darkness, she watched the shadows from the fire dance across the walls of the cabin. She picked up her phone hoping for a signal, and chewed her lip as she read the all too familiar 'No Service' sign on her screen.

With two deft moves, she brought up Levi Frost's 'Call me ASAP' text message and stared at the screen. Why had he wanted her to call him straight away? Surely it had to be related to Hellyer's escape? She put the phone down and played the few short words from the news reporter standing outside of Saint Joseph's hospital back over in her mind.

The prisoner who escaped had to be Alex Hellyer. It was too much of a coincidence for it to be anyone else. She knew he was a meticulous planner. Leaving his escape until the day before he was due to be transported back to prison made sense. He would be stronger and would have as much time as possible to ensure his escape plan was foolproof. She wondered how he had pulled it off, and then wondered where he was now. Was he still in Vancouver? Had he been recaptured?

Bridgette tried to think positively. No one knew her exact location, not even Renée Filipucci. But her gut tightened as she thought back to how Hellyer had immediately gone after Ron Burns after his release from prison last time. Burns was the detective who had arrested Hellyer years earlier. But it didn't matter to Hellyer that the detective had long since retired. The irony was not lost on Bridgette that Burns had tried hiding out in a cabin two hours north of Vancouver, but Hellyer had still found him.

Bridgette got out of bed and walked to the front door. She slid the slide bolt into place, and frowned as she jiggled the door to test its security. She picked up a chair and wedged it securely under the door handle and then went back to bed.

After pulling the blankets up under her chin, she stared into the fire, reminding herself not to panic. Despite her tiredness, she knew sleep would not come easily. Knowing the only man in the world who wanted her dead was now on the run was turning her holiday into a nightmare.

Friday 7:01 AM

Alex Hellyer sat in the black F150 pickup truck on Ackroyd Road studying the three-storey brick and timber apartment block across the street. The bitch cop lived in a middle-class area of Richmond, about twenty minutes from the city. The streets were leafy and the crime rate was low, but he hoped to add to the crime stats for the area later that morning. He drummed his fingers on the dashboard while he watched the apartment. He figured he would need to find an alternate vehicle before he left the city, but for now, he was satisfied that the pouring rain was providing him with sufficient cover. He had woken early and left the motel shortly before five am. The drive along the route to Richmond he had marked out the night before had been without incident. The pouring rain had reduced everyone's visibility, and the single cop car he had driven past had ignored him.

During his time in the prison infirmary he had built-up a string of contacts from the dark web using the smart phone he had smuggled in. One contact had proven to be exceptional at hacking computers and locating people.

Hellyer likened him to an online private investigator who, for a fee of five-hundred dollars, guaranteed he could provide the address and phone number of almost anyone living in Canada or the USA who wasn't homeless.

Hellyer had paid for the service with the credit card he had stolen from the gun dealer. And now, as he sat opposite the apartment block in Richmond, he was confident the hacker had given him the right address.

The apartment block was typical of many in the area. Framed by trees on its left and right, the ground floor was only partially enclosed and used as parking bays for residents. There was no security, and Hellyer had walked in earlier to look for his target's car. The hacker had informed him she lived in apartment 309, but the allotted bay was empty. He knew from her social media posts the cop drove a '66 Mustang fastback. A distinctive car which should have been easy to spot.

When he couldn't locate the car, he wondered if she was working a night shift. If that was the case, she should be home soon. Disappointed but not defeated, he had driven further up Ackroyd Road until he found a diner that opened early. After a hearty breakfast of sausages, bacon and eggs, which he figured would be his last meal before he left Vancouver, he had driven back to wait for her return.

He slipped his right hand into the pocket of his trousers while he focused on the top floor of the apartment block. He found it difficult to breathe as he caressed the blade of his two-inch knife. His anticipation of what he had planned for her was palpable. He closed his eyes and visualized the shock on her face as she saw him standing in her apartment. With nowhere to run, it would be a sweet reunion. A moment in time where he would be in complete control. He visualized her on the floor in her bedroom, begging for her life. A diesel truck broke his concentration as it drove by.

Hellyer swore and opened his eyes. It was time to get moving. He picked up two small Allen keys from the truck's ashtray. The tiny L-shaped metal tools were no thicker than a matchstick and had been purchased along with a metal file from a Walmart the previous day. He held them up, marveling at his handiwork in filing them down. Just under an hour's work had transformed them into instruments that were now ideal for picking locks.

He hadn't picked a lock in ten years, but he was confident he hadn't lost his touch. A bit like learning to ride a bike really; once you'd mastered it, you never forgot. He placed the two picks in the pocket of his jacket and then examined his outfit. He was still wearing the guard's uniform from yesterday. The uniform was now devoid of any patches and emblems that identified the wearer as a prison guard. Although removing the patches had left some marks, he was satisfied he could pass as a delivery driver at a casual glance.

Hellyer leaned across and picked up a cardboard box from the passenger seat. He had found it in the dumpster when disposing of the gun dealer's body. Always thinking ahead, he realized the foot square box was perfect for his needs. After placing an unused towel from the motel in it, he had resealed the box with packing tape, confident enough in his disguise as a delivery driver.

The rain showed no signs of abating and he had waited long enough. He turned up the collar of his jacket and opened the truck's door. After checking for traffic, he dashed across the road. Once inside the apartment's lobby, he loitered, pretending to be waiting for an elevator while he scoped out the surroundings. There was a rear exit and a set of stairs at the back.

Hellyer hated elevators. He was happy enough in confined spaces, but the thought of not being in control from the time the doors closed to the time they opened again bothered him. The stairs were his best option and would also help him avoid tenants.

Hellyer carried the box up the stairs and paused momentarily on the third floor landing. After getting his bearings, he walked casually along the gray-carpeted hallway, checking the number on each apartment door as he went.

He felt his heart racing when he reached apartment 309. He had dreamed of this moment ever since he had regained consciousness after she had shot him on the hospital rooftop. As he gazed at the small brass numbers on the door, he wondered if she was inside. Her car not being in its parking bay was no guarantee she was out. She owned an old car. Perhaps it was in the shop getting repaired? Perhaps she had parked it elsewhere?

He stood staring at the door's security peep hole while debating his best approach. He had no plans to announce his presence by knocking on the door. But if he was not quiet when he broke in and the bitch was home, things could get ugly. If she had learned of his escape, there was every chance she could be waiting to unload a magazine of bullets at him when he entered.

He looked up and down the hallway. No one had emerged from their apartments in the few seconds he had been standing in the hallway. Hellyer pressed his ear to her door. He listened for the sound of a TV or radio. Or someone taking a shower. Or blow drying their hair. Or eating breakfast. Or packing a dishwasher. But he heard nothing.

Now reasonably confident there was no one inside, he inserted the first of the picking tools in the bottom of the keyhole and gently rotated it clockwise until he felt a slight pressure. Next, he inserted the second pick above the first and eased it back and forward, raising the lock's pins one by one. It took less than twenty seconds to lift all five pins, and he was satisfied he had made little noise in the process. Hellyer turned the first pick clockwise until he heard a soft click as the lock's bolt retracted. After looking left and right again, he turned the handle and opened the door.

Hellyer took one step forward and stood in the short hallway, scanning the living room in front of him. The room was sparsely furnished with a single black leather lounge that looked like it folded out into a bed. There was a small dining table with four chairs, and a flat screen TV on a cabinet. Hellyer pulled out his gun as he moved forward. He hoped not to have to use it. Guns were effective, but his small knife was so much more intimate, and he could draw out her death as long as he wanted. He stopped again and listened, but couldn't hear anything except a small whine coming from the refrigerator.

Now in the middle of the living room, he scanned left and right. The kitchen was off to his left and empty. He moved forward and checked the bathroom and bedroom before returning to the living room. The apartment was empty. Hellyer let out a long breath and relaxed a little. Although disappointed the bitch was not home, the opportunity to spend time alone inside her apartment gave him a rush. He would be thorough. First, he would go through her wardrobe to get a feel for the kind of clothes she liked to wear. Next, he would rummage through her underwear drawer and cosmetics to learn more intimate details about her. Finally, he would examine each family photo to learn as much as he could about her background. He would savor every piece of information he learned about Bridgette Cash. It would all help to elevate his euphoria when he finally took her life.

Hellyer retrieved the box from the hallway. Once inside the apartment again, he locked the door and switched the light on. The walls were all painted white, and the furnishings were mostly dark or black. He wondered if she owned the apartment and this was her taste, or whether it had come furnished this way when she had rented it. Hellyer moved to his right to study a large print of a dandelion on one wall. The photographer had captured the closeup just as two of the flower's petals were being carried off on a breeze.

He knew little about Bridgette Cash except that she was intelligent and very good at her job. As he looked around the room, he got the sense she was a minimalist. He moved over to the floor-to-ceiling curtains and opened them a fraction. There were two pot plants and a small wrought-iron table and chair on the tiny balcony. Beyond the balcony, he had a view of the street and could see his truck in the distance. He let go of the curtains, walked back into the bedroom and sat on her bed. After closing his eyes, he tilted his head back slightly and sniffed the air. She wore perfume. It was understated, much like the woman herself, he thought.

Hellyer enjoyed the moment and allowed himself a tiny smile as he fingered the blade of the knife in his pocket. This was where he would end her life. He pictured her corpse lying on the bed in a pool of blood. Once again, he found it difficult to breathe as he allowed his imagination to run wild with the possibilities of what he would do to her.

The sound of another truck broke his thoughts. Hellyer moved back into the living room and thought about his truck. The bitch could be hours away from returning—perhaps not even until late in the evening. He was patient and willing to wait, but his truck was too close to the apartment block. If she spotted it on her way home, there was every chance she would make the connection if it had been reported stolen. He decided he would move it shortly and then return to enjoy his time here alone.

He walked into the kitchen. It was unremarkable, just like most kitchens. Modern stainless steel appliances including a dishwasher. Everything neat and tidy. No dirty dishes in the sink and nothing out of place. Hellyer opened the door to the refrigerator and peered inside. The shelves were almost bare, except for some cheese, ketchup, and olives in a bottle. Hellyer frowned. He expected to see milk, or orange juice, or other food items you associate with day-to-day living. He moved to his left and opened the cabinet door underneath the sink. He clenched his teeth as he lifted the lid on a white plastic garbage bin and glanced inside. The bin was empty. Hellyer rushed back to the bathroom and made a quick search of the cabinets before looking up at his reflection in the mirror. He was not sure what kind of cosmetics she used yet, but everyone owned a toothbrush… and it was missing.

He swore out loud as he headed back to the living room. Hellyer stood with his hands on his hips, staring up at the ceiling while he thought about the development. The bitch was unlikely to be just on night-shift. Was she away for a few days or longer? It was hard to tell, but she definitely was not living here at present.

Hellyer spent a few more minutes searching the apartment for any information that would help him understand where she might have gone, but found nothing. Apart from one small compendium that contained old bills and insurance documents, the place was empty. He figured as a minimalist, she would keep all her records online or on her laptop, which he assumed she had taken with her.

The thought of spending hours rifling through her clothes and possessions to understand more about her lost its appeal. He needed to find her first. He would contact his colleague who had found her address. Perhaps he could find her current location as well.

Hellyer took one last look around the apartment as he picked up the box. It would have been a fitting place to finish her, but he had to find her first.

As he pulled the front door closed behind him, he heard someone coming out of the apartment next door. Hellyer spun and knocked on Bridgette's door just as a woman in her late sixties with long gray hair in a ponytail emerged into the hallway.

Hellyer pretended not to notice her as he knocked a second time.

From behind him, he heard her say, "She's not home."

Hellyer turned and forced a cheery smile as he responded, "Good morning, ma'am. Will she be home later today?"

The woman shook her head. "She won't be back for a week. But I can I take the package for her. I live next door and I can give it to her when she returns."

"I'm sorry, ma'am, but it has to be signed for by the owner."

The woman frowned. "Well, that's not going to work, is it?"

Hellyer thought for a moment and then asked, "I don't suppose you have a forwarding address for her? If it's in the city somewhere, I can get my company to redirect the delivery."

The woman shook her head. "She's on vacation up in the mountains. One of those bed-and-breakfast cabins near Hope."

Hellyer frowned. "Well, my company doesn't deliver that far, so I guess I'll just have to leave a card for her and take this back to the depot."

"Shame, really."

"Yes, but I could lose my job if I don't follow the rules."

The woman smiled. "Well, we don't want that, do we?"

Hellyer allowed himself a small smile as he watched the woman walk toward the elevator. A bed-and-breakfast cabin near Hope was not a lot to go on, but it was a start, and a lot more information than he had had sixty seconds ago.

Friday 8:07 AM

Levi Frost shook the rain off his jacket before stepping into Bridgette's apartment block. He had never met Renée Filipucci, but as he scanned the lobby, he saw only one other person, a woman in her late twenties. Dressed in a dark gray business suit, she had her head down and was staring at her phone.

He walked up to her and said, "Renée?"

The woman looked up and said, "Hi. You must be Levi."

"Sorry I'm late. The traffic's all backed up because of the rain and it took longer than expected to get here."

Filipucci waved him off. "I had the same problem and only just arrived myself."

"Have you heard from Bridgette yet?"

Filipucci grimaced. "I've tried again this morning, but every call is going through to voicemail. It's like she's fallen off the planet."

"I called our operations team. They told me there are two cell towers down near Hope on account of the storms."

"Did they say when they'll be back online?"

Frost shook his head. "No. There's a lot of flooding up there at present. It could be days, apparently."

"Well, let's hope we find a clue to where she's staying in her apartment."

As Filipucci pressed the button for the elevator, Frost said, "Thanks for doing this, Renée. I really appreciate it."

"I gotta say I'm getting worried. This guy Hellyer sounds like a monster."

"I hope we're overreacting. He may not be going after her at all…"

"But we can't afford to take that risk," said Filipucci as she stepped into the elevator. After pressing the button for level three, she added, "The only thing that comforts me is if we don't know where she is, he won't either."

Frost knew from experience how resourceful Hellyer was, but said nothing.

When the elevator opened on level three, Filipucci pointed to her left and said, "BC's apartment is this way."

Frost followed Filipucci along the hallway to apartment 309.

As she opened the door, Filipucci said, "Bridgette is a real neat freak. Hopefully, this won't take long."

Frost followed Filipucci inside and said, "I can see what you mean," as he looked around at the minimalist decor.

Filipucci let out a short laugh.

"If we were doing this at my apartment, we could be there for a month and still not find what we're looking for."

After switching on the light for the living room, Filipucci added, "Why don't I take her bedroom and the bathroom. You can look here and in the kitchen."

Frost let out a breath. He didn't feel comfortable

searching his partner's bedroom, at least not on his own, and responded, "Sounds like a plan."

"I guess we're looking for any clue as to where she's staying?"

Frost nodded. "Anything, really. A note on a pad, a printout in a rubbish bin. Anything at all."

Filipucci responded, "OK, I'll let you know if I find anything," and disappeared into the bedroom.

Frost did a slow three-sixty spin as he examined the living room. He could smell faint traces of the perfume Bridgette seemed to wear most days. He felt like an intruder as he counted off one table, four chairs, a couch and a TV on a stand. He thought Filipucci was right when she said this wouldn't take long as he opened the two drawers of the TV stand. The contents took about thirty seconds to inventory. Two board games, a pack of playing cards, several spare TV cables, some appliance instruction manuals, a corkscrew and two ballpoint pens. But that was it. No brochures. No travel guides. No notepads. Not even a scrap of paper. Frost closed the drawers and moved back to the middle of the living room.

With nowhere else to search, he called out to Filipucci, "Nothing in the living room," and moved into the kitchen.

Frost headed for the rubbish bin under the sink first. If there were any clues, this was where he expected to find them.

Frost grimaced as he lifted the bin's lid. He knew the search was now likely to be a bust as he stared down at a fresh bin liner. He went through the motions of searching each drawer and cabinet in the kitchen, but was not surprised when he could not find anything.

Just as he closed the last cabinet door, Filipucci appeared behind him.

"Did you find anything?"

Frost shook his head. "Not a thing."

"Same in the bedroom and bathroom. Her laptop is missing, which isn't surprising."

"She's a digital native. Most everything she does is on her laptop, which is why there's nothing here."

Filipucci asked, "So what do we do now?"

"This is a bust. I'm gonna head into the office and call the agents for all the cabins that are rented out in the Hope area. Fingers crossed I get lucky."

"Do you want a hand? I've got some time owing me. We can tag-team and it will cut the time in half."

Frost shook his head as they headed for the door. "You may not get the answers we're after. The first thing I'll be doing when I introduce myself is let them know I'm from the Vancouver police."

"That should get their cooperation."

Frost said, "As soon as I find something, I'll let you know," as they emerged into the hallway.

"Likewise. I'll keep trying her number…"

Filipucci was interrupted by a woman in her sixties who stood in the middle of the hallway glaring at them.

She demanded, "What are you doing here? This is private property. I've a good mind to call the police."

Frost withdrew his badge and calmly responded, "No need, ma'am. I am the police. In fact, I'm Bridgette's partner, Detective Levi Frost."

The woman's eyes widened as she responded, "Oh, I'm sorry. I didn't know."

"That's alright, ma'am."

The woman frowned. "Is everything alright?"

Frost played down his response, "There's been a development in a case Bridgette and I have been working on. We're just trying to find out her whereabouts."

"Oh, you won't find her here. She's on a week's vacation."

"Yes, we're aware of that. We were hoping to get an address of where she's staying."

Filipucci chimed in, "She didn't tell you where she was headed, did she? We're trying to get a phone number to contact her."

"No. Only that she was going to be staying in a cabin near Hope. I'm watering her plants for her while she's away."

"Well, thanks anyway, Ma'am," said Frost. "We'll keep trying her cell number."

"It's a pity I didn't get her address. It would've come in handy. First for the delivery man and now you…"

"Delivery man?"

"Yes. A delivery man was here earlier to deliver a package. I said I could take it for her, but apparently she needs to sign for it. He asked for a forwarding address and…"

"What did he look like?"

The woman frowned. "The delivery man? Why is that important?"

"It probably isn't, ma'am. But I'd still like a description, if that's possible?"

"Well… he was about thirty, I guess. He was wearing a blue uniform and he had a slim build. The woman paused to look Frost up and down before adding, "And he wasn't as tall as you."

Frost felt his gut tighten. "Was he clean shaven?"

The woman nodded.

"And what color was his hair?"

"It was brown I think. But what I did notice were his eyes. They were very pale blue."

"How long ago did you say this was?"

"Well, not long at all really."

Frost bolted for the stairs, leaving the woman and Filipucci staring after him.

The woman turned to Filipucci and demanded, "What on earth is going on here?"

Friday 8:42 AM

After searching the building and the immediate surrounds, Levi Frost returned to Bridgette's apartment block, drenched and out of breath. Frustrated that he hadn't spotted Hellyer anywhere in the area, he ignored the pool of water he was making in the middle of the foyer and hit speed dial on his phone.

To his relief, Delray answered the call on the second ring.

"I've got a meeting in three minutes, Levi, so this will have to be quick."

"I'm at Bridgette's apartment block. I'll fill you in on the details later, Chief, but I'm positive Alex Hellyer was here less than an hour ago."

The sharpness in Delray's voice was not lost on Frost as he asked, "Are you sure?"

"I just spoke with Bridgette's neighbor. A delivery driver was here earlier this morning to deliver a package to her apartment. It was definitely Hellyer and…"

"Hellyer was the delivery guy?"

"She gave me a good description," said Frost. "Even down to the uniform. The height and build made me suspicious, so I asked her what color his hair was. She said it was brown but he could have dyed it."

"He certainly had time to change his appearance."

"It was when told me his eyes were pale blue that I knew it was him."

Frost could hear his boss let out a gasp. "Son of a bitch."

"According to the neighbor, he left a few minutes before eight. I've searched the apartment block and the surrounding neighborhood, but I can't find any sign of him."

"Have you called this in?"

"Yes, while I was searching the building. A couple of patrol cars are now in the general area looking for him, but I haven't heard anything back yet."

"We'll need to get a team on this and interview everyone in the apartment block."

Frost grimaced. "I agree, Chief, but I don't think it's going to help much."

"Why?"

"He's going after her, just like he did Ron Burns. And he knows she's not here."

"The neighbor?" said Delray.

"She told him Bridgette wouldn't be home all week… and it gets worse."

"How does it get worse?"

"Hellyer asked her for a forwarding delivery address for the package. She told him Bridgette was up in Hope at a cabin."

Delray swore and then went silent.

Frost added, "Boss, I'm really worried. We need to get word to her."

"So you've had no luck contacting her?"

"No. One of her best friends and I have been calling and leaving messages, but so far she hasn't answered. I heard from the ops team this morning that two cell towers are down in the Hope area."

"The storms there are much worse than here. They've got a lot of flooding."

"I suspect that's why we can't get a message through to her."

"So he's one step ahead of us."

"That's my read on it. I think he's got an hour's head start," said Frost.

"In this weather, by the time he clears the city, it will still be two hours before he gets to Hope."

"I'd like to go after him, Chief."

"This is not our jurisdiction, Levi. I'll call the Hope police chief now. They'll have to manage this."

Frost shook his head and tried to hide his frustration as he responded, "I'm worried, boss. They've got an emergency up there. I can't see them giving too much focus to looking for an escaped felon."

"We don't have the authority, Levi."

Frost gritted his teeth. He knew Delray was right, but that didn't make it any easier to swallow.

Delray added, "We'll get a team out there to examine Bridgette's apartment. Maybe we might learn something."

"Chief, I think that's a long shot. I came here this morning with Bridgette's friend, Renée Filipucci. She has a key to the apartment and there was no sign of a break in and nothing has been disturbed, but I'm sure he's been inside."

"So what do you have in mind?"

"I was planning on coming back to the office to call the agents for all the cabins in the Hope area to see if I could track down which one she's rented."

"No need. I'll get one of the detectives who's already here onto that."

"Then in that case, I'd like to drive out to Hope. Bridgette needs to know what's going on and we need to make sure she's safe until Hellyer's recaptured."

There was silence for a moment before Delray responded, "I'll let the Hope police chief know you're on your way and we'll call you as soon as we find the location of her cabin."

"Thanks, Chief."

"Make sure you call in on the police chief before you start your search."

"Will do, Chief."

"And Levi…"

"Yes."

"You're just there to find Bridgette. No vigilante stuff, okay? You leave Hellyer to the local police."

"Got it, Chief."

"Keep me posted, okay? I don't want two of my team going off the grid."

"You have my word."

"I'm late for my meeting, but this is more important and I need to make some calls. Call me when you get to Hope."

Frost promised he would and disconnected. As he sprinted out of the building, he made a mental note to call Renée Filipucci as soon as he got to his car. He would inform her of the change of plan and then use the driving time to plan his next move. Hope only had a population of six thousand people. He figured someone had to have seen Bridgette in her distinctive car. Unable to rid himself of the nagging feeling that Hellyer had an hour's head start on him, he hoped he wouldn't be too late.

Friday 8.51 AM

The rain didn't let up. After tossing and turning for most of the night, Bridgette had risen just after first light. Although the flood concerned her, it was the persistent thought that Alex Hellyer had escaped and she could be his next target that weighed on her mind. As she sat in the Pooles' kitchen finishing breakfast, she decided now was the time to tell Monica of her decision.

"I walked around the island earlier this morning."

Monica frowned. "In this weather? Why would you do that?"

Bridgette glanced down the hallway toward Amy's room. Although she was positive Amy couldn't hear them, she lowered her voice anyway. "It's not safe for you and Amy if I stay here any longer. I need to get off the island."

Monica picked up her cup of coffee and came around the bench. As she sat down on a stool next to Bridgette, she said, "We'll ride this out, Bridgette. There's no need to panic. The flood waters will drop and…"

"It's not the flooding I'm worried about…"

Monica put her cup down. "You mean the guy on the TV? The prisoner who escaped?"

Bridgette nodded.

"You think he's going to come after you?"

Bridgette grimaced. "Possibly."

"But surely you're safe here?" said Monica with a shake of her head. "At least until the flooding subsides."

"You don't know what he's like. I can't afford to take that risk."

"How much has the water risen over night?"

"About two feet."

"Is the footbridge under yet?"

"Almost," said Bridgette. "The water is lapping underneath the boards. Right now it's my only way off the island."

Monica got up and walked over to the kitchen window. She stared out into the storm that had reduced visibility to about one hundred feet, and said, "If this rain keeps up, the footbridge is going to go under too. I can't see the point in leaving right now. Surely you're safer here than anywhere else?"

"The man who escaped. His name is Alex Hellyer. He's murdered at least three people that we know of…"

Monica's mouth fell open. "He's killed three people?"

Bridgette nodded. "That we know of. But possibly more."

Monica closed the door to the hallway and then sat down next to Bridgette. "I seem to be missing something here. I know you're a cop, but why would he becoming after you?"

Bridgette sighed. "It's a long story. Hellyer used to be a drug dealer and was convicted of the murder of one of his enemies, another drug dealer in fact. Only the man was not dead. He had faked his own death and then disappeared after leaving a trail of evidence that pointed to Hellyer."

"So, they put Hellyer in prison for a murder he never committed?"

Bridgette nodded. "Don't feel sorry for him. He'd already gotten away with two murders that we know of by then, one of them being his own father."

"He murdered his father?"

"He was only a boy at the time. Apparently, he set their house on fire while his father was sleeping, but nothing could ever be proven."

"Wow."

"After sentencing in the drug dealer's murder case, they sent Hellyer to a state correctional facility. Early on in his prison sentence he was attacked in the shower block. He feigned a brain injury and spent the next nine years living in the prison hospital."

"The safest place to be in a prison, I guess."

"Yes," said Bridgette. "He smuggled a smart phone in and spent hours each day secretly searching the Internet trying to find out where the other drug dealer had disappeared to. Eventually, he tracked him down and then ordered a hit man to take him out."

Monica's eyes widened. "He did all that from prison?"

Bridgette nodded. "You'd be surprised what prisoners get up to behind bars. Anyway, he made sure the man's body was left in a location where it would be easily discovered. As soon as the authorities realized the man's real identity, they had to release Hellyer from prison."

"So, let me get this straight," responded Monica with a furrowed brow. "Hellyer was framed for a murder he didn't commit and then put in prison. And then he has the guy whom he allegedly killed, murdered anyway and gets away with it?"

Bridgette nodded.

"Unbelievable."

Bridgette shifted on the stool and then said, "You need to know that Hellyer is fixated on revenge. It seems to be an overriding emotion. As soon as he got out of prison, he went after the police detective who had arrested him ten years earlier. That's where my partner and I came in. We arrested Hellyer after a shootout on the roof of the Saint Joseph's hospital in Vancouver."

"Which was where he escaped from."

"Yes. He was shot during his arrest and required surgery. During his recovery, they held him under guard in a secure room within Saint Joseph's. He was due to be sent back to prison today."

Monica shook her head again. "This guy is a real psychopath."

"Now that he's escaped from hospital, I'm afraid he's going to do the same thing again."

"Only this time… you think he's coming after you."

Bridgette nodded. "I can't stay here. While I'm on the island, all three of us are in danger. I plan to get to Hope and alert the police but, most importantly, you and Amy will be safe." Bridgette paused. She could see by the resigned looked on Monica's face that she would not object.

"The longer I stay here, Monica, the more danger there is for all of us. This is my one chance to escape and I need to take it. If something happened to you or Amy, I would never forgive myself."

"We're going to be completely cutoff soon. Surely we're going to be safe."

Bridgette grimaced. "We can't afford to take that risk."

Monica was silent for a moment. After glancing at the closed door to the hallway, she said softly, "I don't know what to say, Bridgette... I think it's crazy you walking off the island in the middle of this storm, but..."

"Hopefully it won't be long before he's recaptured. I'll hang around in Hope until then, and then I'll come back and get my car."

"Is there anything I can do to help?"

Bridgette shook your head. "I don't think so. I'm going to swing by the cabin and pickup my backpack and then I'll be on my way. Can you say goodbye to Amy for me? I don't feel comfortable explaining to her what I'm doing right now."

"Sure, I understand."

Bridgette managed a smile. "I'd like to come back and finish the holiday when this is all over, if that's okay?"

Monica smiled too. "I would like that very much."

"I best be going."

"At least let me walk you to the bridge. That's the least I can do."

"Sure."

"Let me go tell Amy that I'm heading back to the cabin with you for a moment. I'll let her know that you've gone when I get back."

Bridgette breathed a sigh of relief as she watched Monica head down the hallway. She was not looking forward to the long and wet walk into Hope, but she knew it was the best decision under the circumstances. She was convinced she would be a magnet for Alex Hellyer and the quicker she got off the island and away from the Pooles, the better.

Friday 9:16 AM

The roar of the storm made talking almost impossible for Bridgette and Monica as they ran to the footbridge under the umbrella. Bridgette had put on her hooded rainproof jacket for the trip, but it was proving almost useless as she felt rainwater dripping down the back of her neck.

As they came through the trees and stared at the footbridge below, Monica shouted, "I can't believe this rain. I think it's even heavier than last night!"

Bridgette responded, "I agree," but her focus was elsewhere as she studied the bridge. The boards, which had been above the waterline an hour ago, were now almost covered. As she watched sticks, branches and other debris pile up against the railing, she knew she needed to move fast if she had any hope of getting across it before it went under.

Monica put a hand on her arm and shouted, "We need to be careful going down this slope. With all this rain, it's going to be lethal and we could easily end up on our butts or worse."

Bridgette heeded Monica's advice and trod carefully as

they walked down the sixty-foot slope. She had never been this close to the bridge before and was surprised by how long it was. Even though the river was only about twenty feet wide when not in flood, the bridge itself was almost double that length.

"We're just in time," yelled Monica. "In another half an hour this will be completely under."

When they reached the bridge, Bridgette pushed against the hip-high timber railing and said, "It seems solid enough."

Monica reassured her. "Clint built it to last. The bridge is the least of your problems."

Bridgette let out a sigh as she looked across at the cluster of trees beyond the bridge on the other side. Getting across seemed straightforward, but she was not about to assume anything.

Never one for long goodbyes, she looked back at Monica and said, "I best be going. Thanks for everything, Monica. And the umbrella! I really appreciate it."

Monica gave Bridgette a firm hug. "Good luck today, Bridgette, and stay safe. I appreciate what you're doing for me and Amy."

Bridgette turned to face the structure again. She swept her hair off her face and steeled herself for the day ahead as she gripped the hand railing.

After a deep breath, she took a step forward and immediately felt the icy cold water swirling around her ankles. She fought the urge to look down as the chill from the water began rising through her body.

After she had taken a three steps she heard Monica shout, "I'll stay here and watch you until you get to the other side."

Bridgette gave her a thumbs up signal with her free

hand as she inched forward. Although she wanted to get off the bridge as soon as possible, the last thing she needed was to slip and fall. She murmured, "Slow and steady," as she gripped the rail again with her free hand.

After a few steps, Bridgette got into a rhythm. By the time she was half-way across, she could feel the icy water swirling around her calves. Despite the rising water, she started to gain confidence. It was instantly shattered when Monica screamed, "Bridgette, stop! Stop!"

Confused, Bridgette turned and looked up river. She saw a wall of water hurtling towards her. Knowing she didn't have time to get off the bridge, she wrapped her arms around the railing and braced as the wave crashed down on her.

Bridgette felt a searing pain in her chest as the wave crushed her against the railing and the umbrella went tumbling into the waves. She felt the air rush out of her lungs as the force of the water broke her grip and she tumbled over and over like a rag doll as the river swept her downstream. In the murky darkness, she had no idea which way was up or down. Her lungs were screaming for air. She had only been in the water a few seconds, but already she felt her body shutting down. Disorientated and starved of oxygen, the darkness closed in. The river was like a beast. Relentless. Its grip overpowering and without mercy. She felt her senses go numb and her body relax. Was this a dream? Would she wake up soon?

She felt like she was floating. Abruptly, she broke through the surface of the water, coughing and spluttering as her lungs sucked in oxygen. Flailing her arms, she fought back against the Beast as it tried to suck her under again.

She tried to swim towards the river bank, but the current was too strong. She felt her body pick up speed as she hurtled around a bend in the river. She saw a tree down across the river about forty feet in front of her. The main trunk was only partially submerged, and she felt a whoosh of air escape from her lungs as her body slammed into the trunk. Any hopes she had of climbing onto it were dashed when she felt her backpack snag on a branch. She spluttered as she tried to keep her head above water but the current tried to drag her under.

She could almost hear the Beast calling to her from within the roar of the torrent, *'You're mine now, it won't be long…'*

With her head jammed up against the main trunk of the tree, and the right strap of her backpack pinning her to the branch, the force of the current tried to rip her in two.

She focused all her energy on her left arm and drew it in close to her body. In a single motion, she moved it upwards and pressed against the trunk of the tree. She took a deep breath and used what little strength she had left to twist her body as the river tried to suck her back under. Now sideways against the current, she held her breath and lowered her right shoulder.

She felt her body shift slightly against the backpack. This was the moment of truth. Her one and only shot at survival. After closing her eyes, she took another deep breath and dropped down. With her head now fully submerged, she felt her body twist further against the backpack. Now with a sliver of hope, she kept on pushing until her right arm came free and she slid out of the strap. Now at the mercy of the Beast again, she was sucked under the trunk and down river once more. She could hear a hammering inside her head as her brain screamed for oxygen.

The Beast whispered, *'I'm not done with you yet,'* as she

picked up speed again. She counted in her mind; *'one, two, three,'* as she tumbled over and over, desperately trying to reach the surface. She got to fourteen before her head popped out above the water. Coughing and spluttering, the simple act of breathing had never felt so sweet. She found it a little easier to stay upright without the weight of her jacket and back pack, but she was still at the mercy of the current.

Above the roar of the rain, she thought she could hear a name being called. "Bridgette! Bridgette!"

She wondered if it was the Beast calling her as she came around another bend in the river, but then realized it was Monica standing on the jetty.

Monica held out a long pole just above the water line and screamed, "Grab this! Grab this!"

Bridgette flailed her arms and kicked her feet, but she was thirty feet from the pole and still at the mercy of the current.

Monica screamed again. "Swim! Swim! Swim!"

Bridgette felt her vision closing in. As everything turned to gray, she didn't know whether it was the pouring rain or the Beast having his way.

Bridgette closed her eyes and kicked again as Monica continued to scream.

She tried to lift her arms out of the water, but her strength was gone.

She could hear the Beast whisper, *'You're mine now,'* as everything went black.

Friday 11:12 AM

Hellyer completed the trip from Vancouver to Hope in a little over two hours. It had rained the entire way and he had driven carefully to avoid any possibility of an accident in the treacherous conditions. He had seen several cop cars on the trip, but they had all been preoccupied with minor road accidents, and had ignored him.

Now, as he cruised around Hope while the rain continued to pour, he stuck to the speed limit and obeyed every road rule. He had spent the first half hour scouting the main town area to get a sense of the layout. With a population of just over six thousand, it didn't take him long to build a mind map of the area. Hope was just what he expected; a small, sleepy country town. So small that even the library and museum were listed as tourist attractions. He learned the first Rambo movie had been shot in Hope and was now the main tourist draw card. But with the storm showing no signs of easing, the roads were quiet. Most locals seemed to have hunkered down to wait it out, which suited him fine.

Despite Hope not being somewhere he cared to live, he had taken a moment to admire the scenery. Nestled in the junction of the Fraser and Coquihalla rivers, with views to the Cascade Mountains, he understood why some people chose to live there. But that moment quickly passed. He had a job to do and was confident the small size of the town would work in his favor.

He set himself the target of finding the location of the bitch cop's cabin before sundown, but he ran into problems almost immediately. With many of the townsfolk worried about flooding, half the shops and businesses were closed. Logic dictated the cop probably stopped for gas or groceries before heading to the cabin, so he focused on those first.

Convinced it would only be a matter of time before he got a breakthrough, he pulled up at a curb next to a Shell gas station at the end of the main street. Someone must have seen her. Someone would remember her.

Hellyer lowered the driver's window just a fraction to study the layout. This was his fourth gas station for the day. There were only eight petrol pumps and no customers at present, which was how he liked it. There was one guy in the main store area and two guys working in the garage next door. He spotted three security cameras, which was three too many for his liking. He decided he would walk in to avoid the security cameras recording the number plate on his truck, and switched the engine off.

After pulling the brim down low on his baseball cap, he opened the phone he had stolen from the guard and scrolled to the photos section swiping to the most recent one.

After searching the bitch cop's social media page the previous evening, he had taken screenshots of two images. In one, she was standing in front of her Mustang. In the other, she was with a friend at a party. The photo of her with the car was good enough as it was, but the photo with the friend had to be doctored for his ruse to work.

Hellyer had spent half an hour taking photos of himself in his motel room in different light sources and at different distances from the camera. He kept comparing the pictures he had taken with the photo of the cop with her friend, trying to emulate the same lighting and distance from the camera. Once satisfied he had a good enough image, he cropped the image down with the phone's photo editing software and then superimposed it onto the photo of the cop at the party.

While the phone's photo editing software was not great, with patience he was able to manipulate the image until it looked like he was the friend standing next to the cop at the party.

Satisfied the photo would do the job again, just as it had done at the last three places, he got out of the truck and sauntered into the gas station.

A bell above the door tinkled as he walked in. The store sold everything from cookies to car polish and even had a hot-food bar and coffee machine. Ignoring the store's offerings, Hellyer continued to the counter at the rear, and put on his best smile for the clerk who was a man in his early twenties with a goatee beard. The man closed the magazine he was reading and said, "Help you?"

"Hi there," said Hellyer and then added, "I sure hope you can," as he withdrew his phone from his pocket. He showed the clerk the image of him standing next to Bridgette at the party. "I'm looking for my sister. She came into town yesterday, but she's not answering her phone."

The clerk leaned forward a little to study the image. Hellyer quickly swiped the phone screen with his finger to bring up the picture of Bridgette with the Mustang.

"This may help. This is her car."

The clerk shook his head. "I haven't seen her, but I wasn't rostered on yesterday." He scratched his head before adding, "Jimmy said he saw a really cool looking Mustang yesterday. I wonder if it's your sister he was talking about?"

Keeping up his friendly appearance, Hellyer responded, "Jimmy?"

The clerk nodded. "Jimmy's one of our mechanics. I think he's out back in the shop. Hang on, I'll see if I can find him."

Hellyer could barely contain his excitement as he watched the clerk disappear through a rear door.

Not wanting to get ahead of himself, he waited patiently until the door opened again. The clerk returned with a man in greasy gray overalls. Jimmy was about twice the age and size of the clerk.

Jimmy came up to the counter and said, "You're looking for your sister?"

Hellyer smiled and said, "Yes. Bridgette's staying in a cabin up here somewhere. She was going to text me the address this morning but her phone's been a bit flaky of late and I haven't received it yet."

Jimmy shrugged. "We've got cell towers down on account of the storm, so maybe it's not her phone that's the problem."

Hellyer grimaced. "Yeah, maybe." Keen to get to the point, he added, "So, you might have seen Bridgette yesterday?"

Jimmy nodded. "You said she drives a Mustang?"

Hellyer showed Jimmy the picture of Bridgette standing with her car. "This is Bridgette, and this is her car. A '66 Mustang."

Jimmy pointed a greasy index finger at the screen.

"That's definitely her. She was in here yesterday. And what a sweet car. You don't see many in that condition these days."

Hellyer did his best to keep his voice even as he asked, "Did she say where she was headed?"

Jimmy nodded. "Yeah. She was heading out to the Pooles. They live out-of-town a ways. They have this cabin that they rent out." Jimmy frowned and then added, "Only…"

"Only what?"

Jimmy looked at the clerk. "I think they're flooded in. I don't think you can drive up there right now."

The clerk agreed, "Yep, they're definitely cut off."

Hellyer nodded. "Well… that is a concern. Can I at least get the address?"

Jimmy grimaced. "I guess, but you'll need to hang around here for at least a day or two until this rain stops and the floods ease."

"That's fine, Jimmy. I don't have much planned."

Jimmy looked at the clerk. "You got a pencil and paper? I'll draw a map."

While the clerk hunted in a drawer for some paper, Hellyer looked at Jimmy and casually asked, "So tell me, Jimmy, where's a good place to stay in Hope?"

Friday 11:57 AM

Bridgette no longer felt the freeze of the water turning her body blue. She opened her eyes and blinked, but nothing came into focus. She could see shapes... shades of light and darkness. She heard her name being called over and over. But it all seemed distant, and she closed her eyes again.

She felt herself floating as she drifted back off to sleep. She no longer cared about the Beast, or the rain, or the river. Wherever she was, dead or alive, it didn't matter anymore.

She heard her name being called again and opened her eyes. The shapes were still there. Two of them. She blinked several times and then felt her world begin to spin. Feeling like she was stuck in a vortex, she closed her eyes again and suppressed the urge to vomit.

The voice kept calling. "Bridgette... Bridgette... wake up!"

Bridgette opened her eyes again and stared up into the faces of Amy and Monica Poole. They were both kneeling beside her. As her vision came into focus, she could see relief spread across their faces.

Bridgette tried to speak, but no words came out of her mouth.

Monica soothed, "Lie still, Bridgette. There's nothing to worry about. You're safe."

As she closed her eyes again to fight off another wave of nausea, she heard Amy whisper, "Is she going to be alright, Mom?"

Monica whispered back, "She's going to be fine. She just needs some time."

After the nausea passed, Bridgette opened her eyes again. She tried to speak, but her brain seemed disconnected from her body. After several attempts, she managed to croak, "Where am I?"

"You're back at the house," said Monica.

"You don't remember us carrying you back?" asked Amy.

Bridgette managed a feeble, "No," in response.

Monica leaned forward. "We thought we were going to lose you. When you came around the bend in the river, I felt for sure the current was going to suck you downstream."

"I remember trying to swim to the jetty," said Bridgette.

Monica nodded. "You got lucky. Where the two branches of the river converge the currents get all messed up." She paused and said with a smile, "You may not remember it, but I was shouting at you. Telling you not to give up… and you didn't."

Bridgette closed her eyes again. In an instant she was back in the river, freezing and fighting against the powerful pull of the current. "All I remember is I was exhausted."

Monica squeezed her arm. "You did a great job. You grabbed a hold of the pole and I was able to drag you out."

Amy added, "You really don't remember?"

Bridgette shook her head. "I could see the pole and I could see Monica. I started to swim and then everything went black. That's the last thing I remember."

"I dragged you up onto the bank near the jetty and checked you were breathing," said Monica. "You threw up a ton of river water and then just wanted to sleep, so I went and got Amy and we carried you back to the house."

Bridgette grimaced. "I don't remember any of that."

"Once we got you back here, we laid you out in front of the fire, got you out of your wet clothes, and covered you in blankets. You've been sleeping ever since."

Bridgette turned her head and saw the peaceful glow of the fire.

Now realizing she was in the Pooles' living room, she asked, "How long have I been out?"

Monica looked at up at a clock on the wall. "Over two hours."

Bridgette went to sit up, but the room started to spin again. As she lay down, she groaned, "I shouldn't be here. You're in danger and…"

"Amy, Bridgette needs some dry clothes," said Monica as she turned to face her daughter. "Can you go to the cabin and bring some back, please?"

Amy made a face, "Aww, Mom, do I have…"

Monica raised her voice a little as she insisted, "It's going to be awhile before Bridgette will be well enough to walk that far. So you'll be doing her a big favor."

Amy shrugged and got to her feet. She looked down at Bridgette and asked, "Is there anything else I can get for you while I'm there, Bridgette?"

"Thanks, Amy, but I can't think of anything right now."

They watched Amy slink off to the mudroom and put

on her coat and boots. It was only after the rear door to the house slammed shut that Monica said, "I haven't told Amy anything about the prisoner's escape. And for now, I want to keep it that way."

"I understand. I'm really sorry. I didn't want to get you in the middle of…"

"You've done nothing wrong, Bridgette. You did your best to make us safe and nearly drowned in the process."

"But we're all in danger. I'm trying not to be paranoid, but I'm sure he's going to come after me."

"I have a gun."

"A gun?"

Monica nodded. "A shotgun."

Monica got to her feet and hurried down the hallway. Two minutes later, she returned carrying a single barrel shotgun. Bridgette was not an expert with shotguns, but it looked like a 12 gauge. She knew a 12 gauge would make a mess of almost anything that was in its path. Bridgette could tell by the awkward way Monica held the weapon that she was not comfortable with it.

"I keep it locked in a cupboard in my bedroom. I don't like guns, but it was Clint's and I can't part with. I've found a few cartridges. We'll hunker down here and keep this next to us while we ride out the storm. If he comes, we'll be ready."

"This isn't your fight, Monica."

"Life is full of curve balls." Monica shrugged. "This is just another one."

"You shouldn't be in the middle of this."

Monica grimaced. "You don't know for sure that he's coming for you. And even if he is, hopefully by the time he figures out where you are, this storm will be over and you'll be back in Vancouver."

"But there's always a chance…"

Monica shook her head. "Let's talk about it later. The storm's still raging and we're completely cut off now that the footbridge is under water."

Bridgette felt a shiver run down her spine. "I remember the wall of water when I was on the bridge… I tried to hang on, but it was too powerful."

Monica closed her eyes for a moment as she shook her head. "I've never felt so sick in my life. I felt so helpless when I saw you get swept away. I tried to chase after you along the river bank, but the current was moving so fast. I knew my only hope was to cut back to the jetty. Clint always kept a long pole there for maneuvering the boat around in the water. I figured I might be able to use it to help you before you got sucked into the main part of the river again."

Bridgette shook her head. "It never occurred to me that a flood like that could generate a wall of water. It was almost like a small tsunami."

"I read somewhere that can sometimes happen with floods. A dam breaks upstream, or two tributaries converge and you can get a giant wave. I've gotta admit I didn't think about it either until I saw it coming. But by then it was too late. It moved so quickly…"

"I thought I was going to die," said Bridgette, flashing back. "I got snagged on the branch of a tree that had fallen across the river… it kept trying to suck me under."

"Is that where you lost your coat?"

Bridgette nodded as she sat up. "The irony is that branch might have helped save my life. The coat was heavy, and it was almost impossible for me to keep my head above water… it was a little easier to float once I was out of the coat."

Monica looked up at a clock on the wall. "It's midday, and Amy will be back any minute. I've got a pot of vegetable soup that I'm going to thaw out. You're safe here, so just rest."

Bridgette was relieved that the room was no longer spinning, and the fog was clearing from her brain. She reached out a hand and touched Monica's arm. "I haven't thanked you yet, Monica. You saved my life."

Monica waved her off. "You'd have done the same thing for me or Amy in a heartbeat." She paused and then added, "You really think he's going to come after you?"

Bridgette decided now was not the time to downplay the danger. "He's capable of almost anything. We can't be too careful." Her eyes widened, and she screamed, "Amy! She's outside!"

Monica swore as she realized she had allowed her daughter to go outside on her own. "Oh my, God. What have I done!"

As she sprinted towards the mudroom, the door opened. Amy, still dressed in her coat which was dripping wet, frowned and said, "Why are you guys yelling my name?" Her mouth fell open as she stared at the shotgun. "Mom, why do you have a gun?"

Friday 12:41 PM

The trip out to the Pooles' took Hellyer almost an hour. While Jimmy's map had been helpful, Hellyer had to make two detours to get around floodwater. He had tried approaching the island from the north road, but the dense forest of trees leading down to the river made his reconnaissance almost impossible. He gave up trying to find a way onto the island from that position and headed to the southern end. After turning off the highway, he followed the side road that led down towards the river.

Hellyer pulled the truck to a halt about one hundred yards in from the turnoff. He left the engine running to stop the windscreen from fogging up as he stared through the sheeting rain at the side road that had disappeared into the swollen river in front of him. He knew the flooding was bad, but he had hoped the road to the island would still be above the river level. He frowned as he studied the water course he had to cross. He watched as a small plastic drum bobbed up and down in the churning, muddy water as it was swept downstream. The windscreen wipers weren't coping well with the heavy rain. Even though his visibility was poor, the unbroken expanse of black cloud suggested the storm was not about to break anytime soon.

His mood matched the color of the clouds as returned his focus to the river in front of him. He guessed the river was somewhere between fifty and sixty yards wide. He tried to imagine how far below the waterline the bridge that led to the island was, but it was impossible to tell.

Hellyer considered the situation. He hadn't come all this way only to be foiled by a fast running river. He glanced up at the house on the other side. The house was too big to be called a cabin and he knew she must be staying somewhere else on the island. His gaze shifted to the circular driveway in front of the house. Through the trees and rain, he could just make out her Mustang parked out front. He nodded to himself—she was definitely here, somewhere. He would find out where soon enough, but first he had to figure out how to get on the island.

Hellyer had used the trip out from Hope to think about how he might get across the river. He had hoped flooding would be minor, but the scene in front of him told him otherwise. He would need a boat or a canoe at least. Glancing upstream at the surging water, he decided a canoe wouldn't be stable enough. He would need a boat—something small enough that he could transport, but stable enough to cope with the rapids. It would be a risky crossing, but the prize was worth it. Hellyer studied the river as he watched more rubbish wash downstream. There was no way he could fight it. He would need to launch well north of the island and let the boat be carried downstream on the current. He could steer the boat across the river as he went. Finding a place to land would also be a challenge, but he would worry about that later.

Hellyer fingered the tip of the knife blade in his pocket as he thought about his next encounter with her. He hoped it would be in the cabin. He would kill anybody else he found on the island first. Then it would be just the two of them. Just the way he wanted it. The setting couldn't be more perfect. Nobody would hear her screaming above the roar of the storm. He envisaged hours of uninterrupted pleasure. Intimate moments with just her and his knife.

Hellyer closed his eyes. He could hear her screams and whimpers as she begged for mercy. The picture of her cowering in a corner of the cabin, on her knees, begging for it all to be over, sent a tingle down his spine. He sighed as he envisioned the small blade sinking deep into her stomach. Over and over, he would stab her. But he would be patient. He would take his time, savoring the experience until he and the cabin were covered in a beautiful sea of red.

Hellyer opened his eyes and stared at the clock on the truck's dashboard. He needed to keep moving if he was to find a boat and be back here and on the island before nightfall.

He took one last look at the river and then focused on the jetty and the wooden boat tied to the mooring. The car and the boat strongly suggested she was still on the island and he wanted to keep it that way. He checked the reception on his phone—there was still no signal. His mood brightened as he realized she was likely cut off with no way of communicating with the outside world.

Hellyer reached into the storage area behind the seats and removed the rifle. Ignoring the sheeting rain, he stepped out of the F150 and walked down to the water's edge focusing on the jetty on the opposite side. He raised the weapon and looked through the rifle's telescope at the boat. He shifted the aim of his rifle slightly to his left and then to his right, but realized he didn't have much of a target as most of the boat's hull was hidden behind the jetty. After lowering the rifle, he shuffled along the water's edge about fifteen feet and raised the weapon again. He blinked rain from his eyes and focused the scope on the hull just above the waterline and fired one shot. Even with the powerful scope it was impossible to tell if he had hit the boat or not. It felt like the shot had hit higher up and towards the bow. Not what he wanted. He lowered the weapon slightly and moved it a fraction to his left, targeting the middle of the vessel just below the waterline. The boat bobbed up and down on a line of rope that tethered it to the jetty. He waited until he figured out how far it rose and fell and then fired three more shots in quick succession. While the blasts were audible to him, he didn't think anyone sheltering inside the house would have heard them above the roar of the storm. Hellyer lowered the rifle and nodded once to himself as the boat began to list.

Satisfied his job was done, he turned and walked back to the truck. Although he was saturated, he didn't hurry. After climbing into the cabin, he stared back at the boat as he shut the truck's door. The vessel was now tilted at a thirty-degree angle and sitting lower in the water. He guessed it would take a few more minutes to sink completely, but that was precious time he couldn't afford to waste watching.

Hellyer looked up at the house and said, "I'll be back soon."

After putting the truck in reverse, he pushed the island to the back of his mind as he reversed back up the lane. He needed to steal a boat, and this would be his sole focus for the next few hours.

Friday 12:58 PM

Levi Frost started his car and let the motor run for a moment to warm up the interior. He stared through the windscreen at the pouring rain while he contemplated his next move. As he switched on the windscreen wipers, his cell phone buzzed in his jacket pocket. He held his breath as he pulled out the device, hoping it was Bridgette finally returning one of his calls. He grimaced in disappointment as the screen showed it was his boss, Felix Delray.

"Hi, Chief."

Delray, never one for pleasantries, responded, "Where are you?"

Frost stared up at the Cascade mountains in the distance. Through the rain they were almost invisible. "I'm out front of the Hope Police Station. I got here about twenty minutes ago."

"You sitting in your car?"

"Yep. How can you tell?"

"I can barely hear you over the roar in the background. I assume it's still raining there?"

Frost glanced out the windscreen. "It's crazy. I've never seen anything like it. The town's folk are really worried about flooding."

"I can imagine. So have you seen the Chief of Police yet?"

"Not exactly. With all the flooding that's going on, they're stretched to the limit. They've got a junior officer manning the station, but that's it. Everyone else is out attending to flood emergencies. I've registered my attendance, and asked for the chief to contact me when he can, but that could be days."

"Well, that's all you can do."

"I can't see myself getting much help here. They're really under the pump."

"You may not need their help after all—we've got a hit on Bridgette's location."

"That was quick."

"We only had to contact five agencies before we got a match."

Before leaving Vancouver, Delray had arranged for one of the other detectives to call the online booking agencies in the Hope region. He figured Bridgette's cabin booking would be registered on a database somewhere, and it would be easier to track her down that way rather than going door-to-door asking questions. Delray continued, "She's staying in a cabin about ten miles out of town. It's actually on a small island in the middle of the river. I'll give you the address."

Frost opened a notebook and said, "Let me have it."

Frost listened while Delray gave him the address. After writing it down, he said, "I'll head out there now. There's nothing else for me to do here."

Delray cautioned, "I've been listening to the news

reports. Like you said, there's a lot of flooding out there, so you need to be careful. If she's that far out of town, she may already be cut off."

Frost nodded to himself as he watched the rain continue to pound his windscreen. "It could be a long day."

"And remember, no heroics. You're there to find Bridgette, not to catch Hellyer."

"Got it, Chief."

Delray said, "Just find her and make sure she's safe," before disconnecting.

Frost glanced up at the mountains again as he put his car into gear. Getting anywhere near Bridgette's location in this weather would be challenging. He decided now wasn't the time to be relying on his phone for directions; he needed a proper map and supplies to last him a day or two. His first stop would be a general store he had spotted half-a-mile back. As he hung a left onto Princeton Way, his thoughts returned to his conversation with Delray. He would honor his promise to focus on finding Bridgette, but he wondered what he would do if he encountered Hellyer? He clenched his jaw as he thought about the people the psychopath had maimed and killed. There was no way he would be letting him walk away.

The drive out to the island had taken Frost far longer than he had expected. Easing his car to a halt, he frowned as the side road in front of him disappeared into the river. He kept the engine running as he studied the foaming torrent. It seemed to have a life of its own as it rapidly transported a motley mixture of logs, tree branches, and rubbish downstream. He knew this was as close as he would get—at least by car.

Frost's gaze was drawn upwards to a white house nestled amongst trees on the opposite side of the river. Even though his visibility was poor in the driving rain, he did not need to consult his map—this was the address Delray had given him.

He contemplated his options while he stared at the house. There was no way he could get onto the island from here.

He had seen enough and put his car in reverse and backed up the side road until he reached the highway. After pulling a U-turn, he traveled slowly about a hundred yards back up the road until he reached a bridge that spanned the Fraser River. He pulled off onto the shoulder just before the bridge and switched the engine off.

Frost picked up an umbrella from the passenger seat and tried to open it while exiting the car. His maneuver was less than successful, and he swore as the deluge soaked him before he got the canopy fully open.

After brushing water from his jacket, he walked out onto the bridge and stopped when he got to the mid-point.

Frost looked back up the highway. He hadn't seen a car in almost twenty minutes and figured he was probably safe standing there for a while.

He turned to his right and looked back up the river. The view from the highway bridge gave him an uninterrupted view of the island.

He allowed himself a smile as he looked up at the white house. The rain eased off a fraction and gave him a glimpse of a midnight blue '66 mustang parked in the circular driveway out front. Even though the car was a good two hundred and fifty yards away and difficult to see in the rain, he had no doubt he was staring at Bridgette's car.

Keen to phone Delray and tell him he had located his partner, Frost pulled out his phone, then cursed as he stared at the screen; he had no signal.

Frost mused about his next move. His primary goal was to contact Bridgette and make sure she was safe. But with no cell phone reception, he had to find another way to contact her. Getting onto the island was going to be next to impossible without a boat. He assumed Bridgette was still staying in her cabin as his gaze returned to the house. He squinted up through the trees at the rest of the island studying each clump of trees, looking for any other dwellings, but he saw nothing.

Frost frowned as he contemplated what to do next. So near and yet so far. Walking around the island seemed like a long, futile exercise in the miserable conditions. But maybe the smaller tributary of the river narrowed enough somewhere so that he could jump across. Or maybe the cabin was close enough to the river that he could call out or signal her. It seemed like long shot, but no better options came to mind.

He peered over the edge of the bridge at the water below. He guessed the water level was only about four feet below the bridge deck now, but with a mass of trees and other debris backing up against the structure, it was hard to tell. Frost looked up at the lagoon where the two branches of the river rejoined. He guessed the lagoon was only about eighty yards in front of him. He squinted through the rain at what looked like a small timber jetty on the island side of the lagoon. The structure looked to be coping well with the flood, and he guessed it normally sat well above the waterline.

Frost let out a long breath. The idea of spending the day walking around the island looking for the cabin was not appealing. But right now, it didn't seem like he had any other options.

He took a moment to take in the vista while he steeled himself for what was ahead. He tried to imagine the island on a sunny day. He pictured the river as a gentle water course separating the tiny island from the surrounding countryside. He understood why Bridgette had chosen it. The seclusion and separation was just what she needed. It was a refuge. A place where you could switch off, rest and recharge. He took comfort as he noted the owners had wisely built the house at the top of the rise and well above the river's flood line. It would take a flood of biblical proportions before the house was in danger. He wondered what his partner was doing right now. He pictured her relaxing in front of an open fire, oblivious to the fact that Hellyer was on the loose and possibly after her.

His mood darkened as he thought about Hellyer again. Could he be here already? Hellyer couldn't request information from the travel agencies like the police could. Still, Frost knew he was intelligent, cunning and resourceful. His stomach churned as he recalled incidents from Hellyer's past where he had tracked down victims, even after they had gone into hiding.

Frost peered through the tiny rivulets of water that ran off his umbrella as he scanned the riverbanks to his left and right. He looked among the trees for any sign that he wasn't alone, but it was impossible to see anything clearly more than fifty yards in front of him.

Frost scowled as he glanced down at his phone screen again—still no reception. He turned and headed back to his car. He would need to be careful. Getting wet or slipping and falling into the river were the least of his worries.

Friday 2:07 PM

Hellyer pulled up across the street from the 'Boats and Bait' store and left the engine running. He had spotted the store earlier in his reconnaissance of Hope. After using the sleeve of his coat to un-fog the side window of his truck, he stared through the rain at the front of the store. Located on elevated ground in an industrial area on the outskirts of town, the single story white clapboard building didn't look as though it had been painted in decades. Hellyer glanced at the time on the clock on the Ford's dashboard. It was only just after two in the afternoon, and yet the lights inside the store were off and the place looked deserted. He studied the U-Haul storage depot next to the boat shop. The main office was also in darkness and the place looked closed. He would need to inspect the boat shop more closely, but he assumed the business owners had all gone home early to prepare for the possible flooding of their houses.

After zipping up his coat and pulling his cap down low, Hellyer switched the engine off and jumped out of the truck. He was thankful he could shelter under the shop's front awning after sprinting across the road through the downpour. While pretending to window shop, he checked for security cameras inside the store while he tried opening the main door. The front door was locked and the place definitely looked deserted. He walked to the left-hand side of the store and pressed his face up against the shop's large front window and stared inside. Despite the store's darkness he could see the layout well enough. Hellyer swore under his breath. The shop seemed to specialize more in camping equipment than boats. The only two boats on display were both aluminum and too heavy for him to maneuver on his own.

Not easily dissuaded, Hellyer moved to the corner of the building and peered down a driveway that led to a rear enclosure. The enclosure was only accessible through metal gates that were secured by a link chain and padlock. The two gates were about six feet high and clad with rusting iron. Ignoring the water that swirled around his boots, Hellyer walked down the driveway to investigate further.

Peering through the small gap between the gates, Hellyer studied the enclosure. The area was about ninety feet wide and sixty feet deep and set out like a car yard, except the business was selling boats not cars. He smiled to himself as he counted off ten boats. Nine of them, a mix of aluminum and fiberglass hulls, were lined up on boat trailers in a neat row. But it was the tenth boat, an inflatable Zodiac dinghy, at the back of the enclosure that caught his attention. It was much smaller than the other boats and locked in a twelve by twelve cage. From his vantage point, he figured the dinghy was about eight feet long and five feet wide. It was perfect for his river crossing. He thought it would be easy enough to transport in the truck, provided he could carry it. He was not sure how much a Zodiac weighed, but the carry handles on each side suggested it was manageable.

Hellyer had two problems to overcome. The first was getting into the enclosure itself and the second was getting inside the locked cage. The first problem would be easy enough to solve, and he figured getting into the cage would be only slightly more problematic.

He had seen enough and sprinted back to the truck. After pulling a U-turn, he stopped in front of the store and then used the truck's side mirrors to reverse up the laneway. When he was about a foot from the gates, he stopped the truck and glanced back at the street. Confident no one was watching him, he inched the truck back until it was hard up against the two gates. Ignoring the grinding sound of metal on metal, Hellyer continued to back up until the chain snapped and the gates popped open.

He left the motor running and sat for a moment using the rear-view mirror to scan the boat lot. He focused on the cage. Unless he shifted the boats out of the way, there was no way he could get the truck close enough to spring the lock. Moving the boats or trying to pick the cage's lock in the pouring rain would take precious time he preferred not to waste. He shifted his gaze to a small timber workshop next to the cage. Perhaps the key to the cage was inside? If not, he hoped he could find a set of bolt cutters or something similar to make quick work of the cage's lock.

Ignoring the heavy rain, Hellyer got out of the truck and strode across the compound. The workshop had a sturdy wooden door, but the padlock on it looked flimsy. He raised his right foot and kicked at the door with a stomping motion. The lock held firm, but the screws holding the lock's clasp to the door gave a little. He repeated the kick and the door burst open. Hellyer walked inside and looked around. The workshop had a long wooden bench running down its left-hand side, a pile of boxes and some fuel cans stacked up neatly on the right. He could see no sign of a key for the cage so he focused on the workbench. Hellyer noticed three outboard motors in various states of disassembly, along with a pile of spanners, screwdrivers and wrenches. He debated turning the light on to get a better look at the tool collection, but decided there was enough light coming in through the open doorway to conduct his search. After rummaging around for close to a minute, the only tool he found that he thought might be useful was a hacksaw. He picked it up and moved closer to the door to inspect it. He swore as he noticed the teeth in the middle of the blade had worn away to almost nothing. Hellyer dropped the hacksaw back on the bench and bent down to search the shelf underneath.

The shelf mostly contained spare parts, but something at the far end caught his eye. Hellyer picked up the implement. Even in the dim light, he knew this was the tool he wanted. The pry bar was about two feet long and had a hook on one end and a flanged tip at the other. He knew if he could work the implement's tip in through the shackle section of the lock, he could spring it open.

Hellyer didn't seem to notice that he was soaked to the skin as he strode out of the workshop to the cage.

He murmured to himself, "This should work," as he grabbed the cage's lock. Holding the lock steady with his left hand, he guided the wedged tip of the crowbar through the lock's shackle.

Satisfied the bar wouldn't slip out, he gripped the hoop

end of the bar with both hands and pulled down. It took less than two seconds of exertion before the lock snapped and dropped to the ground. Hellyer pulled the gate open. Moving quickly, he disconnected the outboard motor from the rear of the Zodiac and carried it back to his truck. He lowered the tailgate and pushed the motor in before sprinting back to the cage.

After grabbing the zodiac by two of its carry handles, he lifted it off its wooden stand. The dinghy was heavier than he expected, but manageable. Half carrying, half dragging the vessel, he maneuvered it to the back of his truck. Realizing the boat was too deep to fit under the fiberglass cargo cover, he used the pry bar to wrench the the cover away from the hinges that held it to the truck.

As he slung the cover to the ground he realized the boat and motor weren't both going to fit in the cargo area and transferred the motor to cabin. He then loaded the zodiac onto the cargo tray and pushed it forward as far as he could. He stood with his hands on his hips and swore as he realized the boat was too long for the truck and that part of it would overhang the rear tray. He knew there was a real risk the boat would fall off the truck on the way back to the island if he drove at speed.

It was a risk he couldn't take, and after sprinting back to the workshop, he returned with a length of rope, a fuel can and life jacket that he had seen earlier. He lashed the rope through the dinghy's carry handles and tied it off to two anchor points in the cargo area. Satisfied the boat was now secure, he stowed the fuel can and life jacket and then got back into the truck.

With his work here done, Hellyer drove a few feet forward before stopping again to swing the gates shut. After re-threading the chain through the gate as best he could to make it looked closed, he drove off. He kept checking his rear-view mirror every few seconds for any sign he was being followed. Two minutes after leaving the outskirts of Hope, he breathed a sigh of relief. Now certain no one was following him, he focused on the road ahead as he drove through the downpour back to the island.

Friday 3:48 PM

Monica had protested that Bridgette should stay in the house, but Bridgette had been insistent when she realized what was different about the dream. It was the sounds of the explosions. Four in total. Distant but close together.

She was convinced the sounds were not thunder. She had not heard anything more than low rumbles of thunder in the distance since the storm had started. Now, as she trudged through the trees in her waterproof jacket, she was positive the sounds she had heard in her sleep were real. She had not said anything to Monica. Thunder was often confused for other sounds, particularly vehicles backfiring and gunshots. But there were few cars on the road in this weather and it didn't seem likely that what she had heard was a vehicle. Could it have been gunshots? If so, where did they come from? And why? No one in their right mind would be out hunting in this.

Bridgette shivered. Even among the trees, she felt exposed. Monica had insisted she take the shotgun. She had protested at first, but now she was glad she had the weapon. Scanning left and right, she headed towards the jetty.

While the rain had eased a little, Bridgette's visibility was still restricted. She walked on, aware that if Hellyer was coming after her, he could already be here. She did the math in her head. If he had escaped mid-morning yesterday, he'd had plenty of time to steal a vehicle and make the trip.

But how quickly could he find her? That was the question. She had only told a handful of people that she was heading to Hope. And no one knew her exact address, not even Renée Filipucci. Even if Hellyer had found out her home address, she was confident there was nothing in her apartment that would give away her current location. She should have been breathing easy. Cut off from the rest of the world, the odds of him finding her before the storm was over were remote.

And yet, she couldn't shake the nagging feeling in her stomach. The sense of foreboding was overwhelming, and she knew she shouldn't ignore it. She paused as she came to the edge of the tree line and stared down at the river. The water level didn't seem to have risen too much since earlier that morning, which she took as a good sign. Bridgette gazed out across the water to the riverbank on the other side. She looked for signs she was not alone, but saw nothing. She was glad she had the shotgun as she made her way along the riverbank.

Bridgette frowned as she neared the jetty. Something was different. It only took her two more steps before she realized the boat was missing.

Bridgette wanted to hurry, but running with a shotgun in such slippery conditions was risky. She walked as quickly as she could and paused a few feet short of the jetty to study the scene in front of her.

She had expected to see the boat still attached to its mooring and semi-submerged. But there was no sign of the vessel.

Bridgette took a few cautious steps onto the jetty and peered into the murky brown water. But it was impossible to see anything.

After sweeping wet streaks of hair off her face, she walked further along the structure. Keeping a firm grip on the shotgun, she studied the murky water again, but still couldn't see any sign of the vessel. She wondered if the boat had broken free of its mooring or if the non-stop rain had finally taken its toll—sinking the boat where it had once floated.

Bridgette pulled on the boat's tether rope. It was tied by a knot to one of the jetty pylons, but it now trailed out through a whirlpool of currents into the lagoon.

She focused on the currents where the two branches of the river converged. The merged flow rapidly sucked everything in its path downstream towards the concrete bridge that spanned the highway. She lifted her gaze to the bridge and estimated the water level was only about two feet below the structural girders that held up the span. The girders had become a log jam with not enough clearance to allow the motley mix of sticks, branches and other debris caught up in the flood to flow down river.

It looked like an ugly version of a dam wall a Beaver might build. She cocked her head to one side as she studied the muddied entanglement. She could see several flat wooden sheets covered in mud caught up in the maze. At first she thought it might have been a siding from a building.

But as she studied the sheets in more detail, she realized she was looking at sections of the boat's hull.

Bridgette's heart sank. The boat had been Clint's pride and joy and she knew the news would upset Monica. She wondered again what had caused the boat to disintegrate. Tethered to the jetty, it was out of the main currents that were sweeping debris down from upstream. If it had simply filled with water, surely it would have sunk next to the dock? Bridgette looked around, wondering if this was the work of Hellyer? Could he be on the island already?

She pulled on the rope again. It felt heavy, almost as if it was snagged on something. Bridgette laid the shotgun down and gripped the rope with both hands. A small section of the boat's wooden hull quickly broke the surface as she reeled it in. It took under a minute for her to reel the section back to the jetty and hoist it up onto the deck. She bent down and studied the fragment. It was roughly triangular in shape and about three feet across at its widest point.

The mooring rope was still attached to the boat's stainless steel tow bolt and hadn't been cut. Bridgette frowned as she inspected the section. There was a small hole in the panel towards its bottom edge. It was round and smooth. Definitely man-made. She wondered what the hole was for and why nothing was attached to it.

Bridgette flipped the panel over and studied the hole from the other side and then touched it with her finger. As she felt the rough splintered edges of the hole, her eyes widened. She had her answer.

Remaining as calm as she could, she tossed the timber section and rope back into the river and retrieved the shotgun. Without looking around, Bridgette walked off the jetty and headed back to the house, wondering how she was going to tell Monica.

Friday 4:02 PM

Hellyer used the trip back to plan how he would get onto the island. It would not be easy. At first he thought he could cross the narrower of the two channels. At only fifty feet wide, logic dictated this was his best option. But as he mulled over his earlier visit, he recalled the water in the narrower channel was far more turbulent. He decided the wider channel was less likely to tip his boat over, and that would be his best option. Next, he had to figure out where to launch from. The woods surrounding the island were dense, and trying to drag a dinghy through it could take hours. He decided he needed to head further upriver and find a less-wooded spot that was close to the road. He would allow the current to carry him downstream, using the motor to steer him to the island when he found a suitable landing point.

Happy enough with his plan, Hellyer changed into low gear and cruised up the road that ran next to the Fraser River. He had only gone about half a mile upriver from the island before the woods started to clear. With a clearer view of the river, he was surprised at how much the water had risen and how close to the road the flooding was now.

Hellyer pulled off the road when he saw a clear path through the trees. Not wanting to risk getting the truck stuck in the muddy conditions, he stopped as soon as he was far enough off the road to work without being seen.

After dragging the dinghy down to the waterline, he studied the swollen river for a moment before he went back to the truck to collect the boat's motor. The river was still running swiftly, but he didn't think it was as bad as it had been earlier in the day. In less than ten minutes, Hellyer had the motor on the back of the dinghy, fueled and ready for launch.

Hellyer shielded his eyes from the teeming rain with his hand as he studied the river again. There appeared to be less debris than earlier, which he took as a good sign, then he looked downriver toward the island. There were no obstacles that he could make out, but he figured with half a mile and several bends to navigate, he needed to prepare for the worst.

Satisfied that he was as ready as he ever would be, he looked down at the motor. It was small and only designed for use on calm waterways. Even though the boat was small, he expected the fast and choppy conditions would affect its maneuverability and make it difficult to steer. He would need to plan his turns well in advance.

The river was about ninety yards wide on account of the flooding. He planned to steer the boat into the middle of the river as quickly as possible and then maneuver the vessel, using the current to his advantage to navigate the bends in the river before hopefully finding a suitable landing spot on the island. Hellyer knew the consequences if he couldn't get the dinghy to turn quickly enough, or if it capsized. He had traveled over the highway bridge on his return and had seen the mass of debris that had been caught up against the crossing. He knew getting entangled in it would bring a swift and ugly death.

Hellyer pushed the thought of drowning to the back of his mind and checked the motor was securely clamped to the thick plastic panel that functioned as the boat's stern. Satisfied everything was ready, he pushed the boat out into about a two feet of water. The current was not as strong at the edges of the river, and he managed to keep the boat stable while he lowered the propeller into the water. After jumping in and starting the engine, he decided he would remain close to the edge until he got a feel for the boat's maneuverability. He set the throttle to about half power and moved the tiller left and right to test the steering as the boat picked up speed. The boat seemed stable enough, but the steering was almost non-existent.

His efforts to stay close to the shoreline were in vain. In less than thirty seconds, the dinghy was sucked into the middle of the river. Hellyer gritted his teeth as he pushed the throttle to its maximum position and then tried using the throttle arm to steer again. In the raging current, there was almost no perceptible change in direction. He swore as he realized how bad the steering was going to be. As he hurtled around the first bend in the river, Hellyer thought through his options. He needed a new plan and refused to contemplate the possibility of drowning.

The boat lurched sideways as it was tossed about on the rapids. Hellyer felt his body lift off the seat and come down hard with a thud. He ignored the sharp pain that shot up his back as the boat rounded the second bend in the river.

Energized by an ordeal that would terrify most people, Hellyer could now see the island about four hundred yards in front of him. He squinted as he focused his concentration on a point in the river where the island split the watercourse in two. Within seconds, he had a new plan. The plan no longer included selecting where he landed, or landing the dinghy without damage. It was not foolproof, but it was the best he could muster in the conditions.

Hellyer focused on the fork in the river as he closed to within two hundred yards of his target. The rocky landmass beyond was about sixty feet wide and almost as high. Hellyer noticed the current didn't separate into two streams, but crashed into the island like a wave crashing onto a rocky cliff face before separating. He guessed he had about thirty seconds to prepare. There was no point in trying to steer, so he grabbed the handle grips on either side of the dinghy and knelt down.

Through gritted teeth, he braced as the torrent increased the speed of the dinghy before smashing it against the rocks. The force threw him forward, and he lost his grip as his body slammed into a limestone crag. He groaned and reached up to grab at the crag as he felt the boat being sucked off the rocks. Now aware of a throbbing pain in his right shoulder, he focused on maintaining his grip and pulling himself out of the water.

Hellyer knew the next few seconds would determine whether he lived or died. If he slipped back into the water, it would be over quickly. Ignoring the pain, he pulled himself upward until his body was half out of the water. After taking a couple of deep breaths, he hauled himself onto the boulder, willing himself on until he was clear of the river. Hellyer lay face down and sucked in deep breaths, ignoring the rain that continued to pound his body. He let out a groan and waited for the pain to subside a little. After composing himself, he sat up and looked down at the river just a few feet below. One section of the Zodiac had quickly deflated. He debated whether he should try and haul the boat out of the water or let it wash downstream. Hellyer gingerly rotated his shoulder. It stung when he raised it above his head, and he knew he had his answer as he watched the vessel wash off the rocks. He stood cautiously and braced his legs for balance before looking up at the rock face he had to climb. The slippery conditions would make it difficult enough, but after what he had just been through, it would be near impossible.

Undeterred, he let out a roar to celebrate his achievement of making it onto the island.

Satisfied with his progress, he muttered, "Not long now, bitch," and then reached up to grip the next boulder.

Friday 4:09 PM

Bridgette looked around to make sure no one had followed her and then knocked on the door to the mudroom.

Monica appeared a moment later at a small window next to the door. Bridgette could see the relief on her face as she unlocked the door. "Thank God you're back. I was worried sick."

As Bridgette stepped inside to remove her jacket, Monica asked, "Did you find what you were looking for out there?"

"Kind of."

Monica frowned. "Kind of?"

Bridgette sensed her host's change in mood. She could see by her furrowed brow as she re-locked the door that she was worried, and Bridgette couldn't blame her.

"Can we go sit in the living room? I've got a few things to tell you."

"This doesn't sound good," said Monica with a sigh. "Let me go check on Amy first."

Bridgette walked back into the living room and laid the

shotgun down on the floor. She moved over to the fire to warm herself while she thought about how she would break the news to Monica. Her host was a straight up and down person, and Bridgette knew she could handle the truth, so she decided on the direct approach.

A moment later Monica reappeared. "Amy wants to join us, but I told her to wait in her room until I call her."

Bridgette nodded and said, "I think that's wise."

As Monica settled into a chair she said, "I figured out why you went outside. It wasn't thunder you thought you heard in your sleep, was it?"

Bridgette grimaced. "No."

"You think it was gunshots, don't you?"

Bridgette nodded.

"Do you think he's here?"

Bridgette let out a long breath. "I have no definitive proof…"

Monica nodded. "So tell me what happened."

Bridgette explained how she had walked down to the jetty and noticed the boat was missing. The distraught look on Monica's face was not lost on Bridgette. She knew the boat had belonged to Clint and had enormous sentimental value.

She gave Monica a moment to compose herself before she continued. "At first I thought it may have simply sunk, but I couldn't see any sign of it next to the jetty. I looked further out into the lagoon. Everything was being sucked downriver towards the bridge…"

Monica nodded.

Bridgette swallowed and added, "I noticed large pieces of the boat were caught up with all the other debris that was tangled up at the bridge…"

Monica looked away as tears filled her eyes.

Bridgette felt helpless as she said, "I'm sorry, Monica."

A few seconds went by before Monica spoke. "I never liked that damned boat. But after Clint passed, I just couldn't part with it."

Bridgette waited until she felt Monica was ready to continue. "The mooring rope was still attached to the jetty. I pulled it in and there was a small section of the bow still attached to it."

Monica frowned. "The hull fractured? Surely it would just sink next to the jetty?"

"I examined the bow fragment. There was a small hole in it. It was smooth and perfectly round, which I thought was odd. So I turned it over and looked at it on the other side…"

"I'm not sure what you're getting at?"

"The hole was rough and splintered. I've seen similar holes before as part of my job."

Monica's eyes widened. "A bullet hole?"

Bridgette nodded. "Almost certainly."

Monica frowned again. "But how does a hole up near the bow sink the boat? That doesn't seem possible."

"I'm pretty sure I heard four shots. I think the other shots probably hit much closer to the waterline. And if they were close to each other, they could have split the hull."

Monica said absently, "It was an old boat. Clint was always worried about the frame. He said the hull had a split just above the waterline that needed repairing. I guess a couple of well-placed bullets would be enough…"

"Also, I'm fairly sure the shots came from the other side of the river."

"Why do you think that?"

"You tethered the boat to the right side of the jetty,

which meant the right or starboard side of the hull was facing out into the river."

Monica nodded. "That's how it was always tied up."

"The fragment of the bow was mainly from the right side of the boat. The bullet definitely hit that side."

Monica stood up and started pacing. "Which means the shot did come from the other side of the river."

"I think that's a fair assumption," said Bridgette.

Bridgette gave Monica some time to process everything before she added, "As soon as I realized what it was, I threw the panel back in the river."

Monica's eyes widened as she asked, "Why would you do that?"

"I couldn't see any sign of him hiding out. Maybe he was there, and maybe not. But if he wasn't and he comes back, leaving that fragment of the hull on the jetty would make it obvious that we knew the boat had sunk."

Monica sat down and stared into the fire. "He's trying to keep you from getting off the island, isn't he?"

Bridgette nodded. "That's the only explanation I have."

Monica looked up and held Bridgette's gaze. "He's going to try to get onto the island, isn't he?"

Bridgette grimaced. "I think that's a reasonable assumption."

Monica turned white as she mulled over the development.

"I'm sorry, Monica. I had no idea my stay was going to turn out like this."

Monica stared at the fire. Finally, she looked up. With a clenched jaw, she said, "Well, we have two things going in our favor."

Bridgette raised an eyebrow. "Two things?"

Monica nodded. "If he didn't see you at the jetty, then he doesn't know that we know he's here."

"I agree. And what's the second thing?"

Monica stared at the shotgun and responded, "He doesn't know we're armed."

Friday 4:12 PM

After parking his car on the lane near the flooded car bridge river crossing, Levi Frost made his way through the trees and undergrowth along the bank of the narrower of the two river channels towards the northern end of the island. He had hoped for a lucky break. A break that would allow him to find a place to cross the river, or at least get him close enough to get a warning message to Bridgette. But that break had eluded him. His hopes of getting onto the island had soared when he had come across a large tree that had fallen into the river. The tree's trunk had spanned almost the full width of the river. Frost had stood for over ten minutes, contemplating his options as he studied the river conditions.

At first he wondered if he could swim out to the tree, straddle its trunk and then crawl along it to the other side. But the more he thought about the idea, the less he liked it. He was not a particularly good swimmer, and the current was strong. Even a small miscalculation would mean disaster.

He had continued his walk. The rain made it slow going. The density of the trees and undergrowth towards the northern end of the island made it impossible for him to trek next to the riverbank, forcing him to detour up onto a ridge line. Now, as he emerged into a clearing at the far end, he found himself with a panoramic view of the island and the river below.

Frost let out a sigh. This was the end of the trek for him. With no way onto the island, he would need to make his way back to his car and come up with a Plan B.

Although mindful of his mission to find Bridgette, Frost was thankful for the rest. The steep climb in the wet conditions had been taxing, and he felt gutted that he was no closer to finding a way onto the island than he had been two hours ago. He pulled out his cell phone to check for a signal and swore as the words *No Signal* were still stubbornly displayed on the screen.

Frost stared through the rain at the view in front of him. From his vantage point, he could see almost the entire island. Even in the miserable conditions he was able to make out the island's teardrop shape. The dense woods at the northern end fell away abruptly at an almost vertical sixty-foot-high cliff face. Frost watched for a moment, almost mesmerized by the power of the floodwater as it battered the cliff face before violently splitting in two like a block of wood being cleaved by a sharp axe. The storm was throwing its very best at the island, but despite its ferocity, there was still much to admire about the river as it wound its way through the Fraser Valley.

Frost closed his eyes for a moment and let out a long breath as water dripped off his chin. Every square inch of clothing on his body was saturated, and he could feel water squelching in his boots. The long trek back to his car would be miserable and made worse by the fact he had nothing to show for his efforts.

Frost opened his eyes again ignoring the sting of the rain on his face as he focused on the island. From this vantage point, he could just make out Bridgette's cabin, almost completely hidden among the trees. The sturdy wooden structure was only about a hundred and fifty yards from the main house but blended in perfectly with the surrounding woods.

Frost thought about his partner as he studied the cabin. He had previously worked undercover in Narcotics. But after witnessing a seven-year-old boy get killed by a criminal in a hit-and-run as he fled a crime scene in a stolen car, everything changed. Frost had been driving the police car that was chasing the criminal and he had taken the boy's death personally. He had felt responsible and needed time away to recover and figure out whether he could continue as a cop or not.

His break had been months longer than he had expected, but after deciding he wanted to continue and getting the all clear to return, he had opted for a move out of narcotics and into homicide. He thought the change would be good for him. A chance to do something different, to stretch himself and learn some new skills as a police officer. But the transition had been far harder than he'd expected.

Frost originally thought the problem was his pairing with Bridgette, a rookie female detective. He had never worked closely with a woman before, but he soon realized his struggles were far more than just his new partner. He grudgingly admitted he hadn't fully dealt with his own demons as the nightmares continued. Most nights it was the same one. He would wake in a lather of sweat, unable to erase the image of him cradling the broken and bloodied body of the boy while he died in his arms.

Bridgette had understood his grief. She had been working through her own demons, and they had talked about his struggles. It had been okay for him to be weak and vulnerable in front of her. No shame, no judgment.

He had learned to trust her. While they didn't always agree, they had figured out a way to work together. He admired her. She was the smartest cop he had ever worked with by a long shot. She was confident and self-assured, but never arrogant or rude. He liked that about her. He liked a lot of things about her. Frost wondered if he would be this desperate to get a message to his partner if he had been paired with someone else? He hoped the answer was yes, but he couldn't be sure.

In an instant he was back on the rooftop of the Vancouver hospital weeks earlier on the night they had arrested Hellyer. Separated from Bridgette in the blinding smoke from a fire Hellyer started, Frost had come up the emergency stairs and burst onto the roof, unwittingly walking into a hail of bullets from Hellyer's gun. It was only Bridgette's marksmanship that saved him—no question about it. Perhaps that was the reason he was here.

Frost let out a long breath and stared up into the black skies. He ignored the needling rain on his face as he thought about his own demons again. While they continued to haunt him, he was now comfortable talking about them and figured that was the first step to making a full recovery.

He reflected on the last year of his life. So much has changed. His return to work and the euphoria of solving his first murder case with Bridgette had been short-lived as he realized his marriage was crumbling before his eyes. He thought of his soon-to-be ex-wife, Jacinta. She had been his world since his early twenties, but after her affair, he could no longer trust her. They had tried to move on, but within weeks he realized their marriage was over. In the end, his job was all he had to cling to while he worked through his grief.

He lowered his gaze to the cabin again. Not being able to find a way onto the island was a setback, but this was not over. He was determined to find a way to contact Bridgette.

Frost turned to leave, but a moving object on the river upstream from the island caught his eye. At first he thought it was a tree branch bobbing up and down. But his gut tightened as he realized the object was an inflatable boat.

Frost shouted, "No!" and stared in disbelief as the dinghy powered straight ahead on a collision course with the rocky outcrop of the north end of the island. He was not close enough to get a good look at the man who crashed the boat onto the rocks, but as the slim figure emerged from the wreckage and grabbed a boulder to pull himself out of the water, he had no doubt it was Alex Hellyer.

Friday 4:46 PM

Alex Hellyer stared at the cabin from his vantage point in the woods. After scaling the cliff face, he had made his way up through the forest towards the center of the island. He had come across the cabin about ten minutes earlier but had stayed within the cover of the trees, watching and waiting for any sign that this was where the cop bitch was staying.

So far, he had seen nothing. No lights on inside and no movement near the windows.

He had seen a house about one hundred and fifty yards further inland which he planned to check out next. But for now, the cabin was his focus. The cop's neighbor had been clear. It was a cabin she was renting, and this appeared to be the only one on the island. Perhaps she was inside sleeping? Hellyer felt his heart rate quicken as he thought about how he would awaken her from her slumber.

Ignoring the rain, Hellyer sprinted across the open ground to the rear corner of the building. He stood for a moment listening for movement inside, but it was pointless trying to hear anything above the roar of the rain. Keeping his head down, he crept along the side wall of the cabin until he came to a small single pane window.

Pressing himself flat against the cabin wall, Hellyer leaned forward and looked inside. It was dark and he couldn't make out anything beyond shadows. He debated standing there for a few seconds to let his eyes adjust to the darkness, but didn't fancy having his head blown off if the cop woke up at the wrong time. Bending low, he moved under the window and then crept to the front porch. Still seeing no signs of life, he removed his gun from an interior pocket of his coat and crept across the porch to the front door. The door opened inward and was made from aged and weathered timber. He gazed at the latch and figured there was almost no chance of entering without making a noise.

Hellyer checked the rain as a puddle of water formed at his feet. It was falling a little lighter than before but it was still heavy enough that the sound it made on the roof should mask his entry. Hellyer gripped the handle and pushed. To his surprise the door swung open silently.

With his gun up, he scanned the interior before stepping inside. The main room was about thirty feet long by twenty feet wide, but the only sign of life was a tiny glow of embers in the fireplace.

Hellyer noticed a door on the back wall of the cabin and figured it led to a bathroom or similar. He strode through the cabin and flung it open. The room was tiny and functioned as both a bathroom and laundry just as he suspected. No need to explore any further, it was also empty.

"Where are you, bitch?" He stood for a moment in the main living space contemplating his next move. This was not how he had planned it. His dream of spending hours alone in the cabin with her would have to wait.

Hellyer noticed a knitted sweater on the bed. He walked over and picked up the garment. Cradling it under his nose, he breathed in its scent. He smiled as he recalled the same scent in the bedroom of her Vancouver apartment. She was definitely here. This was a setback and nothing more.

Hellyer sat down on the bed for a moment to rest while he planned what he would do next. He assumed she was up at the main house, riding out the storm with the family.

That would present a problem for him, but nothing he couldn't handle. Getting onto the island had sapped his energy so he would stay here for a while to recover while he regained his strength. And then he would make his way to the house, determine how many people lived in it, then figure out a way to get in unannounced. He would shoot them all... everyone except the cop. He would tie her up and raid their refrigerator before bringing her back here.

Hellyer lay down on the bed and looked up at the rafters. The cabin was a small and intimate space, almost like a little chapel, and perfect for what he had in mind.

He would start a fire when he got her back. And then he would show her his knife and make her watch him while he ate. He would tell her of all his plans and let the excitement for him and the tension for her, build.

Hellyer was an artist with his knife. He would take it slow. Be creative and deliberate. He longed to hear her beg. No longer a cop. No longer in control.

He would finally have the upper hand. She would beg for her life and his revenge would be sweet. Something he would savor for the rest of his life. Hellyer glanced out the window. The rain appeared to be easing. He would allow himself half an hour's rest, then it would be time to execute the next step of his magnificent plan.

The next hour in the Poole house was subdued. Amy joined her mother and Bridgette in the living room shortly after Bridgette and Monica had finished their conversation. Despite Amy's questions, Monica had given away little information and insisted they were safe until the flooding subsided. With the TV turned down while they waited for the next news bulletin, Amy had contented herself with reading a book, while Monica spent most of her time at the living room window staring out into the storm. Bridgette sat in front of the fire and thought about what the sinking of the boat really meant.

There was no doubt in her mind that this was the work of Hellyer. Any misgivings she had about exactly which prisoner had escaped from the hospital had evaporated with the discovery of the bullet hole in the fragment of the boat's hull. She was certain he was coming after her. But was he going to attempt to get onto the island now or wait it out until the flood waters had subsided? That was the question she turned over and over in her mind. During the investigation that led to his arrest, she had learned a lot about her nemesis. A psychopath with no conscience, he was hardly likely to wait idly by on the other side of the river.

The sinking of the boat clearly showed his motive was to keep her from getting off the island. As she stared into the coals she tried to put herself in his shoes and think like he did. He would not want to wait. He would want to get onto the island while they were isolated and without any hope of escape. But getting onto the island would require a boat. And not just any boat, but a boat that could navigate rapids. Could he pull it off? Would he risk it?

She was not sure. Hellyer was smart, cunning, and resourceful. While his overriding desire was always revenge, he was calculating in everything he did. Did he have what it took to cross the river and risk drowning? That would take courage, and that was not who he was. Hellyer was more like a jackal or a hyena than a lion. He was a predator; someone who would take advantage of the weak and vulnerable, only striking when there was little or no risk to his own personal safety.

While she had doubts he would make it onto the island before the floodwaters subsided, she couldn't rule it out either. The next few hours would be critical to their survival. She had to plan for all possibilities. If he was waiting for the waters to subside, they had time to plan. But if he intended to take risks to get onto the island as soon as he could, their preparation time could be much shorter.

Bridgette sighed. She knew he would want as much control as possible. He would want to set a trap, to corner her and give her no way to escape. Her stomach churned. The more she thought about it, the more certain she was that he would take the risk.

Monica interrupted her thoughts. "Listen! The rain is stopping."

Bridgette lifted her head. Preoccupied, she hadn't noticed that the roar from the rain had subsided. The occasional soft pop from the wood in the fireplace was the only sound that now punctuated the silence.

Bridgette and Amy both moved over to the window and stood next to Monica.

As they stared at the gray clouds, Monica pointed, and

said, "Look to the north. That's definitely blue sky breaking through there!"

Bridgette immediately thought about Hellyer, while Amy cheered.

They stood for a moment staring at the changing skyline before Bridgette asked, "How long do you think it will be before the floodwaters start to subside?"

Monica frowned, and responded, "I'm not sure. Why do you…" but stopped as she realized the motive behind Bridgette's question. She signaled Bridgette to follow her into the kitchen as Amy returned to the sofa to continue reading her book.

When they were alone, Monica whispered, "What are you thinking?"

Bridgette murmured, "I'm not sure if he'll try to get onto the island while the river is still in flood, but I know as soon as the floodwaters subside he'll be making his move."

Monica let out a long breath. "I have no idea how long it will take. The waters might rise further, or they could fall away quickly. I just don't know."

"We need to keep watching the weather forecast to see if there is more rain coming or if this is the last of the storm."

Monica nodded. "I agree."

"I think I'm going to take a quick walk down to the jetty."

Monica frowned. "Whatever for?"

"I'd like to get a baseline height of the river. Then I'll check it again at dark. That way we'll be able to get a rough gauge of whether it's rising or falling. If it's falling, we need to know how quickly."

"But what about Hellyer? What if he's out there and see's you?"

"It's a risk I'll have to take. We need to know how long we've got." Bridgette paused for a moment and then added, "The river may hold him at bay for now, but that's not going to last for long and we need to know how much time we have, if any."

Monica grimaced and then said, "You better take the shotgun."

Friday 5:37 PM

Frost made quick work of the trip back to his car. He sprinted where he could and only walked where the forest was dense. His mind kept turning over the ugly possibilities of what Hellyer might already be doing on the island. He tried to suppress the nightmare images and forced himself to focus on what he needed to do next as he raced along the riverbank.

He kept checking his phone, but the display continued to stubbornly register no signal. As he walked and ran, he made his plans. He would drive back towards Hope, continually checking his phone for a signal. As soon as he came into range, he would call the Hope Chief of Police and brief him on the situation. Now that the rain had stopped, he hoped he could wrangle the help of at least one or two officers to get him onto the island to rescue Bridgette before it was too late.

He would also call Delray and give him the bad news. There was nothing Delray could do, but if he didn't get the cooperation he needed from the local police, his boss could at least make some phone calls to get the help he needed.

Out of breath he emerged on the side road, jumped into his car and started the engine. He detected movement on the opposite bank out of the corner of his eye as he threw the car into reverse.

He looked across the flooded river crossing and focused on the figure of a tall, slim woman making her way towards the jetty.

He shook his head. "I'll be damned."

In an instant, he was out of the car and running towards the waterline, yelling, "Bridgette! Bridgette!"

She froze as she looked across the river, scanning left and right as she searched for his location.

Frost began waving his arms. "Over here!"

Frost guessed Bridgette was about ninety yards away. With daylight waning, he couldn't make out her facial features, but he knew she was surprised as she yelled, "Levi? Is that you? How did…"

Frost exploded, "He's here! He's on the island. You have to find somewhere safe."

"What? Are you sure?" He could hear the panic in Bridgette's voice.

"I saw him in a boat earlier. He's landed on the north side of the island. Do you have a gun?"

Bridgette held up the shotgun. "Yes. It's the owner's and…"

"You need to get back to the house now! Barricade yourself in. I'm going to get help. There's no cell reception here, but as soon as I get back into range, I'll call the local…"

Frost didn't need to finish his sentence. Bridgette was already sprinting back towards the house.

He felt bile rise in his throat as he watched her disappear into the woods.

As thoughts swirled around in his mind about how much life had unraveled for them in the last twenty-four hours, he murmured, "Stay safe, Bridgette," and then bolted for his car.

Bridgette sprinted back through the forest towards the Pooles' house, praying that she wouldn't be too late. Unlike the trip down to the jetty, where she had been watchful, this time she didn't care as Frost's words, 'He's here,' kept playing over and over in her mind.

She would never forgive herself if anything happened to Monica and Amy and did her best to block out the possibilities of what she might find back at the house as she emerged from the trees.

She kept a lookout for Hellyer as she sprinted across the rear garden and screamed, "Monica! Monica!" before pounding on the mudroom door.

Monica Poole opened the door almost immediately. "I didn't expect you back quite so soon. Is everything alright? Did you…"

Bridgette closed and locked the door behind her. "He's on the island…"

Monica stammered, "What! How do you…"

Bridgette held up a hand. "I'll explain later. Right now, we need to make sure every door and window is locked tight and get everyone into one room and bunker down. Where's Amy?"

Monica's face went pale. "She went to her room. When

you left, I checked the doors were all locked just like you told me and…"

"Go get her and meet me in the living room. We can't afford to be separated now and we need to plan what we do next."

"OK," Monica said, then disappeared down the corridor.

Bridgette raced through the kitchen to the living room and then opened the breach of the weapon to check there was a shell in the chamber.

As she snapped the barrel shut, she heard a scream. Bridgette felt a cold shiver run down her spine as she turned to see Monica frozen in the hallway staring into Amy's bedroom.

Bridgette tightened her grip on the weapon and strode down the hallway.

As she reached Monica's side, her host howled, "She's gone. He's got my baby."

Bridgette moved past Monica into the doorway of Amy's bedroom. She had never been in the room before. It contained a single bed, a student's desk, a dressing table and a built-in wardrobe. It was painted a soft lemon color, but Bridgette noticed none of the decor. She moved quickly through the room. First checking the wardrobe and then the rest of the room for clues. There was no sign of a struggle, but that meant little. If Hellyer had threatened Amy with a gun or a knife, she probably wouldn't have given him any resistance.

Bridgette noticed the curtains fluttering on the breeze and felt her chest tighten as she approached the window. She pulled back the curtains and struggled for breath as she stared out through the open window. She studied the garden and the woods beyond for a moment, but saw no sign of either Amy or Hellyer. Bridgette lowered her gaze to the flowerbed four feet below the window. The blooms were trampled and she didn't need to think too hard to understand what had happened.

She looked back at Monica who was shaking on the floor.

Monica tried to speak as Bridgette came to comfort her, but the words came out incoherently.

Bridgette barely had a moment to contemplate what had happened when the silence was broken by a ringing sound coming from the kitchen.

At first, the ring was soft, but then it rose in its crescendo.

Monica's eyes widened. "That's the cabin phone."

Bridgette placed a firm grip on Monica's arm as she attempted to get to her feet.

"Let me take it. We know it's me he wants, not Amy."

Bridgette walked into the kitchen and let out a deep breath as she picked up the receiver of the ancient handset. She could hear Hellyer's heavy breathing and Amy sobbing in the background.

The silence continued for over ten seconds before Hellyer said in a relaxed tone, "I assume I'm speaking to you, Bridgette? If it was the brat's mother, she would be screaming down the phone at me by now."

Bridgette swallowed hard, but didn't respond immediately. She wanted Hellyer to divulge as much information as possible before she spoke. He would be after a trade. Her life for Amy's, except she had no confidence he would keep his part of the bargain. If she didn't play her cards right, all three of them could be Hellyer's captives in a matter of minutes.

Finally, she said, "I'll come quietly. But you've got to release Amy first."

Hellyer laughed, and then hissed, "What do you take me for? Some kind of idiot? She's tied up on a chair here and I'm not releasing her until I have you here, tied up, and under my control."

Bridgette responded calmly, "She's only a girl and can't get off the island. How far can she run?"

Hellyer growled, "You've got two minutes. The cabin door is open and I'll be inside with the girl. You walk in unarmed, and I'll think about letting her go. Anything other than your full cooperation and I promise you I'll cut her from ear to ear and you can watch her bleed out."

Bridgette racked her brains to think how to buy more time.

As an afterthought, Hellyer said, "Two minutes and not a second more. If you're not here by then, I'm going to start cutting strips off her arms. If you don't believe me, just lean out her bedroom window. I'm sure you'll hear her when she screams."

There was a moment's silence before Hellyer added, "And tell the Brat's mother to stay in the house. If I see any sign you haven't come alone, she'll get her daughter back in pieces."

The line went dead. Bridgette looked up at Monica, who was now just inches from her side as she asked, "Is she okay?"

Bridgette swallowed. "He's got her tied up in the cabin, but I think she's okay for now."

Tears welled up in Monica's eyes. Her bottom lip quivered as she asked, "Oh my God, what are we going to do."

"Have you got all the shotgun shells?"

Monica nodded. "They're in my pocket."
"We need to move fast. I'll tell you my plan on the way."

Friday 6:02 PM

"Did you hear any of the conversation," asked Bridgette as they rushed through the house.

"Not really," said Monica.

"He wants to make a trade. Amy for me. Only I know he has no intention of keeping his promise. This is just his way of getting me to go to the cabin."

After stepping out of the mudroom and into the rear garden, Bridgette raised a hand to signal Monica to stop.

"He's threatened to harm Amy if I'm not there in two minutes, so we need to make this quick."

As Monica dissolved into tears again, Bridgette placed the shotgun on the ground and then gripped her by the shoulders.

"Monica, you need to hold it together!" Bridgette leaned in close and added, "I can't do this on my own."

Monica held Bridgette's gaze and nodded once. "You're right. I have to be strong for Amy. What do you need me to do?"

"He's going to leave the front door to the cabin open.

He wants to watch me walk up the path, and then he's promised to let Amy go when I arrive. But I don't think that's going to happen. He'll want to keep Amy as well, so I want you to circle wide through the woods with the shotgun and approach the cabin from the far side. Get as close to the side window as you can and look for an opportunity when he's not next to Amy."

Monica blinked. "Opportunity?"

Bridgette nodded. "To shoot him. Can you do that?"

Monica grimaced. "I've never shot an animal, let alone a human, but…"

"Hellyer is neither human nor animal—you'll be doing the world a favor."

"OK. But what happens if he doesn't have a gun? What if he's only got a knife? Do I still need to shoot him?"

"I'm fairly sure he will have a gun, even if he doesn't show it. We can't trust him. If you get a shot, take it."

Monica let out a breath. "OK."

"And one more thing… don't be waiting for him to be separated from me. As soon as you've got a clean shot where Amy's not in the firing line, you take it."

Monica frowned, "But I don't want to hit you as well."

Bridgette tightened her grip on Monica's shoulders. "You can't think like that! We have to save Amy and we have to take him down. If your aim is true, he'll cop most of the blast. This is all about the three of us surviving and this is the best plan we've got."

Bridgette let go of Monica and bent down to pick up the shotgun. After straightening up, she held Monica's gaze and added, "You can do this," and then handed Monica the weapon.

They stared at each other for a moment before Monica

said, "Thanks, Bridgette. You're putting your life on the line for my kid."

Bridgette put on a brave smile. "Be as quiet as you can going through the woods. It's getting dark, so be careful. We don't want you tripping while you're carrying a weapon."

Monica gave Bridgette a hug with her free arm. "I'm worried about you, too. What if he shoots you?"

Bridgette didn't want to go into all the gory details of what Hellyer did to his victims and simply responded, "He's not interested in shooting me, Monica, trust me."

"I'd better be going."

Bridgette said, "Good luck," then watched her host disappear into the woods.

Bridgette counted off thirty seconds in her head before she stepped out onto the trail that lead from the house to the cabin. She breathed in deeply to calm her nerves as she began the short walk. She didn't think Hellyer would be hiding anywhere close by to ambush her so she used the time to plan what to do next. He would be confident she would come to him on his terms while he had Amy. She tried to picture how the confrontation might go down, but knew from bitter experience events rarely played out the way they were planned.

She figured Amy would be tied to a chair. Probably in the middle of the cabin, close enough to the doorway that Hellyer could see outside. Hellyer was cunning. He would want to get her inside and tied up as quickly as possible. Bridgette knew the only way she could give Monica a clean shot was to keep her distance from Amy. She had to figure out a way to draw Hellyer away. He would probably have a gun and she didn't put it past him to shoot and wound her if she didn't fully cooperate.

Bridgette swallowed as the cabin came into view. She

could see light flooding outside and knew the door was open.

She could feel her heart beating through her chest as she approached. She hoped Monica was in position and wished they'd had time to figure out a way to signal each other. Bridgette moved off the pathway and into the open area in front of the cabin. She circled around until she was in front of the cabin and about fifty feet from the front door. Her heart skipped a beat as she saw Hellyer inside with a knife pressed against Amy's throat.

Amy was tied to a chair just as she had pictured, but Hellyer also had a piece of material wrapped tightly around her mouth to prevent her from screaming.

Amy's eyes widened as she realized Bridgette was close by and started mumbling through her gag. Bridgette didn't allow herself to be distracted as she focused her gaze on Hellyer and began summing up the situation. She could see no sign of a gun, but knew that meant nothing. Right now he had a knife at Amy's throat and that gave him all the power he needed.

She stopped ten feet short of the cabin's porch. They stared at each other for a few more seconds before Hellyer broke the silence. "Well, well. Good of you to join us, Detective Cash."

More silence followed before Hellyer said in a relaxed voice, "Where's the little bitch's mother?"

"I told her to stay back at the house and wait for Amy," she lied

Hellyer nodded. Bridgette was not sure if he believed her as he demanded, "I'm going to need you to step inside, detective."

In as even a voice as Bridgette could muster, she

responded, "The agreement was that you would let the girl go first."

Hellyer sneered, "I'm just one slice away from ending this little bitch's life. Get your ass in here now!"

Bridgette's eyes darted momentarily to the right of the cabin. As darkness closed in, it was impossible for her to tell if Monica was in position. She had to assume she was and wracked her brain to think of a way to draw Hellyer away.

"Untie her and I'll come forward."

Hellyer growled, "One slash, detective. That's all it will take."

Bridgette called his bluff. "You do that, and you'll be dead before sunrise."

Before Hellyer could respond, Bridgette moved to the edge of the porch to throw him off guard. She estimated she was now about fifteen feet from Hellyer and Amy. Close enough to be shot at if Hellyer produced a gun, but not close enough that she was at his complete mercy if all he had was a knife.

Bridgette added, "Untie her and I'll come to the door."

"Not going to happen. I'm going to count to five and..."

"You know it's me you want. She's just a kid. Let her go and you can have me."

Bridgette swallowed as she watched Hellyer's knife hand at Amy's throat. Her heart went out to the young girl who was hyperventilating. To her relief, Hellyer pulled the knife away from Amy's throat and cut the bindings that held her to the chair.

"She can go into the bathroom. But if you don't come straight away, her mother will need a plastic bag to take her home in."

Bridgette nodded. "We have a deal."

She prayed Monica was in position and winced as

Hellyer gripped Amy by the hair and dragged her through the cabin and out of sight.

A moment later, Bridgette heard a door slam.

Hellyer called out, "She's in the bathroom. Your time is up!"

Bridgette took a deep breath and walked up onto the porch. Her heart seemed to rise higher into her throat with each step. She couldn't see completely into the cabin from her position and wondered if he had double crossed her. But she was heartened when she could no longer hear Amy's whimpering.

She walked as far as the cabin's doorway before stopping again.

Hellyer walked back into the middle of the cabin and stopped. Bridgette breathed in deeply and tried to calm herself as she stared at her nemesis who now had a gun pointed at her chest.

As a sneer spread across his face, as he murmured, "It's time."

Friday 6:05 PM

Bridgette gulped as she stared into the barrel of the gun.

Hellyer demanded, "I won't ask again. Get your ass in here now, or I'm going back to the bathroom. I swear I'll only need fifteen minutes and she'll not only be dead but unrecognizable."

Hellyer ogled Bridgette up and down before he grinned and added, "And then I'll come after you. You can't get off the island and you won't be able to hide for long."

Bridgette held her breath as she moved gingerly forward. She stopped just inside the doorway and scanned the interior of the cabin. She was relieved to see that Amy was not in the room. Bridgette desperately wanted to check the side window to see if Monica was outside, but resisted the urge, knowing that even a momentary glance might tip Hellyer off that she was not alone.

Hellyer dropped the aim of the gun from her torso to her knee and said, "Start walking bitch or I'll blow your knee out."

Bridgette's brain was screaming, *'where is Monica?'* as she stepped forward. She wondered if Monica had tripped and fallen as she stared at Hellyer who was still a good twelve feet from her. He signaled for her to move to a chair he had set up near the fireplace.

Bridgette gulped again as she stared at the chair. It was facing the fireplace. She knew Hellyer would want her seated in the chair with her back to him before he approached.

Hellyer growled, "Get moving."

Bridgette ambled forward. Nine steps. Not long enough to make a proper plan, but it was all she had. She deliberately stopped behind the chair and gripped its top rail.

As Hellyer barked at her to sit, she pivoted and flung the chair across the room. It was more instinct than plan. Reckless and unlikely to succeed. But it was all she had and she was not going down without a fight. Bridgette dropped into a crouch as the first gunshot was fired. The expected searing pain of the bullet entering her body never came. At first she thought Hellyer's aim might have been wide, but as her brain registered the sound of shattering glass accompanying the gunshot, she realized it was Monica who had fired.

She lifted her head just in time to see Hellyer lurching sideways as he fired his weapon blindly at the window. Bridgette pressed herself to the floor as Hellyer crouched behind the table and fired at the window a second and third time.

The room went quiet for a moment before the silence was shattered by a second boom from the shotgun. This time, Bridgette saw the flash of the weapon and realized Monica was standing directly outside the window. She held her breath as Hellyer squeezed off multiple rounds in Monica's direction before he fled out the front door and into the night.

Bridgette's first thoughts were for Monica. Had she been

hit? She rushed to the window and peered into the darkness but could see no sign of her host. She shouted, "Monica! Are you there? Are you okay?"

It felt like the longest few seconds of Bridgette's life before Monica emerged from the shadows. Shaking uncontrollably, Monica walked forward, her eyes constantly darting about. She stopped a few feet from the cabin window, cradling the shotgun.

"Have you been hit?" asked Bridgette.

"I don't think so," answered Monica as she loaded another shell into the shotgun. "Where is he now?"

"He fled the cabin. Let's get you inside. You'll be safer in here."

Monica stood rooted to the spot. Tears flowed down her cheeks as she asked, "How's my baby? Is she alright?"

Bridgette soothed, "He locked her in the bathroom. I think she's okay."

Without replying, Monica rushed around to the front door of the cabin. Bridgette held her breath as she watched Monica stride through the cabin and open the door to the bathroom. She breathed again when Amy emerged and fell into her mother's arms.

While Amy sobbed in her mother's embrace, Bridgette moved back to the doorway and peered into the darkness.

She could see no sign of Hellyer as she closed the cabin door behind her.

After checking the door was properly locked, she turned and said, "Girls, I need you to give me a hand."

Bridgette strode to one end of the dining table and added, "We're not out of this yet, not by a long shot. We need to push this over to the window and upend it. Right now we are sitting ducks if he circles back."

Monica nodded. "You're right."

Out In The Cold

The three women dragged the heavy table across the room and tipped it up on one end. Bridgette pushed the table top back against the window opening and stepped back. The table covered all but the top third of the window. Not quite the full covering that she had hoped for, but Hellyer would be firing from above head height unless he found something to stand on.

For the first time since the ordeal began, Bridgette felt her body relax a little. She turned and gave Amy a brief hug and said, "Are you okay?"

Amy nodded. Through tears she responded, "I think so. I just want this to be over."

Bridgette stepped back to survey the damage. She barely heard Monica's question, "So what do we do now?"

Pointing to a trail of blood that led across the room towards the door, she responded, "Look? He's been hit."

Levi Frost slowed his car again. Only half concentrating on the road, he murmured, "Bingo," as his cell phone showed a one-bar signal. Frost pulled off to the shoulder and immediately hit speed dial to call his boss.

Delray answered on the third ring. "Tell me you've got good news."

Frost switched the engine off. "Not really, boss."

Delray growled, "What does that mean?"

Frost summarized what had happened since his last call to Delray. He got no further than telling him he had witnessed Hellyer land on the island before Delray exploded into a string of expletives.

After calming down a little, Delray added, "So what happened next?"

"He scaled a cliff face at the northern end of the island and then disappeared into the woods."

"Where are you now?"

"I'm in my car and about halfway back to Hope. There's still no cell signal out there. I've been checking while I drove back and picked up a faint signal two miles back. I tried calling the Hope Chief of Police again, but only spoke to the deputy. He was sympathetic, but he said it's unlikely they can get anyone out there for at least another eight to ten hours."

"Why the hell not?"

"The flooding has been bad, boss. The cell coverage wasn't great, and the deputy kept cutting in and out, but it sounded like three people have drowned downriver. I've driven another couple of miles closer to town before calling you and…"

"So what are you planning to do now?"

Frost stared through the windscreen at the closing darkness. "I'm not sure. I was thinking about getting a boat…"

Delray interrupted, "Trying to get onto an island in the dark across a flooded river is suicide, Levi."

Frost grimaced. "You're probably right." He let out a breath and said, "Right now, we've only got two things going for us."

"And what are they?"

"The rain has stopped. I'm going to head back to the island. Sooner or later, the water level will drop. There's a footbridge which I spotted on the way back. It's mostly underwater right now, but if the river drops quickly enough, I should be able to use it to get onto the island."

"Well, that's something I guess. And what's the second thing?

"When I was returning to my car, I saw Bridgette

standing on the jetty on the other side of the river. I managed to…"

"You saw Bridgette? Was she okay?"

"Yeah. Hellyer had only been on the island a short time by then. Anyway, I got word to her about what was happening. She then bolted back to the house."

"Do you know if they are armed?"

"Yeah, the owner has a shotgun."

There was silence for a moment before Delray responded, "Well, that's something, at least."

"She won't go down without a fight, Chief."

"That she won't."

There was silence for a moment before Frost said, "If you can keep the pressure up on the local police for help, I'd appreciate it."

Delray responded, "Got it."

Frost started the car. "I'm going to head back."

There was a pause before Delray responded, "Levi… all that instruction I gave you about staying out of this and leaving it to the local police?"

"Yeah."

"That's out the window. You get a shot, you take it."

Frost was already pulling a U-turn as he shouted, "I just hope I'm not too late."

Friday 6:27 PM

After closing and locking the front door, Bridgette pulled the cabin's three chairs together in a tight circle in the middle of the room and then arranged them to face the table she had placed as a barricade in front of the window.

After they had sat down, there was silence for a moment while they collected their thoughts. Bridgette found it hard to believe they were all still alive. Her respect for Monica was growing by the minute. She glanced at her host who had seemed on the verge of a breakdown just a short time ago at the house. But she had pulled herself together for the sake of her daughter.

She took a deep breath as she reflected on Hellyer's last few minutes in the cabin and how lucky she and Amy were to still be alive. She knew what Hellyer wanted to do to her. Hours of torture while he wielded his small knife. She shuddered as she thought about it and was relieved when Monica broke the silence.

"How are you feeling, Amy?"

Amy shivered as she responded, "I'm okay."

Bridgette frowned. She knew Amy was traumatized and got up from her chair and retrieved her spare coat from a peg on the wall near the fireplace.

She handed it to Amy and said, "Here, put this on. We need to keep you warm."

Amy thanked Bridgette as she put on the coat. She looked pale and shaky. It was understandable, and Bridgette felt guilty they were all in this mess. In time, she would encourage Monica to get her daughter counseling to make sure she recovered properly.

With an encouraging smile, Bridgette said, "I'm very proud of the way you're handling this, Amy." Bridgette turned to Monica and added, "Both of you. You saved my life, and I can't thank you enough."

"I almost didn't," responded Monica with a frown. "Working my way through the woods took a lot longer than I expected. By the time I got to the window and saw…" Monica shook her head before adding, "I thought I was too late."

"But you weren't."

Monica closed her eyes while the tears welled up.

Amy pointed at the blood trail leading to the cabin door. "Do you think he's badly hurt?"

"It's hard to tell," said Bridgette as studied the blood pattern. "The blood could be from glass cuts just as much from shotgun pellets."

Monica said, "After I fired the second time, he seemed to… spin sideways, almost like I'd hit him in the shoulder. It was all a blur, but looking back now…"

With her eyes still fixed on the blood pattern, Bridgette said, "Often you don't bleed as much when you've been hit by a shotgun unless a pellet strikes a major artery."

Bridgette thought about the consequences of Hellyer's

wounds as she continued to study the blood trail. If he was badly injured, he would try to find some place to hide and recover until he could get off the island. If his wounds were minor, he would retreat and prepare to come after them again. She thought back to her last encounter with Hellyer on the roof at the hospital. He had used fire as a distraction while he had tried to get away, and it had almost worked.

She looked up at the roof of the cabin and went cold. Even though there had been a lot of heavy rain, she knew a fire would still take hold if it was started on the inside of the cabin.

Monica asked, "What are you thinking, Bridgette?"

Bridgette was not about to share her fears. "I need to go after him."

"What? Are you crazy?" protested Monica.

Amy went to speak as well, but Bridgette held up her hand. "We may have a small window of opportunity. He won't be expecting us to come after him and…"

"But why?" said Monica, holding out her arms.

Bridgette looked at the front door as she rose from her chair. "I'm going to head back to the main house and circumnavigate it. I want to see if he's inside and if so, what he's doing. That will help us plan what we do next."

"And what if he's not there?" demanded Monica. "What if he's hiding in the woods waiting to shoot you as soon as you step out the front door?"

Bridgette shrugged. "That's a risk I have to take."

Monica shook her head. "This is madness!"

Bridgette held Monica's gaze. "You don't know him like I do. Unless he's seriously wounded, he will come after us again. I'm sorry, but that's just the way he is. This is our best hope. We need to stay on the front foot."

The cabin went quiet for a moment.

Monica looked at Amy and then back at Bridgette and said, "Crap. I don't like this. But you're the cop. You better take the shotgun, just in case."

"No," said Bridgette with a shake of her head. "You'll need it here for your own protection. All I'm going to do for now is check the house. Logic dictates that's where he will go. He'll need some sort of light to check and dress his wounds. The house is the ideal location and he won't be expecting us to return any time soon."

Bridgette unlocked the door. "Lock this as soon as I get outside and don't open it until I return."

Before Monica or Amy could respond, Bridgette disappeared into the night.

Bridgette sprinted from the cabin to the cover of the woods. After reaching the forest, she took a moment to allow her eyes to adjust to the darkness while she planned her next move. The walk to the house would take her less than two minutes if she followed the path. She didn't think Hellyer would be waiting to ambush her, but she couldn't afford to take the risk.

She circled wide through the woods and approached the house from the front. There were more windows across the front and she figured it would be easier to see movement inside from this angle. Circling left through the woods, she trod carefully to avoid making any unnecessary sounds. After the roar of the storm, the dull rumble of the flooded river in the background seemed eerily quiet by comparison. It took her close to five minutes to edge her way through the woods before the Pooles' house came into view.

Using a Western Hemlock at the edge of the woods for

cover, Bridgette stopped for a moment to study the house. She could see a table lamp on in the main living area and the glow of the fire, but nothing else. There was no movement inside, and the house was quiet. Bridgette scanned the windows of the other rooms across the front of the house, but they were all in darkness.

She narrowed her eyes and peered at the house's upper level. She had never been up there, but Monica had mentioned it contained a guest bedroom, a small bathroom and her office. Each room looked to be in darkness, but with the curtains drawn, it was hard to tell. Bridgette frowned. She needed a different angle to check each room again to be sure. She looked at her car in the middle of the circular gravel drive. It was the only spot that would give her cover and a different view of the front of the house. But it was fifty feet from her current position. She desperately wanted to sprint across the gravel to her car, but she knew the noise she made would alert Hellyer to her presence if he were close by.

Bridgette looked up into the night sky. The heavy cloud cover shut out most of the moonlight. If Hellyer was watching from the house, he would only see vague shadows in the darkness. She took a deep breath. It was a risk she had to take. After creeping out from the cover of the woods, she tiptoed across the gravel, careful to avoid making any sound. Relieved she hadn't been shot at when she reached her car, Bridgette crouched behind the front fender to study the house again.

She scanned each of the upper rooms, but could see no telltale signs of light spilling out from the cracks between the curtains. She was now reasonably confident there were no lights on in any of the upper rooms. Bridgette switched her gaze back to ground level again and focused on the living room. She still couldn't see any sign of movement and sighed as she realized she would need to check the back of the house as well before she returned to Monica and Amy.

Remaining crouched over, she inched backward until she was under the cover of the woods again. It took her two patient minutes to circle through the woods before the rear of the house came into view. The lights were on just as they had been earlier when she and Monica had left to go to the cabin. Through the sheer curtains, she could see a large part of the kitchen and the meals area. From her vantage point, she could see no sign of Hellyer.

Bridgette frowned. She was positive this was where Hellyer would come to treat his wounds. Realizing she needed a better angle, Bridgette sprinted across the back lawn as far as a Skimmia bush before crouching down again. The new viewpoint gave her a closer look at the house from a different angle, but she could still see no sign of anyone in the kitchen or the mudroom. She listened intently for any sound while she watched for movement inside the house. After about two minutes, Bridgette grimaced and sighed; this was not what she expected.

Unsure of what to do next, she tried to think like Hellyer. If his wounds weren't bad, he could be anywhere on the island planning his next attack. Bridgette pictured the blood trail across the cabin floor as she considered the situation. If he had been hit by glass, it would be excruciating to leave in his body. If his wounds had been made by shotgun pellets they would be hard to ignore and he would need tweezers or something similar to dig them out. Either scenario demanded proper light to attend to his wounds. Tending wounds was not something you could easily accomplish in a forest. But Hellyer was not like any other person she had ever met. When cornered, he acted more like a like a wild animal than a human and she needed to factor that in. Maybe he was just blocking out the pain? Maybe he had returned to his boat and was already making his way across the river to get off the island? And maybe he was just hiding in the woods, waiting for the next moment to strike?

Bridgette felt a shiver run down her spine as she realized Hellyer could be close by watching her right now. She glanced back over her shoulder into the darkness as an uneasy feeling settled over her. She had hoped to find out how badly injured he was. So far, her attempts to get on the front foot had been fruitless. It had been almost half an hour since she had left the cabin and she knew Monica and Amy would panic if she was not back soon.

Bridgette bit her bottom lip. She felt vulnerable without a weapon and was not about to go searching in the dark for her nemesis. If he was out there waiting for her to come to him that would play into his hands. She turned to head back to the cabin, but a nagging feeling in the pit of her stomach bothered her. She looked back at the house again. What if he was inside and badly injured? What if he was lying on the floor or somewhere else out of sight? Bridgette swore under her breath.

The fear of not knowing made the whole situation impossible, and she hated the idea of returning to the cabin without being sure. Bridgette focused on the door to the mudroom as she sucked in a deep breath. After counting to three in her head, she sprinted across the lawn to the rear of the house. Pressing herself up against back wall of the house, she focused on the door that led into the mudroom. It was slightly ajar, which bothered her. She couldn't recall if it had been left that way when she and Monica had left earlier, or if Hellyer had left it open as he entered the house.

Out In The Cold

Bridgette inched along the wall until she could peer in through the mudroom window. Nothing seemed to have changed. Coats were still hanging on hangers, muddy boots were still lined up neatly against one wall, and a set of shelves with storage containers looked undisturbed.

Although she could see no sign of Hellyer, she pictured him standing in the shadows, somewhere inside the house. Waiting to ambush her. Perhaps with a knife. Perhaps with a gun. The thought played on her mind as she gripped the edge of the door and gently opened it.

Bridgette waited another thirty seconds while she continued to peer inside, listening for any sound that would indicate she was walking into an ambush. She heard nothing and rose to her full height. She stood perfectly still for another few seconds and then moved forward until she was in the mudroom doorway before stopping again. After taking a breath, she took a step forward. The background roar of the river faded now that she was inside. She listened to the sounds inside the house. She heard the low hum of the refrigerator, and the odd creak of the timber in the house as it settled after the storm, but nothing else. No sound of anyone breathing. No sound of someone walking across floorboards or on the treads of the stairs.

Bridgette took another deep breath and moved forward a few more steps. She stopped just short of the hallway. The door was wide open, just as she remembered.

Her blood ran cold as she looked down at the tiled floor and counted off six red spots. Bridgette didn't need to bend down to examine them—she knew it was blood. Barely able to breathe, she looked up at the open door that lead into the hallway.

Her first instinct was to turn and run, but she knew six drops of blood didn't answer her question. Hellyer had definitely been here. But was he still inside the house? Had he come and gone or was he holed up somewhere inside? Bridgette contemplated her next move.

Finally, she inched forward. Just far enough to peer into the hallway. Her heart raced as she scanned to her left and right. No sign of him. Bridgette took one step into the hallway and stopped again to listen. Still no sound. She examined the hallway floor, looking for any more drops of blood, and saw three that lead from the hallway towards the kitchen. Holding her breath, Bridgette crept forward, stopping just short of the open doorway that lead into the kitchen and meals area.

She tried to calm her breathing as she studied the scene before her. The first aid kit was open on the kitchen island counter top. The counter was strewn with bloody red rags. Almost certainly clothing Hellyer had found and ripped up to clean and dress his wounds. She scanned as much of the rest of the living area as she could see. The chairs around the colonial dining table seemed to be in the same position and nothing else looked disturbed.

Bridgette crept through the kitchen and stood in the archway that lead to the living room. She expected to see Hellyer positioned ready to shoot her, or lying on the floor in agony if his wounds had been serious. But there was no sign of him.

With her heart racing, Bridgette walked across to the polished oak stairway that lead upstairs. She glanced behind her before she turned to study each tread of the stairs. She couldn't see any blood spots, but that was no guarantee Hellyer hadn't gone upstairs.

Bridgette decided not to walk up the stairs. She had heard Monica come down them earlier that day and they had squeaked under her weight. If Hellyer was upstairs, he would almost certainly hear the noise, and she was a sitting duck if he confronted her. Best to retreat to plan her next move.

As she walked back through the kitchen area, Bridgette retrieved a flashlight from a drawer. She took one last look around before leaving and froze as she saw a slip of paper on the dining table. She frowned. The paper hadn't been there when she and Monica had left for the cabin; she was sure of that.

Bridgette crossed to the table and peered down at the note. A chill ran down her spine as she read her name, which had been hastily scribbled across the top.

Friday 7:09 PM

Bridgette knocked on the cabin door and said quietly, "It's me. I'm alone."

She took a step back as she heard the door unlock. A moment later, the door flung open, leaving Bridgette momentarily staring into the barrel of Monica's shotgun.

As Bridgette's heart skipped a beat, Monica lowered the weapon and said, "Sorry, I just wanted to be sure."

Bridgette murmured, "It's good to be cautious," and then stepped into the cabin.

Monica waited until Amy had locked the door and then asked, "Did you find him?"

Bridgette shook her head and then gave them a quick rundown of how she had circled the house but had found no sign of Hellyer. She added, "I'm not sure what it was about the house, but I had a feeling he was still inside."

"You didn't go in? Surely not!" stammered Monica.

Bridgette grimaced. "The surveillance seemed a pointless exercise if I didn't."

Amy's eyes widened. "So you went inside?"

Bridgette nodded.

Both women stared at Bridgette for a moment before Monica said, "Did you find him?"

Bridgette shook her head. "I couldn't find any sign of him inside the house, but he had definitely been there. The medicine kit was out on the island bench and there were bloody rags piled up there as well."

"Do you think he's badly hurt?" asked Monica.

"It's hard to tell. There were a few drops of blood on the floor, but it didn't seem like he was bleeding badly." Bridgette opened the note that Hellyer had written to her and then added, "When I went to leave, I found this on the dining table…"

Amy and Monica read the note together.

It seems our reunion will need to be postponed.
Such a pity.
The cabin would have been the perfect spot, don't you think?
We could have had a wonderful time - you, me and my knife.
I count the days, indeed the hours, until we can be together again.
Until then, I will see you in your dreams…

Monica shuddered. "This is creepy. What does he mean? Has he left the island?"

Bridgette grimaced. "I'm not sure. Part of me desperately wants to believe he's gone. And now that he knows we have a gun, that would make sense. But…"

Monica's eyes widened. "You think he's still here?"

"Honestly, I don't know," answered Bridgette, folding up the note. "If he's not badly hurt, he may have decided to cut his losses and leave the island. But the note could also be a misdirection."

"What? Trying to lull us into a false sense of security?" asked Monica.

Bridgette nodded. "Possibly. I don't see…"

Monica interjected, "But surely he wouldn't dare come after us again? Not now that he knows we're armed?"

"I thought about it from multiple angles on my way back to the cabin. We can't afford to be complacent."

"So what do we do now?" asked Monica.

"We need to leave."

"Why? Aren't we safer here with a gun?" asked Amy with a frown.

Bridgette explained how Hellyer had set fire to the hospital as a distraction shortly before his arrest. She didn't feel comfortable frightening Amy, but decided this was the best way to get her message across. She concluded by adding, "He's not easily dissuaded and he could easily do that again here."

"You really think he would try and set fire to the cabin?" asked Monica.

Bridgette nodded. "I know it's wet on the outside, but if he made a Molotov cocktail or something similar and threw it in through the gap in the window, this place would go up in flames in just a few seconds. We would be at his mercy. And I don't want to put us in that position. We can't afford to stay."

Monica shrugged. "Then where do we go?"

"I think we need to get off the island. I don't like the idea of going back to the main house, because I think we'll be just as vulnerable there."

"But how on earth do we get off the island?" demanded Monica. "We don't have a boat and the river is still a raging flood."

Keeping her voice as calm as she could, Bridgette

responded, "On the way back to the cabin, I took a quick detour down to the footbridge. The water has started receding, and the torrent isn't as strong as it was two hours ago. The water level has dropped below the railing and is continuing to drop. It will be up around our thighs, but I'm confident if we hang on to the railing and take it slow, we'll make it across okay."

"This is crazy," retorted Monica. "Don't you remember what happened to you last time you tried to cross?"

Bridgette shook her head. "Actually, it's not crazy. While there's a slight risk we may get hit by another wave, Hellyer will assume we're staying here. This is the last thing he'll be expecting, and that gives us an edge."

Monica responded, "Wouldn't it be smarter to wait until daylight?"

"We'll be safer crossing under the cover of darkness. The only alternative I can think of is hiding in the woods for the night."

"I'm not sure that's any safer than staying here," replied Monica.

"Bottom line is, I don't want to put you two in any more danger. Staying here isn't smart and I wouldn't be suggesting this if I thought we had a better option."

Monica let out a deep sigh and then looked at her daughter. "What do you think, Amy?"

Amy responded, "I kinda like the idea of getting as far away from him as possible. Even if we have to get wet."

Monica shook her head. "I can't believe this is happening to us. Surely we've been through enough." She looked at Bridgette and asked, "So, what's the plan? If he's still on the island, he could be outside waiting for us right now."

"Yes, he could be," acknowledged Bridgette. "But that's

a risk we have to take. I think our best option is to turn out the lights and let our eyes adjust to the darkness. We wait fifteen minutes and then we head out quietly with no sound and no lights. We walk across the clearing until we get to the slope that leads down to the bridge. The first part of the slope is all rock and it will be slippery. I think we need to go down that section one at a time. I'll get you to go first Monica, and then Amy and then I'll follow with the shotgun."

Monica frowned. "We're doing this without a flashlight?"

Bridgette nodded. "Only when we get down to the bottom of the slope do we turn the flashlight on. And then only to get our bearings. Once we reach the bridge, I'll keep the shotgun trained back up the slope. I don't expect it will take us anything more than a couple of minutes to cross the bridge and then we just disappear into the forest and keep walking until we find a farmhouse to raise the alarm."

"What happens if he shoots at us while we're crossing?" asked Monica.

"That's a risk we're going to have to take. It will be dark and he's right-handed, and you think you hit him in the right shoulder. Pistols are notoriously inaccurate unless you're a marksman. If he spots us and starts shooting, I'll return fire."

"Could he be setting a trap for us?" asked Amy. "What if he's waiting for us on the other side?"

"When we get to the bridge, I'll turn the flashlight on and quickly scan the other side of the river as well."

Monica looked at her daughter and said, "What do you think, Amy? This is your decision as well."

"I say we do it," said Amy firmly. "The sooner we get off this island, the better as far as I'm concerned."

Hellyer gingerly rotated his right arm and shoulder as he stared through the woods at the back of the cabin. He could feel the muscles in his shoulder seizing up as the bruising and swelling increased. He was furious with himself for underestimating the girl's mother. He hadn't expected her to come after him, particularly with a shotgun.

Still, it could have been worse. After escaping the cabin, he had gone back to the main house to assess his wounds. Stripping off his coat and blood-soaked shirt had been painful but necessary. He had counted over a dozen shotgun pellets in his right shoulder and upper torso as he cleaned up his wounds. He had also discovered some glass shards in his neck. The shards were easy enough to pick out with a small pair of tweezers he had found in the first-aid kit. But the pellets were embedded much deeper into his flesh and had proven more problematic to remove. They would have to wait. He figured he had twenty-four hours to get them out before they turned septic. For now, his arm and shoulder still worked, and the bleeding had mostly stopped. He could function and that was all that mattered. Hellyer rotated his shoulder again. The Tylenol he had found in the woman's house was barely taking the edge off the pain, but it was enough to help him focus and concentrate.

All in all, he was comfortable enough with the situation he found himself in. Still alive and alone with three victims in his sights was as good as it got.

He had watched the cop bitch go into the house. He thought about following her inside, but he didn't know if she had a gun or not. And with his injuries, he needed to play it smart. He had watched her leave the house again and had followed her at a safe distance down to the river.

He had watched her inspect the water line. He figured by morning, the water would be low enough for them to risk using the footbridge to get off the island. He couldn't afford for that to happen. Now was the time to strike. While they were in the cabin, where he expected they would spend the night.

It was a pity he wouldn't get to spend the precious hours he had planned alone with the cop. Such a wasted opportunity. But sometimes plans had to change. He thought about the mother as he rotated his shoulder again. He would make sure her death was slow and painful as punishment for shooting him. He liked the idea of tying her up and killing the daughter in front of her. Making the daughter scream and beg for mercy would add a layer of psychological pain for her that would bring him ecstasy.

Hellyer flicked on a cigarette lighter and stared down at the supplies he had taken from the house. A bottle of turpentine and some bandaging from the first aid kit were all he needed to create mayhem. He was not worried about the light being thrown from the lighter. He was a good sixty yards from the back of the cabin and he was fairly confident no one would be looking out the tiny high-set bathroom window in his direction. He decided he would wait another hour before moving in. They would be on edge right now, but hopefully, with the passing of time, they would relax a little .

Hellyer flicked the lighter off and focused on the cabin again. He pictured the tiny building ablaze and imagined the screams coming from inside. The thought of the mayhem he would create gave him a tingle in his groin. He felt for the gun in his coat pocket. He only had one bullet left. He hadn't expected to use the weapon at all and would reserve the last bullet for whoever had the shotgun as they came out of the cabin. He would hunt the others down later, if necessary. Hellyer promised himself none of them would leave the island alive as he settled in to wait.

Barely a minute had passed before the lights in the cabin went out. Hellyer frowned. He had expected them to stay on all night. He couldn't believe they were moving, particularly before sunrise. That would be risky and leave them open to an ambush. But why switch the lights off now? It was too early for sleep and he doubted they would sleep anyway.

Hellyer wondered what they were up to as he listened intently. He heard nothing and moved in for a closer look.

Friday 7:13 PM

Bridgette counted off fifteen minutes in her head and then said to Monica and Amy in a low voice, "Are we ready to go?"

"As ready as we'll ever be," replied Monica.

Amy grimaced. "I think I need to pee first. Sorry. Is that okay?"

"A couple more minutes won't make any difference," said Bridgette with a small smile of encouragement.

Monica and Bridgette watched Amy walk through the shadows of the cabin before disappearing into the bathroom.

When she had closed the door behind her, Bridgette said, "How do you think she's holding up?"

With only the glow of the coals in the fireplace for light, Monica's frown was not lost on Bridgette. "She's a tough kid, but she's been through a lot. Frankly, I'm surprised she's functioning at all."

"That's the other reason I want to get us off the island now. The sooner we get away, the sooner she will feel safe."

"I agree."

Bridgette put a hand on Monica's shoulder. "I think it would be wise for you both to get counseling when this is all over. Traumatic situations like this can play on your mind for years if they're not addressed properly."

"Have you ever had counseling?"

Bridgette nodded. "Yes. Part of my reason for coming here ironically, was therapy. My psychiatrist advised me I needed to get away to clear my head."

Monica shook her head. "Only your nightmare followed you."

Bridgette shrugged. "It's an occupational hazard, I guess. But talking it through with a professional helps. You both would…"

Bridgette heard the toilet flush and decided to continue the conversation with Monica later when they were alone. Amy returned and said with a sheepish look, "I'm ready now."

Bridgette picked up the shotgun. She went over the plan, just to be sure they were all clear on the steps ahead. She asked if they had any questions.

Monica said, "I think I would feel more comfortable with you taking the lead, Bridgette. If all hell breaks loose while we're crossing the bridge, your instinct as a cop will be much better than mine for an escape."

Bridgette nodded. "I don't have a problem with that, but if you're last on the bridge, you'll need to be carrying the shotgun."

"I shot the bastard once. I'm happy to do it again," responded Monica flatly.

Bridgette handed Monica the shotgun and remaining shells and said, "The safety is on. Just remember that if you need to use it."

Monica nodded.

Bridgette moved to the front door. In a low voice she said, "We'll walk across the clearing together and then go down the slope one-by-one just like we planned."

Bridgette paused a moment and took a deep breath. "If anything happens before we get to the bridge, sprint to the woods and don't look back. Just find a place to hide until you hear from me again."

Bridgette opened the door and stepped out onto the porch. She signaled the others not to follow just yet. Unable to see anything in the darkness, she stopped to listen to the sounds of the night, attentive to anything that sounded out of place. She stood for a few seconds, but she could hear nothing above the roar of the river. She waved the others to follow her and together they stepped off the porch and crept across the clearing.

Bridgette only allowed herself to breathe again when they had reached the slope. Keen to keep moving, she whispered, "Remember, this is going to be really slippery. Amy, as soon as I get off the stones, you follow straight away."

"OK," whispered Amy in response.

Bridgette took one step forward and immediately felt her boot slip on the mossy stone surface. She realized there was little chance she would make it down the embankment without falling. Going down the slope on her butt was not what she had planned. It would take twice as long, but the thought of falling and hitting her head convinced her she had no choice.

Cursing under her breath, she sat down and began making her way down the slope as quickly and as she could. She ignored the mud on her clothes and the grime on her hands and between her fingers. The focus was on getting off the stones as quickly as possible.

When she got to the end of the stony section, she turned and signaled for Amy to follow.

Bridgette could barely make out the outline of Amy against the darkness. She watched as the young woman crouched and then made her way down the stones just as she had.

Bridgette turned her focus to the other shape, still standing at the top of the slope and holding the shotgun. She wondered what Monica was thinking as she watched her daughter descend.

She thought for a moment about Monica's request for her to go first, and wondered why she had asked for the change. Bridgette wondered if there was more to it than just wanting her to take the lead. Perhaps it was about protecting her daughter? If Monica thought it more likely that Hellyer was still on the island, it stood to reason that she would want to be between him and her daughter defending her with her life if necessary.

The image of Amy clutching her mother in the cabin after she had been rescued flooded into her mind. The relief and gratitude on Amy's face was genuine. She clearly understood it was her mother who had saved her life. While it was a horrible way to re-unite, she felt mother and daughter were re-establishing a broken bond.

Bridgette was brought back to the moment as she focused on the shadows twenty feet to the right of Monica. The shadows all appeared to be trees and morphed into one another in the darkness. Her gut tightened. Did she see movement, or were her eyes playing tricks on her? Bridgette narrowed her eyes as she stared into the darkness and then went cold as she saw a shadow move.

She screamed, "Lookout, Monica! On your left..."

The sound of a gunshot broke the stillness of the night.

In the moment she expected to see Monica collapse to the ground, her host pivoted and fired back. The illumination from the blast only lasted a fraction of a second, but it was enough for her to see the silhouette of Alex Hellyer rushing towards Monica. Bridgette screamed to Amy to head for the bridge as she started scrambling back up the slope. As she climbed she could see the two wrestling for control of the shotgun and then heard a dull thud just as she reached the top of the stones.

She watched in horror as Monica collapsed to the ground. In the darkness she could just make out the shape of Hellyer bending down to pick up the shotgun by the barrel. Gripping her flashlight like a club, she rushed Hellyer. Her nemesis pivoted and swung the shotgun at her like a baseball bat. The wooden stock of the weapon glanced off her shoulder and crashed into her neck as she tried to duck. Bridgette stumbled to her right and felt a sharp pain in her chest as Hellyer's boot connected with her rib cage.

In an instant, she felt weightless as she tumbled backward. She saw an explosion of light as her head hit the stones. A shadow loomed over her. Despite the danger, Bridgette felt her body relax. Her mind willed her to get to her feet, but her body had other ideas. The shadow above her started to spin. Slowly at first, before it picked up speed. She could hear the faint whimpers of Monica close by and the screams of Amy in the distance as she drifted off to sleep.

After the call with Delray, Frost drove back to the island at top speed. Even though the rain had stopped, the road was still slippery, and his car spun out twice trying to negotiate bends going too fast. Thinking he might not be as lucky a third time, he slowed down.

Throughout the drive, he couldn't get the image of Bridgette sprinting back to the house out of his mind.

He shuddered as he thought about Hellyer now being on the island. He wondered if she was still alive, but decided that was a negative way to think. She was tough and capable, forewarned and armed. Frost took comfort from that as he finally pulled up in the same spot on the side road that he had left earlier that day.

Frost walked down to the river's edge and stood in the darkness. He listened for a moment. He could hear no sounds above the roar of the river.

He switched on his flashlight and played it across the water. The river level had dropped a little, but he guessed the bridge was still under a few feet of water.

Frost turned the flashlight downstream and played it over the jetty. No sign of Bridgette. And no sign of Hellyer, either. He was not sure what he'd expected, but he was okay with everything being quiet for now.

Frost turned on his heel. Encouraged by the slight drop in the river level, he hoped he could wade across the river using the footbridge. He had barely taken ten steps before he heard the unmistakable sound of a gun. Frost clenched his teeth. It sounded like it had come from near the footbridge. Before the sound had dissipated, Frost was already at full speed. He knew the difference between the boom of a shotgun and the blast of a pistol. What he had heard was not a shotgun and that meant Hellyer was firing. He heard return fire and braced for the worst as he worked his way through the trees along the riverbank.

Friday 7:24 PM

As part of her studies in criminology, Bridgette learned a little about the torment victims encounter when suffering a violent or untimely death. What a victim experiences in being burnt to death differs significantly from what they experience when dying from gunshot wounds, and it is different again to the experience of drowning. Before starting her studies she had assumed drowning was a peaceful way to die. That you floated off to sleep, never to wake again—at least not in this world.

But after studying the five stages of drowning as part of her course, she realized she couldn't have been more wrong. The first stage was known as surprise or panic. It was the point where the victim realizes they are in imminent danger —submerged beneath water and unable to take a breath.

The second stage follows soon after. In this stage, the epiglottis involuntarily shuts the airway as a defense mechanism to stop water from entering the lungs.

In the third stage, the victim becomes unconsciousness —usually within two minutes of stage one. In this stage, respiratory arrest begins, and the body starts to ingest water. At this point, a victim's only hope of survival is rescue and resuscitation.

In stage four, the victim convulses involuntarily because of a lack of oxygen. The seizures, along with the skin turning blue, mark the onset of clinical death.

In stage five, irreversible damage to vital organs such as the victim's brain, heart, lungs and liver commence.

She had read horrific stories of how some victims had been resuscitated after entering stage five of the drowning process, only to live with significant and permanent brain damage. She figured death for a victim who had entered stage five was a far more merciful outcome.

It became apparent to her that drowning was not a pleasant way to die. Fighting the panic as your body ran out of oxygen and your lungs filled with water seemed like a nightmare she would not want to inflict on her worst enemy.

Since completing the subject, she had barely given the topic a second thought. Like so much else of what she had learned, it was information she kept in the vast data reserves of her mind to call upon if ever needed for an investigation.

Never did she think the process would apply to her. Never did she think for a moment that drowning would be how she would meet her demise.

As she regained consciousness, what she had learned about drowning was the furthest thing from her mind. Bridgette opened her eyes, but the darkness remained. She felt cold and confused—like she was having an out-of-body experience. She floated as if her mind was trying to break free of her body, eager to depart this life for what lay beyond.

Deep within her brain, something fought against the

separation. A battle raged within her. Part of her mind welcomed the peaceful separation that death would bring. But a small part of her brain resisted the temptation and willed her to fight as long as she could. The darkness continued to shroud her, its cold tentacles pressing against her face and body. She was conscious of a raging fire in her throat, a paradox to what the rest of her body was experiencing.

Bridgette's mind reconnected with her body and her senses reactivated. Like an engine restarting, her brain became aware of her surroundings. In an instant, she recognized the darkness that wrapped around her as freezing cold water and the burning she felt in her throat as the hands of someone compressing her windpipe.

Her lungs screamed for oxygen.

Now fully conscious, Bridgette tried to kick out, but her legs wouldn't move. She was aware of a weight on top of her and realized she was being pinned down. She could hear water swirling around her. Not the tranquil sound of water bubbling when she dipped her head underwater while having a bath. This was different. The sound was loud and urgent. She realized she was in the river and then remembered she had fallen and hit her head on the rocky slope. She was not sure how long she had been unconscious but she realized Hellyer must have dragged her down to the river's edge to drown her.

Bridgette could feel Hellyer's fingers tighten around her throat. She thrashed again, but Hellyer's grip remained vice-like. She could feel his knee on her chest, as if he was determined to keep her pinned down in shallow water. Bridgette swung wildly with a clenched right fist, but only landed a glancing blow on Hellyer's back. She repeated the same swing with her left fist, but he ignored that too.

Bridgette closed her eyes again, her lungs were on fire. The coldness of the water evaporated as her mind focused all its energy on her need for oxygen. She tried to shake her head, but in response Hellyer dug his fingers in even tighter.

The two forces in her mind she had experienced just seconds ago returned. The desire within her mind to separate from her body and escape this life was seductive, but the will to fight would not surrender. Knowing she was on the brink of passing out, Bridgette reached up with her hands until they broke the water's surface. She felt her right hand touch Hellyer's face before he pulled away. Bridgette frantically tried to grab his hair.

In response, he tried to push her head deeper into the riverbed.

As she continued to thrash, Bridgette grabbed his hair with the fingers of her right hand, and clenched her hand shut.

She could feel him try to pull away as she held on for dear life. Now with a reference point, Bridgette grabbed at his hair with her left hand as well.

She thought she heard a groan above the roar of the water, but couldn't be sure. Hellyer started thrashing as she pulled back with both hands for all she was worth. In an instant, she felt his weight shift. Bridgette brought up her right knee and connected with his groin. She lifted her head out of the water as he let go of her throat. Oxygen had never tasted sweeter as she took a deep breath. Amid a fit of coughing, she continued to gulp in the night air as she tried to get her bearings. She tried to roll away, but Hellyer lurched at her as she attempted to struggle to her feet and shoved her into deeper water pushing her head below the surface again.

Frost figured he was about two minutes from the footbridge when he heard screaming above the roar of the river. He quickened his pace as best he could in the conditions, but as he closed in on the footbridge all he could hear was sobbing somewhere in the forest on his side of the river. He knew from the tone and pitch of the voice that it was a young woman, probably the same person who had screamed earlier.

Conscious that he could be setting himself up as a target for Hellyer as he searched for the woman, Frost switched his flashlight off and pulled out his pistol. Barely able to see three feet in front of him, he slowed to a walk as he fumbled his way through the darkness. His progress was slow, and he stopped frequently to check that he was still closing in on the girl's sobs.

Her voice ebbed and flowed as if she was on the move through the trees and undergrowth. With every step he took to follow her, he knew that she was moving further away from the river.

Frost frowned as he pushed on. He had heard no other voices and figured she was alone. He guessed the gunshot had caused her to run. Alone and frightened, he knew engaging her wouldn't be easy, and he didn't want to traumatize her any further.

Frost stopped again to listen. The whimpering continued, but he didn't think she was moving anymore.

If Hellyer had captured her, she would be screaming. He wondered what she was doing. Maybe she was tired of running and had found a hiding spot. He debated turning his flashlight on again, but decided against it. He didn't want to startle her, nor did he want to panic her into running again.

Frost guessed he was now a hundred and fifty yards or so from the riverbank. If her mother was still on the island, perhaps she didn't want to move any further away. He worked his way up through the trees, stopping regularly to listen for the sobs, mindful that Hellyer could be close by. He pictured her crouched down, confused and scared. He wondered if she had gone into shock as she tried to make sense of what had just happened.

Frost walked a little closer and then stopped again. In a voice barely above a whisper, he said, "Hello. This is Detective Frost. I'm Bridgette's partner."

The whimpering stopped. Frost knew the girl would be terrified.

Afraid she would run again, he added, "I'm not going to hurt you. I'd like to switch on my flashlight, but I don't want to make either you or me a target."

The girl didn't make a sound. Frost called out again, "My name's Levi. What's yours?"

After a moment's silence, the voice called back, "Amy."

Relieved that she had finally communicated, Frost responded, "Amy, stay where you are. I'm not going to switch my flashlight on just yet, just in case he's out there looking for you. Is that okay?"

Frost let out a long breath when Amy gave him a feeble, "Yes," in response.

After moving carefully through the darkness, Frost stopped when he got to within a few feet of the girl.

"I'm going to hold up my badge and switch my flashlight on for just for a second, just so that you know it's me. Is that okay?"

After Amy gave him the okay, Frost pulled out his badge and held it up next to his face. He switched the flashlight on just long enough to say, "Hi Amy, I'm alone and you're safe."

He heard Amy move the moment the forest became dark again.

Before he could comprehend what was happening, he felt the girl wrap her arms tightly around him.

As she sobbed into his chest, she spluttered, "I think he shot my mom."

Friday 7:37 PM

Bridgette was now in waist deep water. She could feel Hellyer grappling with the collar of her coat as he tried to pull her under water again. Already weakened from the ordeal, she knew her only hope of survival was getting away from him as quickly as possible.

She tried to pull away, but Hellyer's grip on her coat remained firm. Bridgette relaxed her shoulders and twisted around in the water. Wriggling slightly, she managed to shrug off the coat. In the darkness, she quickly separated from Hellyer, but one enemy was replaced by another. This enemy was stronger than Hellyer—more insidious—and no less malevolent.

Now barely able to keep her head above water, Bridgette had no strength to fight the Beast of the river as the force of the current dragged her downstream.

It felt like only minutes since her last ordeal when she had been washed off the footbridge.

The current was not as strong now, but she was still tossed about like a rag doll. With no strength left to fight, she allowed the torrent to have its way. Monica wouldn't be there to drag her out this time. She was resigned to her fate. She had given it everything and was comfortable enough with a force of nature taking her life rather than the murderous intent of a psychopath.

Bridgette thrashed as she struggled to keep her head above water in the swirling torrent. She felt completely disorientated in the darkness. The current tugged at her body. She felt like she was being drawn down into a watery world from which there was no escape. The sound around her subtly changed as the water pushed her around another bend. She tensed knowing she was just seconds away from the tree that had fallen across the river. It had taken almost inhuman strength for her to get out of her coat last time. Strength she did not have now.

Bridgette braced herself for the inevitable. She clasped her hands around her head in a feeble attempt to lessen the blow of the tree striking her body. To her surprise, the impact never came, and she sailed harmlessly under the overhanging trunk with just her knuckles scraping the bark. It was only then that Bridgette realized how far the water level had dropped.

Her sense of relief was short-lived as the rapids hurled her further down river. She became conscious of a light playing across the river in front of her and then heard the unmistakable boom of a shotgun above the roar of the torrent. She figured Hellyer must have taken Monica's shotgun and was now using it to shoot at her. But she wondered why. Her chances of survival were minuscule and with her head barely above water she was an almost impossible target. Perhaps he couldn't bear the thought of her drowning rather than dying at his hand?

Bridgette squinted as the light played over her again.

Out In The Cold

She braced for another shot as she rounded the last bend in the river before the lagoon. She pictured Hellyer running alongside the river bank, somehow holding both a flashlight and a shotgun.

She coughed up water again as the river spat her out into the lagoon.

The torrent subsided noticeably in the larger body of water, but Bridgette still felt its tentacles dragging her towards the bridge. She let out a gasp as she realized she would soon be just another tangled lifeless object in the ten-foot high pile of debris trapped under the bridge.

Bridgette kicked to try and fight her way out of the current. But her kick was feeble. She was frozen and exhausted. No longer able to lift her arms out of the water, she gazed up at the shadowy shape of the jetty. She passed the structure barely six feet from the last pylon, but it may as well have been a mile. For a moment, she was alone and wondered where Hellyer was. She figured if he was still trying to follow her around the river, he would reappear soon.

Bridgette tried to kick again towards the shoreline, but her body refused to cooperate. Without Monica and the pole, there was no way she could escape the current. She rolled onto her back and gasped for air.

As her life ebbed away, she was conscious of the flashlight again. The beam was illuminating the trees on the other side of the river. As the light zigzagged back and forth, she pictured Hellyer sprinting back across open ground towards the jetty. She turned her head slightly as she felt the urge to vomit.

Barely able to keep her eyes open, her will to live was gone. If Hellyer shot her before she became entangled in the debris at the bridge, then so be it. She had fought the good fight and given it her all. She floated on her back and breathed in the cool night air as the current drew her past the jetty. Her body convulsed from the freezing temperature of the water, but she no longer cared.

As she drifted, she felt something sharp smack into the back of her head. As she felt a ringing in her ears something brushed her left arm. It was softer than the object that hit her head. She twisted in the water and realized it was the rope that was tied to the jetty. Before the current could carry her away, she grabbed at it with both hands just above the fragment of the boat hull that it was still attached to.

It took all her strength to hold on as the current tried to carry her away. In the evening gloom, she knew she was not far from the jetty. But with barely enough energy to cling to the rope, swimming to the safety of the structure was out of the question.

Struggling to keep her head above water, Bridgette gritted her teeth. Something deep within her triggered a spark of hope as she realized the taut rope was beginning to pull her out of the main current.

Bridgette peered into the darkness. It was hard to tell how far away the riverbank was. She guessed it was about twenty feet as she kicked with her right leg. She coughed up water again as she saw the riverbank. It definitely seemed closer. Spurred on, she kicked again and again, unsure of where the energy was coming from.

The muscles in her hands and arms began to spasm as she clung to the rope. Bridgette did not attempt to change her grip for fear she would lose hold of her lifeline. Ignoring the cramp in her hands and arms and the cold now permeating her whole body, she kicked again.

She didn't care how far Hellyer was away, she doubled down, continuing to kick with all her might. The riverbank loomed large on her left—a black shadow at least ten feet tall. She closed her eyes and clenched her jaw and kicked again and again until her left shoulder bumped into something solid. Bridgette's feet treaded water until she felt the sharp slope of the rocky bank beneath her feet. It was slippery and difficult to stand on, but it helped her get her head and shoulders out of the river. Her teeth chattered as she checked out her surroundings, looking for a way to scramble up the riverbank. She gritted her teeth again while the unmistakable beam of Hellyer's flashlight played out across the water just in front of her.

Daring not to breathe, she waited, praying Hellyer wouldn't lower the beam of light. If he did, he would see her pressed up against the river bank.

After a few seconds, Hellyer pointed it up toward the main channel of the river and then mumbled something she couldn't hear. The beam bobbed up and down as it searched the river further up the channel. She pictured Hellyer walking along the riverbank holding the torch in front of him as he went. She figured it would not be long before he returned but this was her only chance to get to the jetty before she was discovered.

Friday 7:42 PM

Pulling herself forward by the rope, Bridgette inched closer to the jetty. She kept looking up to the top of the riverbank some eight feet above for any sign that Hellyer was on his way back. She knew his reconnaissance upriver would not take long and he would return at any moment. Bridgette focused on the pylons of the jetty now just three feet in front of her.

"Just a few more seconds," she murmured. That was all the time she needed to make it safely under the jetty. If she hid behind the pylons, maybe she could wait just long enough until Hellyer gave up the search.

Still exposed, she continued her steady progress, praying Hellyer wouldn't turn the beam on the jetty or the nearby riverbank until she was hidden.

She admonished herself to stay calm. One slip and it would all be over. The current was not nearly as strong near the bank, but it was still swirling and if she lost her grip on the rope or her footing, she knew she wouldn't have the energy to recover.

Bridgette continued hauling herself along the rope as the water continued to swirl around her. She tried to ignore the light playing across the river further upstream. It was getting stronger, and she knew Hellyer was not far away. With two feet separating her from the jetty, she heard a creak on the platform and looked up.

To her horror, she saw Hellyer walk out onto the jetty. He carried the shotgun in the crook of his right arm, while making slow, sweeping arcs of the lagoon with the flashlight. Bridgette gritted her teeth, as she heard him mumble, "Where are you, bitch?"

Hoping not to make a sound, Bridgette let go of the rope and dove forward as silently as she could. It was a risky move, but she couldn't afford to be out in the open any longer. She gave a final kick then gratefully wrapped her arms around a pylon. She stood in about five feet of water and as she tried to control her chattering teeth she glanced back at the riverbank. Trying to clamber up the almost vertical embankment would be impossible. The ladder at the end of the jetty was her only hope of getting out of the water. She would have to wait and suffer the freezing conditions for a little longer until Hellyer gave up on trying to find her. She tried to ignore Hellyer's shuffling footsteps above as she focused on the ladder. It was in deeper water and with the swelling current, she knew it wouldn't be easy to get to. She would need to swim from pylon to pylon. There were three of them between her and the ladder, all about eight feet apart.

Bridgette re-gripped the pylon. Her whole body was numb. She figured she had been in the water for over half an hour now. Her uncontrollable shaking and foggy head were both telltale signs she was suffering from hypothermia.

She wondered how much longer she could last as she

heard Hellyer mumble again, "You gotta be out there somewhere," before he turned to walk off the jetty.

Her heart fluttered when she looked up through the tiny cracks in the tread boards. She listened as he stopped almost directly above her. The tread boards continued to creak as he shifted his weight. She watched as he swung the beam over the edge of the jetty and played it up and down the water next to the riverbank where she had been just moments ago.

Bridgette stifled a small cry as Hellyer pulled on the rope she had been holding just moments ago. The night filled with the sound of Hellyer roaring at the top of his lungs. To her horror, she heard him drop into a crouch position. She tried to make herself as small as possible as she hid behind the pylon while Hellyer made a sweeping arc with the beam of his flashlight under the jetty.

Bridgette's heart sank as the beam zeroed in on her pylon and Hellyer growled, "Got you."

Bridgette heard a scuffling sound on the jetty platform above her. She tried to look up between the tread boards to see what Hellyer was doing, but the beam from his flashlight provided little illumination. Heavy footsteps replaced the scuffling as she heard Hellyer race off the jetty. Bridgette shivered. She knew he would be most likely looking for a place on the bank where he could get a good shot at her. She vowed to make the task as difficult as possible.

She peered into the darkness at the end of the jetty. She would still be within range of the blast, but it was her best chance of survival. She focused on the first of the three pylons that separated her from the end of the jetty. Too exhausted to lift her arms out of the water, she used a breaststroke motion and no longer cared about the noise she made. The distance was only ten feet, but in her weakened condition, it seemed like a mile.

She saw the beam of Hellyer's flashlight play across the water in front of her as she reached the first pylon.

After taking a gulp of air, she struck out for the second pylon as the water exploded about four feet in front of her. Startled by the shotgun blast, she kept swimming as the flashlight played across her. Now halfway between the first and second pylons, the beam of the flashlight shifted around a little before it became steady.

Bridgette heard footsteps racing back across the jetty. With the beam now steady and focused on the pylons, she realized Hellyer must have set the flashlight up on the bank to give him the illumination he needed for his next shot.

She looked at the ladder next to the third pylon. She was tempted to swim into the shadows on the opposite side of the jetty. But that wouldn't get her far enough away.

She tried to think like he did. If he only had the shotgun and a handful of cartridges he had taken from Monica he would want to make every shot count and would want to know exactly where she was before he pulled the trigger. Because she was under the jetty and the boards were too thick to fire through, he would need to partially descend into the water to get a clear shot at her. He would probably rest the barrel on a rung of the ladder above the waterline to keep it steady. He would hold the gun with his right hand while he held onto the ladder with his left. It would be awkward but effective. Being right-handed, that's how she would do it, and she figured he would be no different.

He would take his time; after all, she was not going anywhere. The bastard would want to savor every second.

Bridgette realized she only had one option. It was

unlikely to succeed, but better to go down fighting than hiding behind a pylon that only hid half her body.

She focused on the ladder as she swam towards the last pylon. She saw his left foot step onto the top rung of the ladder. With no time to lose, she used every fiber in her body to close the gap. Bridgette felt adrenaline kick in just as Hellyer placed his right foot on the second rung.

The fight-or-flight response it triggered helped her focus. She positioned herself directly behind the ladder and gripped hold of the side rail beneath the water with her left hand, keeping her right hand free. She didn't think he was aware of how close she was as she braced her feet on the ladder and peered up through the rungs. Now just two feet apart, she could see him clutching the shotgun in his right hand as he gripped the ladder with his left. Wrenching the gun free was her best hope of survival, but Hellyer was holding the gun too far away from the ladder for her to make a play for it.

She needed a fresh plan as she watched him clumsily continue his descent. She focused on his left hand as he stepped down into the water. Bridgette made a fist and waited until he was almost waist deep before swinging it down in a hammer action. She heard him yell in pain as her fist crushed his fingers against a rung of the ladder.

She felt her heart skip a beat as he let go the shotgun to grab at the ladder with his undamaged hand. The splash of the weapon as it hit the water buoyed Bridgette as Hellyer collapsed against the ladder. With just the rungs separating them, she knew this was her moment as she stared into his startled eyes. Bridgette focused on his throat.

She had learned about the power of a punch to the windpipe long before she had entered the police academy. Since junior high, she had taken Taekwondo as a sport, rising to the level of state champion. The throat punch, known as a Tiger Claw, was never allowed in competition.

She had thrown thousands of these punches during her martial arts training. Her technique was honed to a point where it was now a reflex action. With just the rungs of the ladder separating them, the punch would normally be crippling, if not lethal. But in her weakened state, she knew she would be lucky to strike even a glancing blow.

Bridgette threw the punch as Hellyer reached between the rungs of the ladder to grab at her hair. She felt her blow glance off the side of his neck as he roared, "I don't care whether I shoot you or strangle you, bitch. Either way works for me."

Bridgette tried to rear back to throw a second punch, but Hellyer had a fist full of her hair and pulled her forward. Almost numb with cold, she barely felt any pain as her face smashed into the ladder.

Before she could react, Bridgette felt his other hand wrap around her throat. She tried to pull away, but Hellyer was too strong.

She could feel his hot breath as he hissed, "It won't be long now. Next time you black out will be your last."

Bridgette felt her world spin as his left hand crushed her larynx. She was so weak now that even being deprived of oxygen for just a few seconds was more than she could bear.

Reaching around the ladder with her right arm, she tried to grip his hair to pull him away. Hellyer bobbed and weaved, desperate to evade her clutches while he continued to choke her with one hand. Bridgette's hand slipped down from his forehead to his face. Closing her eyes, she focused all her attention on her right hand as she cocked her thumb. Bridgette jabbed at his face, searching for his eye socket. She felt his grip on her throat ease a little as he tried to weave out of the way of her jabs hitting its target. She gulped in air greedily and changed tack, pressing her thumb into his throat instead. While her nails were not particularly long, her thumbnail dug deep into his windpipe, causing him to scream. She felt his left hand release from her throat as he attempted to fend her off.

For the first time since entering the water, Bridgette dared to hope as she stretched up her right thumb and dug it deep into Hellyer's left eye socket.

Hellyer roared in pain as he let go her hair and the ladder. She watched for a second as he flailed around in the water before disappearing beneath the surface. Realizing this was her best opportunity to escape, she swung her body around to the other side of the ladder. Desperate to get away, she tried to climb, but her arms and legs felt like jelly.

Hellyer surfaced and began thrashing around in the water just a few feet from her. The climbing process was slow, with her brain having to focus all its energy on moving one limb at a time. She managed to get up four rungs before she felt a hand grab at her left foot but she lashed out with her right foot, connecting with the bridge of Hellyer's nose. She watched him disappear beneath the surface of the water again before she continued her climb.

Her arms and legs weighed a ton but she targeted the jetty, just two feet above her, and willed herself not to pass out as her head began to spin.

She murmured, "Just a few seconds more," as she continued the climb. The splashing in the water below her continued until she reached the top of the ladder. She went momentarily dizzy as she hauled herself off the ladder and onto the jetty.

She felt nauseous as she rolled onto her back and looked up into the dark night sky. Her head spun and she vomited up more river water. Bridgette worked to keep her eyes open, but everything was spinning. She shut her eyes, but nothing changed and she felt like she was falling but couldn't control it. Bridgette felt the cold from the tread boards radiating up through her body. She desperately wanted to get further away from Hellyer, but the spinning disorientated her. Something gripped her lower body as she vomited again. She opened her eyes and tried to lift her head, but her world continued to spin as she drifted off to sleep.

Saturday 8:07 AM

Bridgette opened her eyes and tried to focus, but she could only see blurred images. She shut her eyes again and took a few deep breaths while she tried to figure out where she was. She was lying on her back, but not on the jetty—something softer had replaced the hard wooden tread boards. As another wave of nausea washed over her, she breathed in deeply. When it passed, she tried opening her eyes again. This time, her world came into focus. A shadow appeared in front of her face. She recoiled as she remembered her last encounter with Hellyer.

"Bridgette, it's me, Levi. You're safe… just relax."

Bridgette blinked and stared up at Levi Frost's face.

His soft smile was at odds with his furrowed brow. "You need to rest."

"Where am I?"

Frost raised an eyebrow. "You don't remember?"

"The last thing I remember was lying on the jetty… after climbing up the ladder."

Frost sat down on the bed next to her. "I searched for

you all night. I found you about an hour ago, tucked in under some trees not far from the jetty." Frost frowned and then added, "I carried you back to the main house. You don't remember?"

Bridgette shook her head. "No."

"Well... You'd been out in the cold all night. You were mumbling some weird stuff and I'm sure you're suffering from hypothermia."

"Weird stuff?"

Frost shrugged. "You weren't making much sense." He pointed to the blankets that covered her and added, "I stripped you down to your underwear, and then I laid you out on the bed and covered you up." Frost grimaced and then added, "Sorry."

Bridgette frowned. "Sorry?"

"That I had to get you out of your wet clothes."

"That's perfectly fine, Levi. You couldn't leave me in wet clothes and I really appreciate it."

"We need to get you showered and changed."

"I still feel a bit giddy. Maybe I'll wait a bit."

Frost nodded.

Bridgette tried to sit up. "Monica and Amy!"

"They're safe." Frost grinned and motioned for Bridgette to lie down again. "Monica's got a broken nose and some concussion, but she'll be okay."

"And Amy?"

Frost answered, "She's with her mom, and she's safe too." He then explained how he had found Amy hiding in the forest after she had escaped from the island. "I got her back to my car and locked her inside, and then came back across the footbridge to look for you and Monica."

"So Monica is okay?"

"She was pretty dazed when I found her. I managed to

get her to her feet and across the bridge. The water level had come down a bit by then. When I got her back to the car, I called an ambulance. They were picked up about an hour ago."

"So we have cell reception again?"

Frost nodded. "I came back to look for you while I waited for the ambulance, but I couldn't find any sign of either you or Hellyer. I feared the worst."

"The last thing I remember was passing out on the jetty."

"So what happened?"

Bridgette explained everything she could remember from the moment she had left the cabin with Monica and Amy. As she got to the part of her story where she used the rope to get to the riverbank, she shook her head. "I can't believe I survived that river twice."

Frost grinned. "Someone was looking after you."

Bridgette nodded and then said, "By the time I got to the jetty, I was exhausted. I tried to hide underneath, but he started shooting at me. I don't know where I found the energy to fight him off."

"You had right on your side. I think that always counts for something."

Bridgette frowned. "Did you find him, or did he escape?"

"You don't need to worry about him anymore."

Bridgette's eyes widened. "You arrested him?"

Frost shook his head. "No. He's dead. I went back to the jetty at sunrise. I was still trying to find you, but I found him instead."

"Where?"

"He was caught up in all the debris at the bridge. When I first saw the body... I thought it might be you. It was covered in mud and silt and I wasn't really sure. But, one arm was raised up out of the water... It's definitely a man's arm, so I kept searching for you."

"I can't believe he's dead," murmured Bridgette.

"You don't have to worry about him now. The nightmare is over. Now, it's just a matter of rest and recovery."

Bridgette nodded, but said nothing further.

Frost frowned. "You really should take a shower. You will feel so much better."

"I agree."

"All your stuff is back at the cabin and covered in glass," said Frost as he pointed at a chair covered in clothing. "I had a look in Monica's closet and picked out a few things that you can try on."

Bridgette managed a smile. "Thanks, Levi. That's very thoughtful."

"I'm going to head downstairs and see if I can rustle us up some food while you take a shower. I'm sure you're starved."

Bridgette smiled weakly. "Thanks, Levi. I appreciate it."

"Will you be okay up here on your own?"

Bridgette nodded.

Frost yawned. "I'm actually famished myself. I could seriously go for some bacon and eggs. And I need a coffee or two to keep me awake. How does that sound to you?"

Until Frost had mentioned food, Bridgette hadn't been overly hungry. The mere mention of bacon and eggs changed her mind. "That would be great."

"Once I've got something organized, I'll bring it back up here for you."

"No, I'll come down. I'm sure I'll be okay with the stairs."

"Just take it easy, there's no rush. The river is receding,

and the footbridge is now above the waterline. When you're up to it, we'll go back to the cabin and pack your stuff. I've called this into the local police, but they won't be here for some time. I'd like to drive you to a hospital and get you checked out. After that, we can head back to Vancouver. You can make a statement then when you're good and ready."

Keeping a blanket wrapped around her, Bridgette got up from the bed and took a couple tentative steps. "Have you told the chief?"

"Yeah. He's been out of his mind with worry, but he calmed down when I told him you were back here sleeping and Hellyer was dead."

Bridgette grimaced. "I guess he's going to make me take more leave."

Frost nodded knowingly. "I think that's a safe bet."

They stood about three feet apart, staring at each another for longer than normal. Finally, Frost put a hand on her shoulder, and said, "The chief wasn't the only one out of his mind. I'm glad… I'm glad you're okay too."

Bridgette joked, "It's going to take more than a psychopath and a flood to get rid of me."

Frost smiled at her dark attempt at humor. They held each other's gaze for a little longer before Frost said awkwardly, "I'd better head downstairs."

Bridgette watched Frost leave. She stood in the middle of the room, wondering what had just happened. Frost's concern was understandable and genuine. She replayed their last few seconds over in her mind as she picked up the fresh clothes from the chair. Only a few words had been spoken, yet she felt so much had been communicated. She headed to the bathroom, knowing the moment she had just shared with Frost would play on her mind for days to come.

After finally getting out of the river, Hellyer had been surprised when he couldn't find any sign of the bitch cop. He knew she would be exhausted from her ordeal and he had expected to find her passed out either on the jetty or somewhere close by. He had tried searching for her but the batteries in his flashlight quickly died, making the task next to impossible in the dark. Without a gun, he had hidden among the trees when the big cop returned to continue his search. He waited for an opportunity to strike but the cop had his gun at the ready and the opportunity never arose.

He had followed the cop at a safe distance when he returned to the jetty just before dawn. The cop had stood in the one spot for ten minutes, playing the beam of his flashlight across the debris caught up on the bridge downriver. It intrigued him. What was he looking at? Using the cover of the trees, he had crept as close as he could to listen in when the cop eventually made a phone call.

He could only make out a few words of the conversation, but became curious when the cop uttered the words, "I think he's dead," just before he ended the call.

Intrigued, Hellyer had stayed in his position and studied the bridge. As dawn broke, he could barely contain his glee when he finally saw what the cop had been looking at. When he spotted the arm of a dead man sticking up above the waterline, he had chortled to himself, "Some schmuck has washed up downriver and he thinks it's me."

He knew the island would be crawling with cops later in the day and the smart move would have been to escape while he had an opportunity. But the bitch was still alive. Which was unacceptable. And which was why he had come to the island in the first place. He loathed unfinished business and knew his fury would burn and consume him. She had to die and preferably at his hand. He decided to stay and see what happened.

Using the cover of the woods, Hellyer had continued to follow the cop as he searched for his partner. Now, with the aid of daylight, the cop retraced much of the ground he had searched overnight. It didn't take long before the cop found her in a clump of trees near the jetty. Hellyer had fumed at first. He had walked within a few feet of where she had passed out, but without the aid of a flashlight he hadn't seen her. His anger quickly turned to curiosity as he watched the cop pick her up and carry her back to the house.

After watching the big cop carry his partner in through the front door of the house, he had circled around to the rear of the dwelling to get a better look inside.

Now as he waited, crouched at the edge of the woods, he could see no sign of them. He suspected the cop had taken her upstairs. He remained in the shadows, watching and waiting, while he pondered what he would do next.

Hellyer allowed himself a grin as he reflected on the last twelve hours. After losing his grip on the jetty ladder, he had almost lost his life as the current in the lagoon had dragged him towards the downstream bridge. He had thrashed around as he desperately tried to swim back to the jetty. But the current made the task almost impossible. It was ironic that the rope the bitch had used to save her life had saved him as well. After grabbing hold of it, he had spent twenty minutes fighting against the current before he made it back to the jetty.

After a few minutes, the big cop had reappeared in the kitchen. Hellyer placed a hand in his coat pocket and felt the blade of his two-inch knife as he watched the cop start preparing breakfast. The kitchen was at the back of the house. It would be easy enough to circle around to the front and quietly enter through the front door.

If he could slip inside while the cop was preoccupied with preparing breakfast, he would only need a moment to finish her. Hellyer imagined her sleeping in a bedroom. He visualized cutting her throat and sitting on her bed for a few precious seconds, building a beautiful memory while she bled out. He thought about how he would get away if she cried out. He could always escape out an upstairs window if the big cop heard anything. He was confident the cop would stay and attempt to save his partner's life rather than chase him down.

Being caught was always a risk. He knew that. But the prize that awaited him overshadowed everything else. As he thought about the euphoria he would experience, he could hardly breathe. He watched the cop crack an egg into a frying pan. He had seen enough and set off at a sprint through the forest.

The shower and change of clothes took longer than Bridgette expected. Partly because she had to shampoo her hair twice to get rid of all the mud, and partly because she was still thinking about her last conversation with Frost. She played the words over in her mind as the steaming hot water washed over her. She frowned as she thought about the last look Frost had given her. Was there something in it? Or was she over-reading it? After all, she was vulnerable from her ordeal and Frost made her feel safe.

The confusion continued to play on her mind as she got out of the shower. It was just one look. And what did one look mean, anyway? She liked Frost, but had never seen their relationship as being anything more than professional. Besides, he was going through a messy divorce and he didn't need any romantic complications right now; least of all from his partner. She thought about Delray. Although Vancouver Police frowned on relationships between officers, it was generally tolerated if you weren't working in the same team.

While she got dressed, she decided she was making way too much of it. It was natural for Frost to be concerned for her welfare. And it was natural that there would be some intimacy in their reunion, even if they were just colleagues. She picked up her jumble of dirty clothes from the floor and took one last look in the bathroom mirror. Her hair was still wet and the bruising on her face where Hellyer had hit her was turning purple. She figured she would look worse tomorrow, but at least she was alive. Her thoughts returned to Frost as she got a waft of the bacon and eggs he was cooking downstairs. She thought about what she would say to him when she joined him for breakfast. If she was not careful, it could get awkward.

She decided she would keep it light and murmured to herself, "Let's not make it a big deal of this," as she reached for the doorknob.

As she opened the bathroom door, her blood ran cold as she stared into the face of Alex Hellyer. In the blur that followed, she saw his face light up with a sadistic grin as he grabbed her by the neck and thrust a short-bladed knife at her stomach. Still clutching her wet clothes, Bridgette used the balled mass to deflect the strike as she screamed, "Levi!"

Hellyer hissed, "Not this time bitch," as he drew the knife back to thrust at her again. Bridgette parried with her wet clothes and screamed her partner's name again as the blade swung through the air and buried itself deep into the damp, balled mass.

Bridgette kicked for all she was worth as Hellyer thrust the knife at her stomach a third time. She was conscious of a stinging pain across her left thumb as her right foot connected squarely with Hellyer's groin. Hellyer's eyes widened a little as he staggered backwards out of the bathroom. With just four feet separating Hellyer from the stairs, Bridgette dropped the clothes. In a single fluid motion, she raised her knee to waist height and then snapped her leg straight.

The 'front kick' was one of the first kicks she had mastered in Taekwondo. She had used it dozens of times in competition to put an off-balance opponent on the mat. But this was not a competition and a lot more was at stake if she didn't execute it correctly.

Hellyer saw the kick coming and swayed back, but her kick found its mark, with the ball of her heel connecting with the right side of his chest.

Bridgette heard a rush of air escape from Hellyer's lungs as he stumbled backwards. Rushing forward, Bridgette kicked again using a sidekick and watched as Hellyer tumbled backward down the stairs. He crashed heavily and she saw his head bounce off the timber treads twice before his body crumpled in a heap about halfway down.

Bridgette stood at the top of the stairs, not daring to breathe as she looked down at her nemesis. She was conscious of Frost standing at the bottom of the stairs with a gun in his hand and his mouth open.

He looked up at her. "You okay?"

Bridgette gave a single nod.

"You're bleeding."

Bridgette looked down at the deep gash across the top

of her right thumb and watched as blood dripped from the wound onto the floor.

She shrugged. "I've had worse," and then watched as Frost climbed the first three treads of the stairs to take a closer look at Hellyer. With his gun trained on Hellyer's head, her partner bent down for a closer look before straightening up again.

"He's got a bad gash on his head and he's bleeding…" Frost reached out his left hand to feel Hellyer's neck for a pulse.

After about five seconds, he looked up and shook his head.

"He's dead?" asked Bridgette.

Frost nodded and moved Hellyer's body to one side of the staircase.

Bridgette felt a wave of relief sweep over her body. Unable to control her emotions any longer, she started sobbing and slumped onto the top step.

Moments later she was conscious of Frost sitting beside her.

"You don't need to be strong anymore," he soothed, wrapping an arm around her.

They sat in silence for several minutes before Frost said, "I'm going to carry you downstairs. You don't need to look at this any longer and I need to dress your hand."

Bridgette didn't object. She felt safe for the first time in days as Frost scooped her up. She closed her eyes hoping the nightmare was now finally over.

Epilogue

3 WEEKS LATER

Bridgette was a few minutes early for her late morning coffee catch-up with Renée Filipucci. She had arranged to meet her friend at the Revolver coffee shop in Gastown. Revolver was one of the few coffee shops that consistently made it into the top ten in Vancouver. Bridgette liked the place for reasons other than coffee. Being more of a tea drinker, she loved the atmosphere of the establishment. Revolver was long and narrow, with its coffee bar running down one side of the establishment and a row of tables down the other. The place had a rustic feel and she liked the way the bench seats at each table were suspended by steel pipes from the ceiling, almost like swings.

Bridgette preferred sitting in the back and was pleased that a table in the rear corner was available. After sitting down, she looked up at the map of the world on the wall beside her as she breathed in the smell of fresh, roasting coffee. The map was made entirely out of Flathead nails. They were hammered together in clusters that made up each country and she never ceased to be impressed by the ingenuity and patience of whoever had created the artwork.

She was drawn back to the present when she felt her phone buzz in her pocket. At first, she thought it would be a text from Renée to say she was running late, but instead, it was a text from Monica. It had been three weeks since she had left the island and although she had spoken to Monica several times by phone, she was looking forward to a return trip to see her and Amy. The last call had been two days ago and a relieved Monica had told her the insurance payout for her husband's death had finally come through. Monica was excited about the prospect of finally being debt free and it looked as if her relationship with her daughter was turning a corner too.

Bridgette read the text message.

'Cabin windows have been repaired. Looking forward to having you back to finish your holiday any time you are free!'

Bridgette smiled to herself as she texted back.

'Fantastic! I'll call you soon.'

As she put her phone down, Bridgette looked down at the scar that ran across the top of her left thumb. It had required nine stitches and was only now starting to heal. She thought about the other scars Hellyer had left upon Monica, Amy and herself. Mental scars that would remain with them for the rest of their lives. Even though he was dead, the scar would be a constant reminder of what she had been through. She refused to let him win and hoped Monica and Amy felt the same.

Bridgette looked up as the door to the coffee shop opened. She smiled and gave a brief wave as Filipucci walked in. The journalist gave her a nod and then mouthed, "Have you ordered yet?"

When Bridgette shook her head, Filipucci stopped at the coffee bar and placed their order.

After paying for an espresso coffee and a peppermint tea, Filipucci sat down opposite Bridgette. "Hey, BC, I figured you'd be drinking peppermint tea. I hope that's okay?"

"Hi Renée. That will be perfect. Thanks."

"So how did your psych visit go?

The Vancouver police had provided a psychiatrist for Bridgette. Normally a private person, she would have preferred to work through her issues alone, but her attendance was compulsory after another major trauma incident. She had been pleasantly surprised by how helpful the psychiatrist had been.

"She's happy with my progress. Today was not much more than a check in now that I'm off medication. She's given me another week off, but after that, I think I'll be heading back to work."

Filipucci smiled. "Well, that's good news. So you're off all the meds?"

"Even the sleeping pills. I'm not letting that bastard ruin my life."

"Good for you. I gotta say, I am glad he's dead. It must help with your recovery, knowing he can't ever hurt you again."

"Or anybody else." Keen to change the subject, Bridgette added, "How's your day?"

Filipucci shrugged. "Same old, same old. Publishing

deadlines, but that's a journalist's lot in life." Filipucci cocked her head to one side and then added, "So what are you going to do next week? You must be bored out of your brain sitting around at home?"

"You've got that right," said Bridgette with a grimace. "I'm doing a little gym work now that my hand is getting better, but I'm hoping to head back to Hope to stay with Monica and Amy."

Filipucci frowned. "Is that a good idea? I mean…"

"My shrink thinks it will be good for me."

"Like getting back on a horse after you've fallen off, I guess?"

"Something like that. I'm actually just looking forward to seeing them both. They've been through a lot and I feel guilty I never got to visit Monica in the hospital."

"You can't beat yourself up over that, BC," responded Filipucci with a raised eyebrow. "You were suffering from hypothermia, a bruised larynx and face, *and* you had that nasty hand injury."

"I know. But that's why I want to go see them. There's a lot for us to talk about."

"When you're cleared to go back to work, will you still be doing the same stuff?"

"Hopefully. I've spoken to the chief, and he's keen to have me back in homicide as soon as possible."

"Well, that's good. And will you be still working with Levi?"

"I haven't heard any different, so I guess so."

"Have you spoken to him since leaving the hospital?"

Bridgette flushed. "A few times, but it's mostly been text messages."

Filipucci raised an eyebrow. "A few times? What does that mean?"

"It means... a few times. We've been comparing notes on the case. We had a meal together last night and..."

Filipucci's eyes widened. "You went out on a date with him?"

"It wasn't a date," exclaimed Bridgette. "It was..."

Filipucci leaned in a little. "Level with me, Bridgette, are you sweet on him?"

"He's concerned about my recovery," answered Bridgette with a roll of her eyes. "It was his idea for us to get together and I didn't see a problem with it."

Filipucci she sat back in her chair. "You didn't answer my question and you're blushing like a schoolgirl."

"That's because it's hot in here," said Bridgette, taking off her coat.

Filipucci mused, "I wouldn't blame you if you were sweet on him. I mean, he's a good-looking guy and, well... you're the smartest girl I know and you're easy on the eye. You'd make a great couple."

"We're just colleagues."

Filipucci folder her arms. "Colleagues? Really?"

Bridgette knew the interrogation was far from over. After a moment of silence, she sighed and then said, "When we were in the house and Hellyer attacked me... there was a moment afterwards. Levi picked me up and carried me downstairs. Nothing was said, but I felt..."

She paused for a moment while their drinks were delivered and then continued. "Obviously, I was in a highly emotional state... and I guess it's understandable that I would want human contact."

"But?"

Bridgette sighed. "I don't know... maybe this was different."

"I know you've had boyfriends before."

Bridgette nodded.

"But have you ever been in love?"

Bridgette grimaced. "Not even close."

"Wow!"

Bridgette picked up her peppermint tea. "This is all very confusing."

"So the dinner last night... did you talk about it?"

"Of course not! I'm not even sure how I feel. Right now, I just want to get back into a routine."

Filipucci nodded. "It's going to be hard to work with him if this isn't resolved."

"He's going through a messy divorce," said Bridgette as she sipped her tea. "He doesn't need any more complications in his life right now. And I'm certainly not going to give him any."

"What did John Lennon say? 'Life is what happens to you while you're busy making other plans?'"

Bridgette rolled her eyes again, "Something like that."

"I think you should talk to him about it as soon as possible."

"That's not going to happen," replied Bridgette with a shake of her head. "That might be your style, but it's not mine."

Filipucci placed her hands on the table. "At least promise me one thing."

Bridgette held Filipucci's gaze. "If I can."

"At least be open to the idea. Don't push him away just because you work with him. Good guys are hard to find and the right guy for you might be sitting right under your nose."

Bridgette opened her mouth to say 'No,' but paused. She knew Filipucci meant well and it would be disrespectful to their friendship to dismiss her idea out of hand. "OK."

Filipucci raised an eyebrow again. "OK, what?"

Bridgette sighed. "OK, I'll… keep an open mind."

Filipucci smiled. "Good girl."

They were lost in their thoughts for a moment while they took sips of their drinks. Filipucci stared down at Bridgette's small concentric ring tattoo on her left forearm. It had the words Family, Faith, Friendship and Peace written in it. She pointed to the artwork and said, "You normally get a new word inked into your tattoo after going through a crisis. What's it going to be this time?"

"I'm not getting a word this time," said Bridgette as she looked down at the artwork. "I've only got room for one more word, and I'm not ready to get it added yet." Pointing to the long scar on her left thumb, she added, "Besides, I've got this as a reminder of what I've been through."

"What's the last word going to be?"

Before Bridgette could answer, Filipucci's phone buzzed. She picked it up off the table and cursed. "This is work. I gotta take it. Do you mind?"

Secretly relieved that she didn't have to answer the question, Bridgette replied, "Of course not," and sipped her tea while Filipucci took the call.

After a brief exchange, Filipucci disconnected. "That was my boss," she said with a frown. "I'm sorry, but I gotta get back to work. We've just had a big story come in about corruption in the mayor's office. The boss wants everyone back in the office, pronto."

"No problem, Renée. Duty calls."

Filipucci swallowed the rest of her coffee in two gulps. "You still good for tomorrow night?"

Bridgette remembered Filipucci had been planning a catch-up dinner for a few of their girlfriends tomorrow evening at one of the local bar-and-grills. Normally, it was an attractive offer, but after three weeks of sitting around her apartment, she was keen for a change of scenery. "I'll let you know. I'm going to call Monica. If she's happy to have me come back and stay, I'll probably leave first thing tomorrow."

"OK, no problem. Just let me know."

Bridgette stood and gave Filipucci a hug as they said goodbye. She watched her friend walk out of Revolver. Filipucci could be infuriating at times with her questions, but she had a good heart and Bridgette appreciated her honesty. She replayed their conversation over in her mind as she sat down again. She conceded her friend was right. It would be difficult for her to work with Frost if there were genuine feelings between them. But she was not sure how she felt, let alone how Frost was feeling.

Bridgette sighed. As usual, she was probably over complicating things. She had a lot to think about and the idea of getting out of the city for a few days to clear her head had more appeal than ever.

She picked up her phone and dialed Monica's number from memory to leave a voice message. To her surprise, it was answered on the fourth ring.

"Hi Bridgette, how are you?"

"I'm doing okay, Monica. And you?"

Monica laughed. "Well, my nose will never be straight again, but apart from that, I'm doing okay, too."

"And Amy."

Bridgette could hear Monica let out an audible sigh. "She's started sleeping in her own bed again, which is a good sign, but she's got a way to go yet."

"Well, that's understandable, given what she's been through."

"The sessions with the psychologist are helping. He says

it's a healing process for both of us and it may take twelve months or more."

"I'm sorry I got you guys caught up in that."

"Not your fault, Bridgette. And if there's one silver lining to all this, Amy and I are talking again, just like we were before Clint's death."

"I'm so glad. That must take a load off your mind."

"It does. What with that and the insurance money coming through, I'm really ready to start a new chapter."

"Well, that's great news."

"And what about you, Bridgette? Are you back at work yet?"

"No, I've got another week off and…"

"You must come and stay. Amy talks about you all the time, and we have so much to catch up on."

Bridgette smiled. "You're too kind, Monica."

"The cabin is ready, so come whenever you like."

"Well… would tomorrow be too soon? I'm going out my mind in my apartment."

"Tomorrow would be fine. The sun is shining and the bed's made up and Amy has even restocked the firewood."

"Thanks Monica. I'll be there early afternoon if that's okay?"

"I'm looking forward to it. I won't tell Amy. We'll leave it as a surprise for her."

"Sounds good. I'll see you then."

After disconnecting, Bridgette reflected on how lucky they all were to still be alive. She took a last sip of her tea and then put her coat on. It was just a two-minute walk to the EasyPark where she had left her Mustang, but she was not ready to go home yet. She decided she would make the most of the day and take a walk down to the harbor.

After thanking the staff of Revolver for their hospitality,

she pushed through the door and walked out onto Cambia Street. Bridgette looked up at the cloudless blue sky and then closed her eyes for a moment. As she soaked up the sun's rays, she was thankful her life was returning to normal, and for now, that was enough.

Next in The Bridgette Cash Mystery Thriller Series

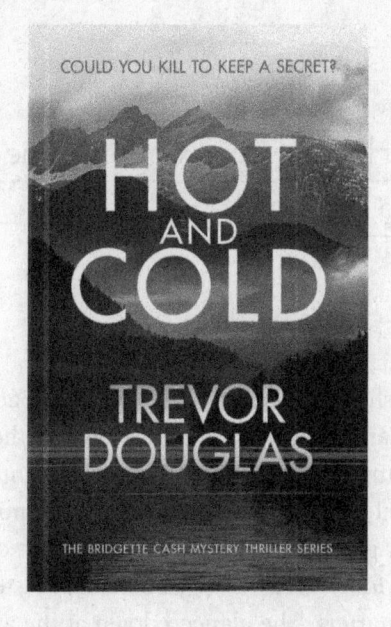

vinci-books.com/hot-cold

A cold case. A deadly conspiracy. Detective Bridgette Cash is running out of time.

When a man is arrested for a long-unsolved murder, Bridgette Cash is brought in to close the case. But as she delves deeper into the investigation, Bridgette uncovers evidence pointing to the man's innocence and a plot involving powerful individuals determined to secure a conviction at any cost. With her life and career on the line, she must unravel the twisted truth before the real killer silences her forever.

Turn the page for a free preview…

Hot and Cold: Chapter One

Bridgette Cash shifted her '66 Mustang Fastback down into second gear and eased the car to a halt in the Vancouver police department parking lot. Her grip tightened on the steering wheel as she gazed up through the misting rain at the four-story glass and brick building in front of her. It had been almost four weeks since she had last stepped inside police headquarters. She glanced down at the angry red line than ran across the back of her hand and thumb and sighed. The knife wound was another permanent reminder of how dangerous her work could be.

After fifteen months in the job she couldn't imagine doing anything else. But she found it almost impossible to switch off, even during her latest recuperation leave.

She gazed up at the building again and frowned as she thought about the meeting she was due to have with her boss in a few minutes. Chief Inspector Felix Delray was a veteran cop and he wouldn't simply take the word of a police psychologist that she was ready to return to work. Bridgette knew he would grill her about her mental state before he made his decision. She nodded once as a concession that she would do the same thing in his position.

She thought over the questions he was likely to ask her. He would probe using all his skills as a police detective to satisfy himself that she was ready to return to the rigors of work and murder investigations. She had seen him interview dozens of suspects. Delray had a conversational tone that was subtle. He would engage her in casual conversation and then slip in a probing question. She wouldn't lie—that wasn't her style—but she would need to choose her words carefully. Although she had stopped taking medication, she still had trouble sleeping and would regularly wakes up in sweats. Bridgette gently tugged at what remained of her left earlobe, a habit she had developed during periods of intense concentration. Unlike her right ear, the bottom of her left lobe was uncharacteristically flat—the legacy of a bullet that had almost ended her life during a shootout in her first murder case. The shootout haunted her for months but she rarely thought about it now.

Bridgette checked her watch—it was closing in on nine AM. Just time for her to make it up to the second floor for her meeting. She sighed as she switched off the engine. Delray only had her best interests at heart, but her worst fear was that she would be assigned desk work until he was satisfied she was ready to return to her role as an investigator. She found desk work soul-destroying. Despite her IQ of one hundred and fifty one, she had never pictured herself as an analyst sitting behind a desk.

After getting out of her car, she buttoned her coat to keep out the rain and then walked across the parking lot. She decided she would head directly to Delray's office rather than her desk in the common area where all the detectives sat. They were all aware of her most recent ordeal and another brush with death. Her peers were all well-meaning, but she wasn't ready to answer questions about her recovery or what she would be doing next. She disliked being the center of attention and figured it would be easier to steer the conversation away from anything personal and onto what she was doing next after she had met with her boss.

The ride up in the elevator gave her a final moment to rehearse her answers before the meeting. She murmured, "Let's get this over with," as the elevator door opened. Bridgette walked down the short corridor to Delray's office and paused in the open doorway. She studied her boss for a moment before knocking. Delray was in his early fifties and had the build of an aging wrestler. His short, dark curly hair was now graying at the temples, giving him an almost distinguished look. He was street-smart and had a loud voice that some of the junior detectives found intimidating. Bridgette smiled to herself. His thick dark-rimmed glasses were perched on the end of his nose, almost defying gravity as he read an open file on his desk.

She knocked once. "Hi, Chief."

Delray looked up and smiled. "Well, well, look who's back. Come in and take a load off, Bridgette."

Delray's office was twelve-by-fourteen and barely large enough to accommodate his desk, two filing cabinets, and three visitors' chairs. Almost every square inch of his desk was covered with paper files. To an outsider, it looked chaotic, but Bridgette knew better. Delray was highly organized and had a sharp mind. Like most Vancouver police officers, he had started in uniform before his promotion to detective. He had risen through the ranks and had developed a reputation as an honest, hard-working police officer who got the job done. Never one for police politics, Delray had been promoted to chief inspector of homicide in his early forties and refused any further promotions, citing he wanted to stay with 'real police work.'

Bridgette knew this was code for he couldn't stand the politics, a sentiment she shared and respected.

They made small talk for a few minutes, with Delray bringing her up to date on the team's murder cases. The office fell silent briefly as Delray leaned forward and clasped his hands together. Nodding towards a file on his desk, he said, "I've read the file from the police psychologist. She seems satisfied that you're ready to return to work."

Delray raised an eyebrow and added, "But I want you to tell me how you're feeling. Are you ready to come back to all this chaos?"

"I am, Chief," said Bridgette with a nod. "I'm bored at home and there's only so much time I can spend at the gym."

"I've been in your position once myself," said Delray as he leaned back in his chair. "You've had a pretty rough couple of months…"

Bridgette nodded again, but said nothing in response. *Here it comes*, she thought.

"Solving murder cases generally doesn't mean risking your life…" Delray paused and held Bridgette's gaze. "But of course, we know that the Alex Hellyer case was different."

Bridgette sighed as she relived the shootout on the roof of a Vancouver hospital several months ago, as she and her partner had tried to arrest Hellyer for murder. They had both come under intense fire from Hellyer as he tried to escape. Hellyer was subsequently arrested, but not before Bridgette had shot him in the chest. The man had almost died on the operating table as the surgeons had removed the bullet. Diagnosed as a psychopath, Hellyer then spent weeks in the hospital under armed guard while he recovered. The night before he was due to be transported back to a normal prison, he had escaped. Despite a state-wide manhunt, Hellyer had evaded capture and had come after Bridgette who was holidaying in a cabin on the Fraser River.

"It's not every day you're hunted down by a psychopath," added Delray. "What you went through would haunt most people for the rest of their lives."

The nightmare had culminated with Hellyer breaking into a house where she was hiding. Bridgette glanced down at the knife wound on her hand as she thought about their final battle. She grimaced as she relived the moment Hellyer had fallen down the staircase and broken his neck as he tried to stab her. "I take a lot of solace knowing he can't hurt me or anyone else ever again."

"You must dream about it?"

"I dream about a lot of things, Chief. But I am sleeping and I'm off all medication."

Delray nodded. Bridgette could see he wasn't convinced and added, "What happened with Hellyer is going to stay with me for a long time. I know that, but I'm not letting it define me. My psychologist thinks I'm ready to return to work and I agree with her."

"Well... that's good to hear," said Delray as he picked up the psychologist's report. "Ultimately, the decision on your return to work is up to me. I've got to decide whether you're up to the rigors of normal detective work, or if I assign you something else to do."

"You mean desk work?"

Delray nodded. "Being chained to a desk isn't your style or mine for that matter... I have something else in mind."

Bridgette let out a sigh of relief. "Thanks, Chief."

"Don't thank me just yet," said Delray as he placed her psychologist's report on the top of a pile of files. "You ever hear of the term 'Hot and Cold'?"

"As in the legal tactic?"

Delray nodded.

"I studied a couple of them during my criminology degree," said Bridgette with a nod. "It's a tactic prosecutors sometimes use when a suspect is charged with multiple murders, but you only try one case at a time."

"You got it. The murder trial for the first victim is known as the hot case, while the trials for any subsequent victims are kept on ice, just in case they don't get a conviction the first time around."

Delray picked up a file from his desk and handed it to Bridgette. "This is one of those cases. We failed to get a conviction on the first murder charge, but we now think we've got enough to go ahead with the trial for the second murder victim."

As Bridgette opened the file, Delray asked, "You ever hear about the murder of Fiona and Tessa Halloran?"

Bridgette shook her head. "Not that I recall."

"It happened about thirteen years ago—long before your time here—so I'm not surprised."

As Bridgette scanned the case summary, Delray continued, "Fiona and Tessa were sixteen-year-old twins. They were murdered in a remote wooded area, just back from the Gulf Beach in north Vancouver. One of them died from blunt trauma wounds to the head and the other was strangled."

Delray continued as Bridgette flipped through the pages in the file. "A guy called Remmy Chilton was charged with their murder two days after the incident. He was a loner and a drifter, and we have eyewitnesses who placed him near the murder scene, close to the time of the twins' death. There was a baseball cap found near the murder scene that was matched by DNA to Chilton."

"Sounds like a fairly straightforward case," said Bridgette as she closed the file.

"You would think so," said Delray with a grimace, "But he got off on a technicality."

Bridgette raised her eyebrows. "So what happened?"

"They lost crucial evidence between the arrest and the trial."

"What kind of evidence?"

"The baseball cap. It was sent to the lab for DNA testing —so far, so good. They found a hair in the cap which was a match for Chilton. But when it came time to return the cap along with other DNA evidence from the crime scene, the cap was missing."

"How does that happen?" said Bridgette with a frown.

Delray massaged his temples for a moment. "Back in the day, Vancouver Police were directed to use a government-appointed facility called VGL for all its DNA and forensic testing. VGL stands for Vancouver Government Laboratory in case you're wondering. It doesn't exist anymore because they were incompetent."

"In what way."

Delray shifted in his seat. "Evidence occasionally went missing, and DNA tests were often thrown out of court because they weren't accurate. Long story short, the place had an incompetent director. It took three years and a government inquiry before he could be fired and the place overhauled. In the meantime, a lot of cases, including this one, suffered."

"But why would you proceed with a court case when your prime piece of evidence goes missing?"

"Richard Temple is the reason."

Bridgette nodded knowingly. Dr. Richard Temple was the senior crown prosecutor for British Columbia. She had heard mixed reviews about his capability, but she'd had little to do with him and didn't offer an opinion.

Delray continued, "You can imagine the media coverage the murder of twin girls generated. There was a lot of pressure on Temple to proceed to trial. But that was a mistake. The missing cap made the jury doubt the chain of evidence."

"Even though they had a DNA match on the hair?"

Delray nodded. "Temple got one thing right, at least. Not trying both murder cases concurrently at least gives us a second shot."

"What a mess."

"It was an embarrassment for the police department and the beginning of the end for VGL."

"So why now? Why wait thirteen years to retry the case?"

"Chilton has been missing. Shortly after he was acquitted, he moved to the USA and everyone lost track of him. Vancouver Police weren't ready to charge him for the second murder so he was free to leave. He worked on boats out of Maine and basically lived off the grid."

"So what changed?"

"He got picked at the border three days ago."

Bridgette frowned. "Trying to re-enter Canada?"

"Apparently, Chilton isn't very bright," said Delray with a shrug. "He claims he didn't know there was a warrant out for his arrest. I've set up a preliminary interview for you with Chilton for two o'clock this afternoon. No one from here has spoken to him yet, and he hasn't been officially charged. I just want to know if he's going to change anything in his story before we formally charge him with the second murder. The murder file has all the background. Let me know if you need more time, and we can postpone the Chilton interview."

Thinking the meeting was over, Bridgette went to rise from her chair, but Delray motioned her to sit again. "We need to discuss one more thing about this case."

"Okay."

"There's a second reason why I chose you for this. This could all get very ugly if it's not handled correctly. Temple has already called the Commissioner. He wants Chilton charged immediately and no mistakes like last time."

"But if the cap is still missing?"

Delray grimaced. "We go without the cap. Temple thinks focusing on the hair found at the crime scene and the eyewitness accounts can lead to a conviction."

"And you agree?"

"I've had a quick look at the case. If nothing else has changed, then yeah, I think we can get a conviction. Temple will have to be upfront with the jury about the missing cap, but the hair is the main piece of evidence, anyway. That's what ties him to the crime scene. And we have photos of the cap at the crime scene and Chilton never denied he owned a cap like the one we found."

As she got up to leave, Delray added, "Temple is leaving the prosecution service to enter politics. The media are going to go nuts again over this case and he will manipulate it any way he can to get positive exposure. I don't expect any problems, but with the politics involved, you never know…"

Hot and Cold: Chapter Two

After meeting with Delray, Bridgette returned to her desk in the common area. As she suspected, she was the focus of their attention, with her colleagues welcoming her back and wanting to know how she was feeling. Bridgette told them she was better, which was mostly true, and looking forward to getting on with her next case. She discussed the Halloran case with several senior detectives, who warned her to be careful. From their experience, Prosecutor Temple played dirty and wasn't afraid to double-cross people, even those who worked on the same side as him.

Bridgette thanked her colleagues for the warning, reassuring them that Delray had said something similar. After switching on her computer and spending a few minutes sorting through a backlog of emails, Bridgette pulled out the case file for the Halloran' murders and read the summary. They had found the twin girls about forty yards from Gulf Beach in the hinterland. Bridgette wasn't overly familiar with the area. She remembered visiting the beach once as a small child when her mother and father were still alive. Her memories were sketchy, but she recalled the hinterland was dense with trees and undergrowth. She decided to scout the entire area the next day to get a better understanding of the murder scene as she recalled the suburb beyond the hinterland was affluent: big houses, large blocks, and well spread out.

After reading the summary, she opted to review the photos of the crime scene before she read any of the reports. She knew from experience that photos told their own story—without bias or assumptions—and she hoped this would help her determine if anything had been missed in the initial investigation.

The photographs were sorted into two folders, one for each sister. She opened the folder for Tessa Halloran. Tessa was found strangled and partly covered with leaves in a thicket. She flipped through the photos, which appeared to be in chronological order. The first images showed Tessa's body in the thicket. There was little to see in the pictures apart from the victim's lower legs. The next series of images showed Tessa after they had removed her body and placed it on a nearby trail. Despite the trauma of death, Tessa's beauty and athleticism were evident to Bridgette.

She flipped through some other notes in the file that revealed Tessa and her sister were both five-feet-ten and played in the state volleyball team. Bridgette pulled a legal pad out of a drawer in her desk and noted their height. Even though she had a photographic memory and would forget nothing she read, the visual stimuli of a note on a page helped her think.

Switching her focus back to the photos, she studied the pictures from the morgue. There were clear strangulation marks around Tessa's neck. The coroner's report detailed the bruising and concluded Tessa's attacker was probably right-handed. She made a note about this and kept flipping through the photos. A photo of the back of Tessa's head intrigued her. It showed bruising and a gash that was about an inch long. Bridgette read the coroner's notes. Dirt and small rock fragments were extracted from the victim's wound and analyzed. Forensics matched rocks in the area to the victim and the coroner concluded the wound was consistent with Tessa hitting her head on a rock in the area shortly before her death.

Bridgette frowned and wrote 'Head wound - Tessa' on her legal pad. Had she been trying to escape her attacker? Had she slipped and hit her head when she had fallen? She would read the investigator's notes later. But it seemed plausible that the killer had overpowered her, strangling her before hiding her body in the undergrowth.

Bridgette checked the time of death before she continued. The coroner had estimated it to be somewhere between three and six p.m. Bridgette leaned back in her chair, her mind abuzz with questions. She wrote several more notes and then turned her attention to the crime scene photographs of Fiona Halloran.

Bridgette studied the face of Fiona. She, too, shared Tessa's beauty, which wasn't surprising. They had found Fiona lying face down on a pathway further up in the woods. Temple had decided to try Fiona's murder case first because of the proximity of the cap and DNA evidence to her body. Bridgette flipped forward in the case file to a hand-drawn map, which showed the location of both bodies in relation to the beach. Fiona was discovered about thirty yards from her sister on a path away that lead from the beach to a nearby suburb. She lay face down in the photos. The coroner's report showed Fiona had a cracked skull from two blunt force blows to the back of the head. Death would have been almost instantaneous. Forensic evidence suggested the murder weapon was a tree branch or similar, though it was never recovered.

Bridgette flicked through the other photos from the crime scene. The wooded area seemed to have lots of undergrowth. She saw potential in a fallen tree branch being used as an improvised weapon. She made a note to check her hypothesis when she visited the murder scene tomorrow.

Bridgette pushed back from her desk again and stroked her left earlobe as she asked herself, *'Why does he strangle one girl and then beat the other to death?'*

Bridgette scratched a few more notes on her pad. The summary report didn't explain why the girls were in the hinterland. They had been holidaying in a house nearby with their family, but the family hadn't realized they were missing. Had they come for a meet-up? Had they been returning from the beach when their killer confronted them? Bridgette checked the coroner's report for Fiona's time of death. It showed the same time range as her sister: between three and six p.m. The coroner couldn't determine the order of the murders or if one person was responsible for both deaths.

Bridgette picked up several closeup photos taken of Fiona's skull in the morgue. The coroner noted the location of the trauma wounds as just behind her left ear and concluded the attacker was likely right-handed if she had been hit from behind while running away. Bridgette made more notes on her pad and then sat back again. She thought it was strange that the coroner was open to the possibility that the same man didn't kill both girls. Had there been more than one killer?

Bridgette doodled on her pad as she considered different

scenarios. There appeared to be no motive for the murders. Were they thrill kills? Just some random opportunity that presented itself? She thought about Remmy Chilton. Had he been following the girls? Was he looking for an opportunity to rape one or both of them? She scanned through the final summary of the investigator's notes. This was the conclusion of the lead detective, Cliff Robertson. She knew little about Robertson other than he had retired six years ago. She made a mental note to ask Delray if she could contact him. It would be worth getting his point of view once she had sifted through all the evidence and interviewed Chilton for herself.

Bridgette then read the coroner's report for each murder victim in detail. Both girls had been wearing T-shirts and white shorts. Their clothing was intact and there were no signs of sexual assault. She checked back over both reports —Chilton's DNA was not found on either body. Bridgette frowned as she wrote the words, 'Was he interrupted?' on her pad. She wondered if someone discovered him and he had fled the crime scene before he could act on his real motive.

Bridgette continued to scan through the photographs and paused when she came to the images of a teal baseball cap. The notes showed the cap had been found just off the trail, eight feet from Fiona's body. She studied each image of the cap in detail. The lab had enhanced two of the photographs to reveal a human hair caught in the inner lining. The baseball cap was an NBA cap for the Charlotte Hornets. She didn't follow the NBA but recognized the cap had the original team logo.

Bridgette swiveled around to her computer and keyed in the words 'VGL laboratory scandal', and pressed enter. The search engine mainly returned news articles covering the crisis period for the organization. Bridgette checked the date stamp for the top articles—most were at least ten years old. She scanned the headlines for each piece. The majority focused on the government's announcement that the Royal Canadian Mounted Police would lead a new facility to replace VGL which was being closed down.

One article caught Bridgette's attention. She opened it up and read the report. It detailed a pattern of behavior within VGL. DNA tests were regularly botched, and forensic evidence had been lost in multiple cases. The article also hinted at the presence of thieves within the organization. VGL lost several weapons, cameras, and phones while they had been in their custody.

Bridgette picked up a photo of the cap again. It looked almost new, and she wondered if it had value as a collector's item, which was why it had gone missing. She started making a few more notes as a voice called from behind her, "Hi, Bridgette."

Her heart skipped a beat as she turned to see her partner, Levi Frost, leaning over the partition that separated their two cubicles. She admonished herself to hold it together as she responded, "Hi, Levi."

Grab your copy...
vinci-books.com/hot-cold

About the Author

Trevor Douglas is a multi-award winning author and the recipient of the gold medal for best crime fiction novel, and the gold medal for the best overall novel in the 2024 Global Book Awards.

Trevor is married with two adult sons and when he is not writing, enjoys bushwalking, watching AFL and discovering the best coffee shops in Brisbane with his wife.

After a long and successful career as an IT consultant, Trevor now writes full time.

Acknowledgments

A note of thanks needs to go to William Ian for the island artwork. Thank you for your patience and such a quick turnaround, it is much appreciated.